Thomas MacKellar

Rhymes atween-times

Second Edition

Thomas MacKellar

Rhymes atween-times
Second Edition

ISBN/EAN: 9783337270278

Printed in Europe, USA, Canada, Australia, Japan

Cover: Foto ©Andreas Hilbeck / pixelio.de

More available books at **www.hansebooks.com**

RHYMES ATWEEN-TIMES.

THE POET'S VENTURE.

I SAT me down to build a boat
And launch it on the sea afloat:
I wrought it with a loving will,
Putting to task my utmost skill:
I gave its form the highest grace
My hand and eye knew how to trace,
And beautified its every part
According to my native art.
I set the mast, and spread the sail
To catch the softliest-breathing gale,
And then I sent it forth to go
Whichever way the wind might blow.
Who knows?   It may be lost at sea,
Or come with treasure back to me.

RHYMES
ATWEEN-TIMES.

BY THOMAS MACKELLAR.

PHILADELPHIA:

PORTER & COATES.

1890.

SECOND EDITION.

Preface to the Second Edition.

THIS edition of *Rhymes Atween-Times*
is sent forth by the author—*firstly*, to
please himself; and, secondly, to win the
approval of readers of pure and gentle in-
stincts.

Some pieces in the first edition have been
transferred to the author's book of Hymns
and Metrical Psalms, and new poems have
been inserted in their stead.

T. McK.

WOODNEST,
GERMANTOWN, PA.
December, 1890.

CONTENTS.

RHYMES OF COMMON LIFE.

RHYMES OF COMMON LIFE.

RHYMES ATWEEN-TIMES.

MEMORIAL ODE.

Recited at the Unveiling of the Battle Monument at Germantown.

I.

IN the far, slow-coming days,
  When war shall nevermore be known,
And men shall sing the heavenly lays
  Of love and peace alone,—
And tatter'd flag and sword and gun
  Adorn antique historic halls,
Or hang as curious relics on
  The antiquary's walls,—
As generations, with untiring tread,
    Along the aisle
    Of centuries shall file,
The children shall approach with reverent head,
And ask in wonderment: What means this pile?
Its eloquent lips will tell to eager ears
The deeds heroic, wrought in olden years,

Of valiant men, who, at their country's 'hest
When by tyrannic hands distrest,
    Left hearth and wife and child,
And toil'd by day in hunger, heat, and cold,
And lay at night wrapp'd in the chilly fold
    Of stormy skies and tempests wild,
      Without a whisper'd cheer
Of faithful wife, or mother's fond embrace,
    So comforting and dear
      To men of noble race,—
The men who lifted up their good right arm
    To shield their land from harm,
      And, uncomplaining, bled
And fell, the conquerors though dead.
Not they who shout are conquerors alone,
For they who fall before the day is won
Are also victors, and the laurell'd crown
Fitly adorns the warrior smitten down.
    No martyr dies
    A fruitless sacrifice;
      Heroic deeds
    Are the immortal seeds,
Nourish'd by blood and tears,
    That yield the fruit of liberty
    And conscience free
Through time's unresting years.

II.

The fragrance of thine old renown,
    O Germantown!
Like precious scents that never pass away,
Fills all the land e'en at this day:
    For o'er thine undulating hills
      The long street ran

Where wise Pastorius and the peaceful clan
Proclaim'd the brotherhood of man,
    And freedom for all from slavery's bonds and ills.
  A century had scarcely mark'd its score,
When through that peaceful thoroughfare
    Ran rivulets of gore,—
  The heart's blood, rich and rare,
    Of men who dared to take
The gage of battle for sweet Freedom's sake.

III.

    The crimson sun
    Rose luridly upon
The hills and vales of Germantown,
    Prefiguring the fray
    That happen'd on the day
When Washington swept down
    Upon the foreign hordes
    That lent their swords
To slay the new-born babe of Liberty.
    No drum was heard,
    No shrill fife stirr'd
The quiet of the chill October morn;
No rustling of the dry leaves of the corn
That stood in serried ranks upon the yellow lea.
    The town lay all asleep,
    While Freedom's little band
Was moving silently, with purpose stern and deep,
    Upon the haughty enemy
    Reposing nigh at hand.

IV.

    Hark the rattle of the shot!
    The booming of the gun!

The cry of quick surprise!
The battle is begun!
King George's soldiers run,
And shouts of victory arise!
While the pursuit is hurrying and hot,
The startled burghers on the long, long street,
Flee fast away with terror-quicken'd feet
O'er the wide fields, while down the travell'd way
Grape-shot and canister spread havoc and dismay.

But, lo! a fog comes murkily down
And midnight gloom o'ershadows Germantown,
And friend and foe, unseeing and unseen,
Strike random blows
Wild and unrestrain'd;
And friends mistake for foes
Their patriot brothers, till the browning green
With kindred blood is stain'd.
The foes, befriended by the darksome dew,
Fly to the fateful house of Chew,—
The fort-like mansion built of massy stone
That stands upon the verdant lawn alone.
Ensconced behind the rocky shield,
Their bullets sweep the open field,
And patriot heroes on the greensward fall,
Slain from windows of the stony hall.

O precious moments lost!
The chieftains of the foreign bands
Bring up their overpowering host
That lay upon the lower lands,
And the outnumber'd patriots
Reluctant beat
A slow retreat,
While firing at the foe the final Parthian shots.

V.

Defeat was victory!
The news ran o'er the land
How bravely fought that little band
Against the veteran hosts that came from o'er the sea;
And freemen grasp'd with firmer grip the brand,
And, trusting in the Lord, determined to be free.

The long, long night of war lay on the land;
But in the seventh year
The Sabbath-day of freedom broke
The darkness drear,
And, freed from tyrant's yoke,
Sweet, gentle Peace dropp'd gifts with plenteous hand.

VI.

The enfranchised country grew apace in strength,
Despite old Europe's supercilious ban,
Until at length
The youngest-born of nations led the van.
And yet a stain upon her forehead lay!
She, who had wrench'd the manacles away
From her own hands,
Still held in captive sway
The stolen sons of Afric's sunny lands.
The wrong begat a curse that grew amain,
Perverting heart and brain,
Till hatred's gall tinged artery and vein,
And friend and fellow scowl'd upon each other.
As once the infant land unkindly
Was smitten by the angry mother,
So now the infuriate Southron blindly
Turn'd in wild wrath upon his Northern brother.

The gates of Hades open'd wide again:
The guns that boom'd on Sumter struck the knell
        Of half a million men,
        Stark dead, or sorely wounded.
A doom more dire than Cain's upon the nation fell:
    The trump of war o'er all the land was sounded:
        From Pennsylvania's mountains
            To farthest Southern shore
        A thousand crimson fountains
            With kindred blood ran o'er;
And many a homestead wept a hero dead,
And Rachels that would not be comforted
        Sat by the desolated hearth.
            Ah! wrathful day
            Well pass'd away
    Forever and forever from the earth!
Ah me! the sin, the unrepented sin,
That brought the avenging time of retribution in!

                    VII.

No son of thine or denizen is he,
        Wherever he may roam,
    Over the wide, wide world, or up or down,
  Who says not, when he dwells again at home,
There is no town in lands beyond the sea
    More beautiful than thou, O Germantown!
Yet pleasant homes nor loving ones could stay
The valiant men who, hastening away
        With hurried step, rush'd to the battle-field,
            And, looking not behind,
        Made their own breasts the shield
            To ward the blows
    Of weapons held by brave, misguided foes,
            Encarnadined

With blood from kindred veins.
Let the page historic tell
The crimson'd battle-plains
Where many a strong man fell:—
Enough to bid the grateful verse
On this auspicious day rehearse
How victory swept the cloud of war away,
And rainbow'd peace athwart the heavens lay.

VIII.

Beneath the peaceful skies,
And with the Father's smile,
We dedicate this pile
To sacred memories
Of men of elder as of modern day,
Whose place of burial, to man unknown,
Is all unmark'd by monumental stone:—
To nameless heroes slumbering in the sea,
The sighing winds their ceaseless lullaby,
Who seem, as 'twere, to need more care of God
Than they who sleep beneath the churchyard sod:—
We dedicate this pile to the dead brave who share
The grassy resting-places of the town,
Enwreathed by loving hands in flowery May
With garlands fragrant, and as Eden fair,
And grander in the Father's eye than monarch's
jewell'd crown.

IX.

The land of all the lands by Heaven most blest!
Who strikes at her doth strike at Freedom's breast.
If she must bleed, let not the blow
Be dealt by children's hands again,

But by a common foe,
The foe of God and freedom-loving men.

O North! O South! O East! O West!
Away with jealousy, suspicion, hate!
Joint heritors are ye of one estate,
Forevermore to hold;
Ample and broad, so fill'd with bread and meat,
The recompense of honest toil,
That ye might welcome all the world to eat:—
A land whose hills are iron, coal, and gold,
Whose valleys run with oil:—
A land of God and gracious charities
That heal the mind and give the sufferer ease,—
Yea, every ill assuage,
From orphan'd infancy to helpless age:—
A land of freedom for right deed and thought,
The just and equal law its only king,
Which none may set at naught.
What would ye more?
What lacks your earthly store?
O happy land! to God thank-offerings bring!
Let the dead past, and all its curse and scorn,
Be buried, with no resurrection morn!
Stand forth, O land, in unity and might,
Loving the good and true, and valorous for the right!
Down to the unreturning depths be hurl'd
All things by God abhorr'd,
And stand thou ever forth a blessing to the world—
To the glory of the Lord!

A BALLAD BY THE SEA.

AT mid of night beside the sea,
   The moon far in the west,
I sigh'd for one long gone from me
Who day by day still seems to be
   A dweller in my breast.

And suddenly a stranger came
   As if from out the tide,
A man of bow'd yet stalwart frame,
Whose face I knew not, nor his name,
   And sat him by my side.

He laid his brawny arm on mine,
   That old man by the sea;
His locks were hoar with age and brine;
His eyes with tender gleams did shine;
   A winsome man was he.

"Comrade!" so spake the ancient man,
   "A good God loves us all.
This world is order'd by a plan
Too broad for thee or me to scan,
   That covers great and small.

Why hug a sorrow to thy heart
   And nurse it till it bite?
Why chafe the wound until it smart?
Why turn against thyself the dart,
   And thine own bosom smite?

In other years—how long ago,
  Comrade, I cannot tell—
In sun and shine, in rain and snow,
When all was calm, when storms did blow,
  I served a skipper well.

I saved his life and risk'd mine own;
  A daughter fair had he;
Before another year had run
The skipper own'd me as a son,
  'My husband!' whisper'd she.

I built a cottage near the shore:
  Next-door to heaven it seem'd;
For love came in the open door,
And from the rafters to the floor
  Its blessed presence beam'd.

The God in whom we trusted sent
  A babe of beauty there,
And as the seasons came and went,
They added, to our glad content,
  Two more as sweet and fair.

I went a voyage o'er the sea,
  My heart still staying home;
O'er many a sea and far country
For wife-sake and our children three
  I was content to roam.

My wandering journey o'er, I sought
  My cot beside the sea,
For love and treasure I had brought,
Beyond my boyhood's wildest thought,
  For wife and children three.

My home of love I stood before;
  The windows gave no light:
Trembling, I knock'd upon the door,
A neighbour only said, ' No more !'
  My heart fell dead that night.

The years pass on, no longer told;
  I leave it in God's hand
To share among His poor the gold
I strove so long to gain and hold;
  And now I walk the strand,

And when the wrecking winds do sweep
  A vessel on the shore,
In my good life-boat forth I leap
To aid the strugglers in the deep,
  As Christ hath done before.

Now, comrade, ere with thee I part
  This only will I say:
Go heal the sorrows of thy heart
(No matter whosoe'er thou art)
  By doing good alway."

A far-off look was in his eyes,
  As if he saw away
Beyond the sea the blessèd skies,
Where no one weeps and no one sighs,
  Where God's belovèd stay.

The ancient man arose and sped
  His way along the sea;
I ponder'd on the words he said,
And pray'd, before I sought my bed,
  To be as wise as he.

THE OLD MAN OF MINNEQUA.

A DAPPER old man came over the hills,
    Came over to Minnequa:
In bearing erect and as prim as a prig;
His whiskers and beard and his long-flowing wig
    The whitest that ever you saw;

A spry little wight, with a queer chapeau
    Of the mythical days of yore;
With hosen of silk and gold-buckle shoon,
And trousers and vest of the skin of the coon,
    As folk of antiquity wore.

To the place of the waters of healing he came
    As the sun sank wearily down;
Seeking to charm away sickness and care,
The old and the young were gathering there
    From cities of olden renown.

" From the ends of the earth, good people, I come,
    From wanderings hither and yon,
To drink again of the health-giving fount,
Where I play'd in my youth at the base of this mount
    Ten thousand summers agone.

" I've drank in the East, I've drank in the West,
    And the farthermost North and the South,
And my feet have traversed the earth around,
But not a drop of water I've found
    So sweet as this to my mouth."

The people made way for the dapper old man;
　To the brink of the fountain he rush'd;
While six dozen men with buckets did dip,
He emptied each vessel with ease at a sip,
　As fast as the waters up-gush'd.

He drank and he drank till the sun went down,
　And he drank through all the night;
And day after day he was drinking still;
And it verily seem'd he never would fill,
　So thirsty the gray old wight.

He drank till he grew much bigger than two
　Of his former self, and soon
The buckles of both of his shoes were rent,
And zigzagging into the air they went,
　Like aerolites shot from the moon.

He drank and he drank till his coat was split,
　So great was the mighty strain;
And the buttons flew off to the regions atop,
Like corks from bottles of new ginger-pop,
　Or Widow Clicquot's champagne:

And they were all turn'd to ethereal dust,
　Thin nebulæ just begun;
And scientists now of our much-learnèd age,
Who scan every dot in philosophy's page,
　Find metals in rays from the sun.

The dippers a-weary then ceasing to dip,
　The drinker dropp'd off in a nap,
And snored so loudly he cracked the air
And burst the bands of the Delaware
　And open'd the Water-Gap.

That noise of noises resounded through
  The atmospherical halls:
It scoop'd Niagara's bottom, and threw
The rocks high up in the ether blue,—
  So came the wonderful Falls.

And into the famed St. Lawrence stream,—
  A distance of many miles,—
Swiftly descended the cloud of rocks,
As from a gigantic pepper-box,
  And founded the Thousand Isles.

Along the banks of Seneca Lake
  It deafen'd the ears of men ;
It split with its invisible wedge,
Driven by some Herculean sledge,
  Wide open the Watkins Glen.

In stellar realms such a racket was made
  Polaris was twisted askew,
And one of the Pleiades fell into fits,
And splinter'd to infinitesimal bits,
  And faded forever from view.

The monkey-tribes in the cocoanut climes,
  Where the summer-time never fails,
Were smitten with such a tremulent fright
That some became hairless and others turn'd white,
  And some were stripp'd of their tails.

The Darwinite lights of this ignorant world,
  Engender'd when time was old,
Aver in our day that the untailèd elves
Were fathers of sages,—perchance of themselves,
  If the fact must squarely be told.

The vast concussion squeezed all the hills
   That held bituminous coals;
The deep-hidden stores of oil oozed out,
And fill'd the cavernous depths thereabout   •
   And subterranean holes.

From far Alaska to Florida sands
   And the tropical Indian isles
The world was stunn'd by the thundering sound,
And men fell down in a sudden swound
   Through seventy thousand miles.

The nations all stopp'd their ears, and they held
   Their temples between their hands,
Till the snoring suddenly ceased one day,
And a most stupendous silence lay
   On all the seas and lands,

Until he sneezed a horrible sneeze,
   A sort of volcanic puff.
Alas! the sneezer was instantly kill'd,
For it seem'd as if his nose had been fill'd
   With a thousand pounds of snuff.

The Indians were holding a grand pow-wow
   In a grove beyond the spring;
The squaws and warriors leap'd at the sound,
And dived six fathoms beneath the ground,
   A very unusual thing.

At the same moment his eyes, shooting out,
   Sped up to the region of stars:
In after ages the Washington man,
Whose curious eyes the firmament scan,
   Announced two moons of Mars.

The skies grew dark and a hurricane blew,
  Bending the trees like a fan ;
And some toppled over, and others were bent,
And others upon their brotherhood leant,
  As man often leans upon man.

The body was borne by the cyclonic wave
  Like a boat on a billowy swell ;
The arms of the wind let him suddenly drop
Upon a broad hillock's velvety top
  That rises before the hotel,

Where his bones were turn'd into trappean rock,
  His muscles to arable clay,
And the lapse of the ages rounded his form,
As all unheeding the sunshine or storm
  The wonder of Minnequa lay.

Now from the porch of the Minnequa House,
  On any clear day, may be seen
His form roughly traced on the hillocky crest,
Like a half-a-mile giant taking his rest,—
  Majestic, reposeful, serene.

The folk who stick to the straight line of truth,
  And go just as far as it goes,
May deem this tale an incredible myth,
Like Helen of Troy, or Captain John Smith,
  But all I can say is: Who knows?

THE BROOK OF WATKINS GLEN.

A WAYWARD rill
   On the top of the mount
Stole softly away
   From its mother-fount,
And, sliding adown the mountain-breast
That gently sloped away from the west,
   It tripp'd along,
     Happy and gay,
   Singing a song
    Upon the way.

Stronger it wax'd, and broader it grew,
   And it gleam'd in the sunlight,
   And glitter'd in moonbright,
And danced in the shadows the great trees threw.

   When its glee was high,
    It struck the ravine
   And fell with a cry
    'Twixt rocks mossy-green,—
     Rocks all ragged,
     Cragged, jagged,
   In wild confusion piled,—
     All fissure-rent,
     Twisted and bent,
   Like chaos itself run wild.

Dashing and plashing,
It rumbled and tumbled,
And danced and pranced
In maddest riot,
Taking a leap
Down many a steep,
Then slowly creeping
And almost sleeping
In pools of heavenly quiet;
And, after its holiday rest,
Plunging again
Adown the glen,
As though in quest
Of something newer,
Better, truer,
Hidden away
In a coming day.

Slow moving through cathedral halls,
    Where solemn reverence holds her seat,
Next plunging down 'twixt narrow walls
    Beyond access of mortal feet;
Now twisting like a snake a-fright,
    Now quivering like a bridal veil;
Now emerald-hued, now dark as night,
    Now brilliant as a peacock's tail;
Now slaking thirst of bird and brute,
    Now sheltering fish at every turn;
Now giving nourishment to root
    Of clinging moss and elfin fern;
Now on the cliff the passer-by
    Charming by its unceasing hum,
Till gentle thoughts that light his eye
    Within his lonely bosom come.

So the brook on sped
  Its varying way,
While the day grew night
  And the night grew day,
And ever, like a restless soul,
It hasten'd to its final goal.
    But cliffs still tower'd,
    And shadows lower'd,
    And rocks stood out
    To hedge about
The path of the struggling rill,
    And it struggled in vain
    Till the clouds gave rain,
    And the torrents fell,
And the brook began to grow and fill,
    And its veins began to swell:
  With the heavenly aid,
    Again it sped
    On its widening bed,
  Its progress all unstay'd,
Until it found its home and rest
In Seneca's enfolding breast.

So, men and brethren! is our life:
The toil, the rest, the peace, the strife,
But school us for the heavenly place
In God's good way and God's good grace.

RAIN IN THE MOUNTAINS.

AQUARIUS took a walk one day
        And Bacchus met him on the way;
They idly chatted as they went
Until they came to Bacchus' tent.
Aquarius set his water-pot
Beside him in a handy spot;
And Bac, as he was wont to do,
Of wine brought out a jug or two.
The water-god,—too many such,—
Imbibed till he had far too much; .
And when to sit upright unable,
He fell asleep beneath the table.
" Now," cries sly Bac, " I'll play a joke
On Minnewaska's temperate folk :
I'll give them water quite enough
To make them cry out *Quantum suff.*"
Aq's water-pot he then upset,
And mount and plain o'erflow'd with wet.
The fogs hid all the world away
From mountain-folk day after day,
Till the hotel all lonely sat
Like Noah's ark on Ararat.

But rain nor clouds nor darkness quell'd
    The joyous life above the Lake;
For still the cheerful chatting swell'd,
    And still the song of gladness brake,—
Until the echoes woke old Aq;
    And, springing up in sore dismay,

He spilt the wine of cunning Bac,
  And took his pot and went his way
To Juno straight, and begg'd her soon
To give the earth a dry new-moon.

In queenly style she made reply,
(A queen could not such suit deny :)
"At ten o' the clock this very night
The moon, in infant robes bedight,
High in the heavens shall hang her horn,
Precursor of a clearing morn ;
And nightly shall she glow more bright
To whispering lovers' fond delight ;
A crystal clearness in the air
Shall make the landscape doubly fair ;
No rain upon the mount shall pour
Save in the morn from one to four."

Then old Aquarius left the queen :
The weeping skies became serene,
And glorious splendors fill'd the earth
Soon as the sweet young moon had birth ;
And vale and mountain, beauty-clad,
Shouted for joy, and man was glad.

LAKE MOHONK.

GIRDLED by the Shongum Mountains,
 Sentinel'd by Eagle's Nest,
Mohonk, daughter of the fountains,
 Seems a gem on beauty's breast.

Like a child that, loved of Heaven,
 Bears the peace-marks of His grace,
By His unseen finger graven
 On the trustful, earnest face,

Thus the rippling Mohonk's seeming
 To my restful eye to-day,
As I sit and gaze, half-dreaming,
 At the waters' gentle play.

Strange that scene so softly quiet
 Follow'd æons of crash and rage,
When the Lord's almighty fiat
 Form'd creation's title-page!

Chaos, darkness, overtumbling;
 Gas mephitic, vapours dire;
Lightning, earthquakes, thunders rumbling;
 All the world in molten fire :—

Twisting, shrivelling, torn asunder,
 Mountains lifting up their crests,
Splitting with the crash of thunder
 Down, far down their rocky breasts :—

Coldness of the Arctic Ocean
  Numbing lands and seas and streams,
Silence follows wild commotion,
  As a sleep succeeding dreams.

Nature travails till He pleaseth,
  And the child of pain is born :
At His word the tumult ceaseth,
  And His light awakes the morn.

Thus the pageant sweeps before me,—
  Chaos, in God's fitting time,
Ushering in the day of glory
  Pictured in Miltonic rhyme.

With no sin of man assoiling,
  Earth a paradise were found ;
Yet, with all of sin's despoiling,
  Beauty lingers still around.

Glory crowns the lake and mountain ;
  Beauty smiles on hill and vale ;
Music of the bird and fountain
  Echoes downward to the dale ;

Winds of balm around me stealing,
  Scented with the fragrant pine,
Giving comfort, strength, and healing,
  More than dwell in oil and wine.

And the worn and weary gather,
  And the glad and hopeful come,
Where the children of the Father
  Catch some glimpses of their home.

Rest, O soul! nor nurse thy sorrow;
　　Garner strength upon thy way;
Take not worries of the morrow;
　　Christ will help thee day by day.

Rest is faithful labour's guerdon;
　　Soon, with spirit brave and strong,
Thou canst bear again life's burden,
　　Singing hope's uplifting song.

A FIFTY-YEARS' VOYAGE.

Mr. and Mrs. William B. Bement's Golden Wedding, Jan. 26, 1890.

A YOUTH and a maiden,
　　Love-welded together
Embark'd in a vessel
　　In sunshiny weather,
To go on a voyage
　　Without knowing whither;
And Hope hung her pennant
　　High up on the mast,
As softly they scudded
　　Or sped along fast.

A crew came aboard
　　As they sail'd on their way,
And chubby-faced sailors,
　　And hearty, were they.
They came aboard singly,
　　Dropp'd down from above,
And got for their living
　　Full rations of love:

A crew well assorted
  Of girls and of boys,
Some paying in beauty,
  The others in noise.

They sail'd in the sunshine;
  They sail'd in the storm;
They sail'd in north countries;
  They sail'd in the warm.
Blow hot and blow cold,
  The vessel went on:
They tugg'd at the oars
  When fair winds were gone.
They touch'd at the islands
  Where gold did abound,
They gather'd the treasures
  That lay all around.
The vessel full laden,
  A storehouse of good,
They lifted the anchor
  And homeward she stood.

Their heads were grown wintry;
  For full fifty years
The good ship had taken
  To compass the spheres.
Now peacefully riding,
  The vessel no more
Shall go out to sea
  Far away from the shore.
And may the Great Master,
  The Lord of the seas,
At last bring her safe
  To the haven of peace.

THE POET ANATHEMATIZETH THE MOSQUITO.

YE agile, fragile, marsh-begotten sprites!
 Ye airy, fairy dwellers by the sea!
Tiny in frame, but mighty in your bites;—
 Big as a goose, what devils ye would be!
Ye stripe-legg'd, gossamer-wingëd imps of spite,
Secret and sly, like thieving sneaks ye light
 With footfall soft on man's unguarded skin,—
His neck, his ear, his finger, or his nose,
Or any part unarmour'd by his clothes,—
 And deftly stick your poison'd lancets in,
And suck his blood until ye wellnigh burst.
 Ye slim, attenuated wretches! ye
 Wing-gifted congeners of the jumping flea!
By all are ye unanimously curst!

No pity do ye show to man or beast,
 To tender infant or to maiden fair,
 Nor reverence pay to winter-frosted hair,—
All are your prey, the greatest and the least.
 Ye Ishmaelitish Arabs! I would know
Your right to run a muck by night and day
And stealthily take the blood of man away,
 From head unwigg'd to unprotected toe.
I'll smite ye, villains! and will give no quarter:
 I'll smoke ye, burn ye, smash ye, break your head;
 Asphyxiate and choke ye with the rage
Of sulphur, pennyroyal, camphor-water,
 Till the last culex lies before me dead,
 Known nevermore save in sciential page.

A QUEST FOR THE SEA-WIND.

LOST, a wind,—a wind from the sea!
　　It wander'd away,
　The weathercocks say,
'Twixt the rise of the moon
　And the dawn of the day.
It may have gone, of its own wild will,
　Away to the far nor'west,
To ramble over some piney hill
　With a mantle of ice on its crest.
It may have fallen unaware
　Into a quiet sleep
In some far palace of the air,
　Or in the crystal deep.
If I but knew its hiding-place,
　I'd rap upon the door,
And make it frisk about apace
　Till it were fain to roar
And wreak its wrath on land and sea,
　And blow the sand amain,
And bend the head of every tree
　Upon the seaside plain,
Until its rage were fully spent
　And it should softly sing
Sweet airs unto our heart's content,
　And health and healing bring.

Where is the wind, the good sea-wind,
　That fann'd us yesterday?
A gift for him whose wit can find
　The truant gone astray.

O man who sitteth in the steeple
  Built beside the sea,
Who in the morning tells the people
  The weather that's to be,
Where is the wind that yesternight
Blew o'er the ocean fresh and light?
Why kept ye not a stricter watch
  While we were all a-dream?
Why did ye not the urchin catch,
  Bind him to morning's beam,
And hand him over to the East,
  Or to the East-by-South,
A prisoner, not to be released
  By any word of mouth
Till sweet September in her grace
  Begins her queenly reign,
And comfort gives to every place
  From Florida to Maine?

But idle is my quest, O man
  That sitteth in the tower!
Though skillful ye the clouds to scan,
  Too hard I task your power.
Yet still I cry, this quiet day,
  Where has the sea-wind fled?
And still I sigh for its soothing play
  About my fever'd head.
      But lo! a faint puff
      Comes shyly along
        O'er the low Jersey shore,
      Merely enough,
      Like a far-distant song,
To stir up the senses with longings for more.
O wind from the sea! come back to your home,
And lift up the waves until they roll proudly,—

Till they break into foam,
  And the surf shall sing loudly:
To the worn and the weary,
  Escaped from the city,
  Show the grace of sweet pity,
And make their souls cheery!

A BATTLE-HYMN.

GOD defend thee, land of nations!
    Mother of the brave and free,
E'en amid thy desolations
  Stronger grows our love for thee.

Comrades! be our motto ever,
  Faithful to our country's trust!
Though we give our lives, yet never
  Shall our mother kneel in dust.

By the love we bear that mother,
  By the duty children owe,
Faithfully by one another
  Stand we till we crush her foe.

Let the hail of bullets rattle,—
  Hostile weapons line the field,—
In the day of freedom's battle
  God Almighty is our shield.

When the cloud of war is riven,
  Peace shall like a rainbow shine;
They who for the right have striven
  Coming ages shall enshrine.

THE OLD MAN OF SKY-TOP.

THE clouds came a-peering
   O'er Sky-Top one day,
And look'd at the lake
   While tripping away.

"Old Man of the Mountain,"
   They halted to say,
"Do you want any water?
   If so, we will stay."

"No! no!" grumbled he,
   "I have more than enough;
Go away! go away!"
   And his accent was gruff.

"Why, what is the matter,
   You crusty old chap?
We'll stir up your bones
   With a smart thunder-clap."

So they fired a volley
   Terrific and dread,
Which startled him so
   That he popp'd out his head

At the point of the cliff;
   And his fear was so vast
That he turn'd into stone,
   And stuck hard and fast.

They threw a fleece veil
  All over his head;
But when it was lifted
  They saw he was dead.

Then off they went packing,
  The nimbus below
And the cumulus high
  And whiter than snow.

They wildly flew over
  The Shandaken hills,
Nor stopp'd till they jostled
  The tall Kauterkills,

And all the wild reaches
  That lie to the Nor'ard,
And Overlook winks at
  From the eye in his forehead;

And there overtaken
  By Night's chilly breath,
With over-much weeping
  They pined unto death.

But the stony Old Man
  Of the Mount shall remain
While the Shawngunks shall stand,
  In sunshine and rain.

In a tempest, 'tis said,
  The old fellow cries,
And tears in a torrent
  Run down from his eyes.

In the silence of eve
  A double-bass word,
That sounds like " Ter-choonk !"
  May also be heard.

And any who listen
  On a high windy night
May still hear him whistle
  With ear-piercing might.

Don't say I'm a rhymer,
  Much given to quiz;
You can see for yourself
  His petrified phiz.

WATKINS GLEN.

O MIGHTY rift! Cleft in the far-off time
    Ere God created man, when darkness lay
Upon the deep; ere yet in swampy slime
Vast creatures gambol'd in their awkward play,
  Or birds flew in the air, or fishes fann'd
Their fins in the cool waters; when the sun
  And moon and stars shone on a silent land,
Void of inhabitant, life unbegun :
  Silent from noisy life alone; for, lo !
The lightning flash, the peal, the earthquake
    shock,
The rush of waters and the crash of rock
  Rack'd the rent world as with an utter woe,
Till God call'd peace and order on the earth,
And man's first home was fitted for man's birth.

O mighty rift! Mysterious whispers fill
   All its profoundest depths, solemn and dread,
   As if intoning requiems for the dead.
Anon I hear the rushing of the rill,
   Quick tripping from the canyon's upper crown,
Merry and musical, leaping adown
   The sudden steeps, and falling fast asleep—
Like children after play—in crystal pools
So quiet as to tempt life-weary fools
   To spurn the gift the good God bids them keep.
Far overhead the craggy walls let through
   Glimpses of heaven serenely fair and bright,
   Promises of rest in upper realms of light
For the brave soul that dares to bear and do.

O mighty rift! Ages have come and gone;
   Strange forms have lived and died, and pass'd
      away,
   Whose stony bones are with us to this day;
And generations long have hasten'd on;
   Nations have risen and set in final night:
But thou, O rifted cleft, remainest still
   In all thy wondrous grandeur, beauty, might,—
A temple built at His imperial will
   To show His wonders who made all things well;
That man, His child, may marvel and adore,
   And say, while filial thanks his bosom swell,
   To God be glory, glory evermore,
Who, thronëd in His high and holy place,
Still shows on earth His glory and His grace.

THE LOVER TO HIS WIFE.

THE sunniest room in all my heart
 I keep, my love, for thee,
And set thee there from all apart,
 A shrine for none but me.

A being thou of mortal mould,
 And yet of heavenly birth,
A world all made of gems and gold
 Could not outweigh thy worth.

The song of birds, the hum of bees,
 A richer fulness takes,
As in spontaneous symphonies
 Thy voice of music wakes.

When morning puts the veil away
 That hid its beaming face,
Thine eyes unto the light of day
 Gives e'en a brighter grace.

My day of toil is light to bear,
 With all its dizzying din,
Because I feel that thou wilt share
 The boon that I may win.

When night in ebon caves ensnares
 The sun with cunning wiles,
My brow a sweet contentment wears
 Beneath thy cheery smiles.

If clouds should dim thy happy day
  And sorrow touch thy heart,
Be mine the hand to wipe away
  The teardrops as they start.

Along the way of life we'll go
  Together heart and hand;
And when our locks grow white as snow,
  Pass to the peaceful land.

"SICK, AND YE VISITED ME."

BEYOND the far Missouri
  The hunted lay in camp,
Crouching from winter's fury
  In wigwams chill and damp;
Men and women and children,
  All of a copper stamp.

The old and young were lying
  In companies and alone,
Fever'd, and sore, and dying,
  Without an audible moan;
Men and women and children
  Stoical as a stone.

Dreading not a betrayer,
  The hapless hidden lay,
But the foot of the armèd slayer
  Had track'd the snowy way,
And men and women and children
  Were scented out as prey.

List to the rifle's riot !
   Hark to the musket's din !
Amid the desolate quiet
   Hell's ravages begin:
Men and women and children
   All safely trapp'd within.

The astounded wretches wonder,
   Gazing with startled eye,
The leaden rain and thunder
   Passing not harmless by :
Men and women and children
   By white men's bullets die.

Say ! shall we lift the pæan,
   And sound it o'er the land !
A band of sickly heathen
   Falling beneath the brand,
Men and women and children,
   At a soldier's grim command !

Though squaw nor babe were pretty,
   Nor warrior bold and brave,
It seems a horrible pity
   To sweep into the grave
Men and women and children
   Without a prayerful stave.

O people of the nation,
   Who cuddle the ebon race,
Why look with detestation
   On folk of coppery face ?—
Men and women and children—
   For these has God no grace ?

THE BELLES AT HATHAWAY'S.

THE billows haste along the strand
 To kiss the footprints in the way
Made by the maidens on the sand
 When sporting in the briny spray.
  O greedy billows! ye should be
  Most sharply chidden.   Why so free
With the belles at Hathaway's—
   The witty belles,
   The pretty belles,
The graceful belles at Hathaway's!

The breezes from the spicy pines,
 The fragrant ferns, and clover dells,
Steal underneath the bonnet lines,
 And kiss the lips of all the belles.
  O breezes! bold and wanton ye
  To take such wilful liberty
With the belles at Hathaway's—
   The witty belles,
   The pretty belles,
The charming belles at Hathaway's.

Amid the mazes of the dance
 The music whispers witching spells,
Enwrapping in delicious trance
 The senses of the wilder'd belles.
  O music! how I envy thee
  Such fond familiarity
With the belles at Hathaway's—
   The witty belles,
   The pretty belles,
. The gentle belles at Hathaway's.

5*

EVERY-DAY INDICATIONS.

THE weather will be rainy, clear,
   Or just a little mix'd,
Unless the brakes get out of gear
   By which the thing is fix'd.

Should there be rain, 'twill fall in drops
   That come down pit-a-pat,
And sprinkle o'er the shingle tops
   Of houses, and all that.

The mercury will not go up
   Unless the day grow hot;
The clouds be but an empty cup
   Save in some local spot.

No barometric fall we'll see
   Unless a fierce cyclone
Whirl in potential energy
   Up from the Torrid Zone.

The sky will don its robe of blue
   Envail'd in cloudlets rare;
And birds will sail the ether through
   Like wingëd ships of air.

The lake like liquid gems to-day
   Will dazzle with its shimmer,
Until the sun shall hide away
   And all the world grow dimmer.

And man another step will take
  Along the way of life :
Some hearts with sudden grief will break,
  Some nobly bear the strife.

The helplessness of babyhood
  Will be its strong defence ;
For mother-hearts hath God endued
  With love's omnipotence.

The maiden fair will list to speech
  Wherein love's witcheries run ;
Affection's depths the words will reach,
  And two hearts fuse in one.

From whom the grave has taken most
  That he had loved the best,
That man will walk amid a host
  In loneliest unrest.

Oft will he speak in lightsome tones
  The while his thoughts arise
And reach out for the absent ones
  That live beyond the skies.

For 'neath a quiet smile may lie
  A sorrow of the soul
That needs a daily victory
  To hold it in control.

A few may run an easy pace
  With self-reliant boast :
But God e'er gives to those his grace
  Who seek and need it most.

And they who bear the battle's brunt,
  And temper'd weapons wield,
Will stand up grandly in the front
  And hold the conquer'd field.

God's rank and file, in battle line
  And truth's divine array,
Will set their camp at day's decline
  Along the King's highway

To that good land, by sense unknown,
  That land whose name is Heaven,
Where Christ doth gather all his own,
  And crowns of life are given.

A SEASIDE NOTION.

PEQUOT! Pequot!
    The Paradise spot
Where ocean embraces the river;
    Right royal is she
    With her foot on the sea,
    As she sits like a queen
    Of exquisite mien:
What prettier name shall we give her?

    While poets have sung
    In the old English tongue
In verses pellucid as water,
    No word could be found,
    In all the world round
    To its furthermost bound,
    Sweet enough in its sound
To give to its loveliest daughter.

King Philip came down
One night to the town
To write a pet name he had got her;
And he traced on the sand
Of the westerly strand
The name of the race
Once lords of the place;
And this was the legend—Pequotta.

Oh! sad to be said,
Before it was read,
The surf coming up, like a blotter,
Expunged the t a
So completely away
That the title was shorn
Ere the coming of morn,
And Pequot took the place of Pequotta.

LUNA AND ÆOLUS.

THE beautiful moon
Had a tear in her eye,
For she wept as the motherly
Summer pass'd by,
To lay down her head
In Eternity's lap
And sleep with her sisters
An unwaking nap.

The Wind-Tyrant whistled,
A-mocking her woe,
Till she flew like a skylark
From regions below.

And the giant went hunting
  In earth and in air
To find the young moon
  In her far-away lair.

He ranged in the darkness,
  He ranged in the day,
And fierce-dashing torrents
  He brought into play!
But Luna, protected
  By heavenly bars,
Far in the up-regions
  Held court with the stars.

Around the high peaks,
  Like a beast out of cage,
He howl'd, but the mountain
  Derided his rage.
He dash'd at the lake,
  Yet his fury was vain,
For its waters took captive
  The torrents of rain.

The strength of the Wind-King
  All futilely spent,
To his cavern, outwitted,
  He sullenly went,
When the moon in her beauty
  Rose sweetly serene,
And new-born September
  Saluted her queen!

THE HOUSE BEAUTIFUL.

A HOME for the sisters of Christ,
    For the mothers in Israel,
Who have borne the worries of life
    So lovingly, long, and well :—
Who have given their beautiful youth
    And the wisdom of matronly days
To the sweet little duties of home,
    In womanhood's winsomest ways:—
In the gentle neighbourly deeds
    And the helpful accents of cheer,
In the charities born of His love
    To the soul of the suffering dear.
But few, in the face of the world,
    Are called to do notable things,—
Yet all have a labour to do,
    The people as well as the kings.
As in the sight of the Lord,
    The mite of the widow is more
Than manifold gifts of the great,
    Grudgingly out of their store,—
So the small daily duties well done,
    And all for the love of the Lord,
More precious than deeds of renown,
    Shall meet with His gracious reward.
And right and fitting it is,
    When age has weaken'd the limb,
To shelter the sisters of Christ,
    As service render'd to Him.
Ye wards of the church of the Lord,
    His arms around you are thrown !

O rest in this beautiful home
Till Christ shall beckon His own
To that far-away home in the skies
That He has gone to prepare,—
The heavenly mansion of rest
Which all His children shall share.

SEND-OFF RHYMES

*On Mr. and Mrs. Richard Smith's departure for Carlsbad,
June 20, 1885.*

SOFTLY-SPEEDED be the gale,
    And quieted the water,
As o'er the summer seas ye sail,
Till old Germania's coast ye hail,
    O Philadelphia's earnest son !
    O Philadelphia's gentle daughter !

Health and comfort be the boon
    Of healing Carlsbad's water,
And may God's heavenly blessing soon
Set heart and nerve in perfect tune,
    O Philadelphia's manly son !
    O Philadelphia's lovely daughter !

Hidden in Bohemia's vale,
    The vale of healing water,
Your tenderest thoughts will never fail
To run along the homeward trail
To all whose hearts forget you not
While biding in their native spot,
    O Philadelphia's friendly son !
    O Philadelphia's kindly daughter !

GARFIELD.

THERE'S darkness over every land;
  The hearts of men are failing;
Man takes his fellow by the hand,
In nearer brotherhood they stand;—
  For all the earth is wailing.

There's sorrow in the hut and hall;
  The bells of death are tolling;
The sun is hidden by a pall;
In whelming billows, over all
  The tide of grief is rolling.

Loved Britain's queen of grace and worth,
  The proudest thrones of power,
The millions high or low in birth,—
Yea, all the peoples of the earth
  Are one in sorrow's hour.

'Tis not that bloody-handed war
  A nation's strength has broken;
No pestilence has swept the shore,
Nor famine left in any door
  Its grim and deathly token.

A cruel, vile, accursèd blow
  The world's great soul has smitten;
It laid a man heroic low,
And lines of deep and bitter woe
  On countless hearts are written.

Up to the Majesty on high
  Unceasing prayer ascended;
And kneeling millions wonder why
A righteous God should let him die
  For whom their prayers contended.

'Tis true, a serpent strikes the heel,
  And man sinks down to perish;
And swift diseases from us steal
The loved and loving, till we feel
  This life has naught to cherish.

Yet, world of weeping! question not
  Whatever God ordaineth;
He cannot err, no matter what
The seeming strangeness of the lot,—
  The Lord Jehovah reigneth!

STEALING FOR LIFE.

HO! send the woman to jail,
  She's only a hungry thief,
With furtive eye and cheek so pale,
  And nothing plenty but grief.
Has she stolen ten dollars' worth?
  What be it if only one?
A wretch so vile shan't walk the earth,
  So hide her away from the sun.
Constable! open the door
  And hustle her into a cell;
Drive home the bolts and fasten her sure,
  Though it seems to her like hell.

Away in a desolate room
  Her children—she has but four—
Are huddled, awaiting mother to come
  With food she can steal no more.
One is a child of seven,—
  The youngest a babe at breast,—
Hungry beneath the frozen heaven,—
  Birds in a storm-beat nest.
There's not a coal on the hearth,
  There's not a crumb on the board,
And this in the time of Christmas mirth,—
  The advent-time of our Lord!

O mothers in this great city,
  With babes in a downy bed,—
O fathers, have ye no pity
  For a mother stealing for bread?
Remember, she is a woman,
  And her babes were starving and cold:
She stole because she was human,
  And not from hunger of gold.
'Twas more in the doing than willing,
  For in want the conscience is dumb.—
A prison for stealing a shilling,
  A palace for filching a plum!

A YEAR OF WEDDED LIFE.

NOW Leaf the First of wedded life
    Has just been written and turn'd over,
And not a blot or stain of strife
    The keenest vision can discover.

Adown the page are lasting lines,
  Invisible save to the writers;
And these shall be as token-signs
  Of God's good grace to the inditers :—

Records alike of joys and cares
  That link true souls more close together,
(For life has hours of damp, cold airs
  As well as days of sunny weather):—

Records of friendships that abide
  Like fragrance in Damascus roses,
Whose perfume, breathed on every side,
  An ever-during charm discloses:—

Records of many a deed and aim
  Born of true love and gentle kindness,—
As quick to praise as slow to blame,
  And showing oft a prudent blindness:—

Of works of ruth for Jesus' sake,
  And helpful words in pity spoken,
To soothe the sorrow and the ache
  Felt by the silent spirit-broken :—

Ay! many a line too sweet and pure
  For the rash inquest of the poet
Is written there:—may each endure
  To cheer their hearts who only know it.

May the New Leaf, more rich and rare
  Than any found in fiction's story,
Be fill'd with records bright and fair
  To the dear Master's praise and glory!

LOST, A HEART.

Has anybody seen a heart
  That somehow got astray
About the springs of Minnequa?
A maiden saw, or thought she saw,
  The wanderer yesterday.

The maiden in the evening glow
  Was drinking at the spring,
And when my pathway she had crost
I found that I had somehow lost
  My bosom's dearest thing.

This heart is not a carnal heart,
  But an ethereal sprite,
That none but love-anointed eyes,
By natural instinct shrewdly wise,
  Can captivate on sight:—

An honest heart, as full of love
  As roses full of scent;—
If it has joined itself unto
Another heart as sound and true,
  Then were I well content.

But till I find if this be true,
  I ask, where did it go?
If one should learn its whereabout,
Beyond an if, a but, or doubt,
  Please let the loser know.

6*

THE FIRST CALLED.

HATH come on him a great and bitter sorrow,—
　　His sun of joy eclipsed by sudden night;
And when came in the tardy-moving morrow,
　　'Twas dark and cheerless to his heavy sight.

The eldest-born,—the idol of his bosom,—
　　In all the bloom of early womanhood,—
Untimely nipp'd like a maturing blossom,
　　Droop'd at his feet as in amaze he stood!

Though heavenly-moulded in her outward seeming,
　　Though heavenly-temper'd in her inner mind,
It enter'd never in his vaguest dreaming
　　That she must die. God help him! he was blind.

Dear pitying friends, his speechless grief partaking,
　　Cross'd her fair arms and closed her loving eyes;
Robed in pure white, the while his heart was
　　　　breaking,
　　They laid in earth the daughter of the skies.

And now he goes among his fellow mortals,—
　　And while he mingles in their busy din
His thoughts are knocking at the heavenly portals
　　To seek an audience with the blest within.

Far in the night, when cheerful men are lying
　　Cradled in slumber silent and profound,
Sad on the couch, his wakeful spirit, sighing,
　　For God's sweet comfort reaches round and round.

Then, in his grief, he names the name of Jesus,
  And on His arm he lays his heavy woes :—
"Not as I will, but as my dear Lord pleases!"
  And in His grace the spirit finds repose.

TO SOMEBODY.

I SOUGHT a diamond on the shore,
  The rarest of the rare :
A gem mine own, forevermore
  Next to my heart to wear.

I sought it far, I sought it near,
  Until my hope grew weak,
And well-nigh turn'd to utter fear
  Lest I should vainly seek.

I stood upon the farther land
  That juts out in the sea ;
A fairy wave stole up the strand
  As if to speak to me.

I bent mine ear to catch the word
  So big with fate of mine ;
My soul with ecstasy was stirr'd
  To hear the name—'twas thine !

WANTED, A COURIER.

WANTED, a courier to go in haste
To the regions far away,
Where wet Aquarius has his seat,
As the olden poets say.
Something is wrong in the water-realm,
Some rascal has broken the jars,
Or open'd the spiggots to overwhelm
The planets and lower stars.
Earth is sitting in robes of gloom
Beneath a dripping veil
Of clouds that crack with a thunderous boom
Over the hill and dale.
The rills infantile swell into streams
And the streams to rivers grow,
And they rush and they gush
Till it verily seems
They threaten all summer to flow.

Now, who will the hasty courier be?
Some maiden fair and fancy free,
And light and airy
As feather or fairy?
Or of mien majestic and port serene,
As the goddess Juno of Homer seen?
Or a youth as fleet as Mercury's heel,
With heart of fire and nerve of steel?
Or a grave old man of mind sedate
With wig and wisdom adorning his pate?
Perhaps a dozen will go together,
E'en though they be not birds of a feather.

How many they be, a dozen or one.
Let them be off by early sun,
And telephone soon the reason why
Things are askew in the upper sky,
That means be taken to catch and tether
The tricksy imps by the clerk of the weather.

THE SINKING OF THE CUMBERLAND.

AT Hampton Roads, the month was March
   In eighteen sixty-two,
A man-of-war at anchor lay,
   Ready to dare and do.

Her wooden walls were good and staunch,
   Her name the Cumberland:
Her crew and officers were brave,
   And Morris had command.

Adown the roadstead slowly came
   The Merrimack, a craft
In armour clad to water-line,
   O'er-deck, and fore to aft.

The mailèd Merrimack bore down,
   As hawk upon a lark,
And open'd all her batteries
   Upon the wooden bark.

The Cumberland, undaunted, join'd
   In battle with the foe;
Her balls, like hail against a wall,
   Went glancing to and fro.

" Surrender!" from the Merrimack
   Arose the stern command:
" No, never!" the commander cried
   On board the Cumberland.

The Cumberland fought to the death,
   Her colours at her mast,
And every man beside his gun
   Stood bravely to the last.

The Merrimack with iron prow
   Stove in the frigate's side;
And as the Cumberland went down
   Her last shot swept the tide.

Her living and her dead alike
   Sank with her 'neath the wave:
Encoffin'd in the Cumberland,
   No king hath such a grave.

For they shall live forevermore
   In story and in song,
While liberty on earth abides
   And man abhorreth wrong.

In water many fathoms deep
   The Cumberland went down:
In water but a fathom deep
   There's room enough to drown:

But he who skulks when duty calls
   May find no drop so slight,
In all the world, which would not drown
   His little soul outright.

THE ECLIPSE AND THE RAINBOW.

'TWAS yesterday, in the afternoon,
   A scene came off 'twixt the Sun and the Moon.
Demure as she seems, and modestly shy,
The Moon conceived a feminine prank
While sporting behind a cumulus-bank.
  On tiptoe stealing, in quick surprise,
    When he came by
She tipp'd the Sun a mischievous rap
    Right in the eye,
That blacken'd the cheek of the fiery chap.
The Sun in anger gave her a cuff,—
    A cuff on the ears,—
Not very severe, but quite enough
    To furrow her cheeks with tears,
Which, drenching the peopled world below,
Made all the rivulets overflow,
Till Earth cried out, in sudden dismay,
That the walls of creation had given away.

Then the Sun peep'd out from the rim of his hat,
And the people all wonder'd what he was at,
As the light-bearing shafts, speeding through air,
  Transmuted the tears of his petulant queen
To rubies and diamonds and amethysts rare.
When the circlet of beauty enveloped her form,
Forgiven, forgotten the quarrelsome storm,
  Her sovereign she kiss'd, and all was serene;
And now, in good temper, they jog on their way,
She queen of the night, he king of the day.

CRAWFORD'S NOTCH.

THE Storm-King stood in the car of his wrath,
  And drave over mountain and vale.
As chaff he swept the rocks from his path,
  And they rattled along like the hail.

The King of the Mount, awaking from sleep,
  Gave the burly invader a blow
That hurtled him down the precipitous steep,
  Far down in the valley below.

The chariot stuck in a granitic crotch,
  The horses threw backward their heels,
And kick'd out the gorge ycleped the Notch,
  And splinter'd the chariot wheels.

The beautiful lake the mountains had kept
  Imprison'd high up in the air
Through the doorway of freedom hastily swept
  And chased the Storm-King to his lair.

THE LITTLE ONE.

SHE flew away from earth below
  Unto the country of the stars,
    And angel-hands let down the bars,
    And led her in before the face
    Of One who, in his loving grace,
  Bless'd little children long ago.

THE RIVER OF RHYME.

OH for a spell of the former time,
When I dwelt beside the river of rhyme,
And the frequent thought would over me steal,
"Shall I dip a bowl of its waters for Neal?"
      To the margin I skipp'd,
         (I was younger then,)
         By a sleight of the pen
      The vessel was dipp'd;
And I drank myself, and I found the bowl
Was a pleasant draught for a thirsty soul;
And when I held it to Joseph to drink,
He look'd at me with a friendly wink,
And said it was good, and wish'd for more
Of the waters that flow'd a-past my door.
So many a time I sent him a can:
"He loved it," he said—and I loved the man,
And I was glad to give him a pleasure
As big as the span of my mind could measure;
         Until the day
When he was call'd from the world away,
         And round his clay
The friends who loved him silently wept.
A chord in my bosom suddenly snapt,
      And I, in indolence wrapt,
Left my mansion untended, unkept,
      Till it were nigh to decay.
Though it be now refurnish'd and swept,
      Yet there too seldom I stay:
But still I love to think of the time
When I dwelt beside the river of rhyme,
Where a tide of music flow'd ever along,
And every breeze was the breath of a song.

7

THE THISTLE-SIFTER.

THE sifter sitteth sifting thistles,
　　Witty as the wisest sybil,
　　Yet as silent as the Sphinx:
Ye players on tongue's silver whistles,
　　Pitch up to your highest treble
　　And tell us what she thinks.

The sifter plies her flitting fingers,
　　Flinging many a fluttering feather,
　　Filament and stamen, too:
Now in the time that never lingers
　　Gather all your wits together,
　　And guess what she will do.

The thistle-sifter still is plying
　　Fingers light, and swift, and nimble,—
　　Scattering the airy stuff
That like the feathery down is flying:
　　Lacking scissors, thread, and thimble,
　　She makes a powder-puff.

EARLY DAY.

HOW slowly and majestically comes the morning
　　sun!
His piercing rays begin to break through all the
　　vapours dun;
The morning-star grows paler, and the feebler stars
　　all hide,
The splendour of the early day extinguishing their
　　pride.

See nature rise with crimson blushes from the bed of
    night!
How silently and gracefully she clothes herself in
    light!
She sits in beauty like a bride adorn'd with jewels
    rare,
And when she speaks, all harmonies are blended in
    the air.

For cheerily, most cheerily the singing-birds awake,
And joyously in multitude their songs of praises
    break:
Soul! canst thou hear them piping thus at daybreak's
    holy hour,
And not be lifted up to GOD by love's attracting
    power?

An indistinct and humming noise now steals along
    the air:
Mankind arise from dreaming beds, and for their
    toil prepare:
Some kneel and humbly pray to GOD, while others
    go their way,
Without a blessing in their hearts, to pass a thankless
    day.

Blest be the LORD Almighty for the cheering morning
    light!
If beautiful the sun of earth when rising in his might,
Ineffable must be the Sun that rules the realms
    above,
Through an eternal day of light, of glory, and of
    love!

THE TEMPEST STILLED.

THE tempest from its airy throne descended in its
  might,
And hasten'd to the earth amid the dark and solemn
  night;
It rush'd in its mad fury o'er the face of Galilee,
When JESUS and his bosom friends were sailing on
  the sea.

Night spread her mantle o'er the skies, and hid the
  gentle light
That teaches mariners to steer their trembling ships at
  night:
The raging anger of the gale had quench'd the
  glimmering spark
Of courage in the breast of all His followers in the
  bark.

Yet JESUS slept in quietude upon the tossing sea,
(For every holy one is safe wherever he may be;)
And to him his disciples came, all wan with anxious
  fear,
And said, "O LORD, hast thou no care that we should
  perish here?"

The LORD arose in majesty amid that scene of dread,
And spake unto the tempest-gale that hurtled round
  his head:
He bade the driving winds be still, the waters rage no
  more,—
And then the heavens became serene, the waves slept
  on the shore.

O fully may the Christian trust the Arm that can
    restrain
The howling of the tempest-blast, the fury of the
    main ;
For when the hour of judgment-wrath the day of
    grace shall end,
CHRIST'S mighty arm will succour all who on His
    strength depend.

MY MOTHER KNELT IN PRAYER.

ONCE, in my boyhood's gladsome day,
    My spirits light as air,
I wander'd to a lonely room,
    Where mother knelt in prayer.

Her hands were clasp'd in fervency,
    Her lips gave forth no sound;
Yet, awe-struck, solemnly I felt
    I stood on holy ground.

My mother, all entranced in prayer,
    My presence heeded not;
And reverently I turn'd away
    In silence from the spot.

An orphan'd wanderer, far from home
    In after time I stray'd;
But GOD has kept me, and I feel
    He heard her when she pray'd.

AUTUMNAL QUIET.

THE beautiful repose of age
　　Pervades the land to-day:
The Autumn, like a reverend sage
　　With years and labour gray,
And pausing in his pilgrimage,
　　Is resting by the way.

Or like a mother, meek of eye—
　　Life's active duties o'er—
Who, when the eventide is nigh,
　　Sits calmly in the door,
And ponders on the things gone by
　　And days she knew of yore.

'Tis Nature's time of quietude
　　Before the day of dread,
When Winter in a wrathful mood
　　O'er all the land shall tread,
The leaves and flowers thickly strew'd
　　Along his pathway, dead.

What though no cheerful song of bird
　　Nor insect's merry trill
Among the barren boughs is heard,
　　There's music round me still,
What time these old brown leaves are stirr'd
　　That wither on the hill.

The rivulets are musical,
　　As hiddenly they flow

Along their gravelly beds, or fall
　　On mossy rocks below;
And sweeter notes in cot or hall
　　Are seldom heard, I trow.

I love the woods in Autumn time,
　　So quiet and so dim,
When sighing winds evoke a chime
　　From many a slender limb,
Until it seems the note sublime
　　Of some angelic hymn.

LOST, SOMEBODY'S CHILD.

SOMEBODY'S child is lost to-night!
　　I hear the bellman ring;
And the earth is frozen hard and white,
　　And the wind has a nipping sting.
I know my babes are long abed,
　　A tender, motherly hand
Laying a blessing on every head
After their evening prayers were said—
　　GOD keep the slumbering band!
Yet somebody's child is lost, I say,
　　This night so bitterly cold,
Some innocent lamb has gone astray
　　Unwittingly from its fold.
"Bellman! ho, bellman, whose child is lost?"
　　And I grasp my staff and cloak;
But the ringer over the wold had cross'd
　　Before I tardily spoke.
The neighbours soon gather, and far and near
　　We pry into ditch and fen,

Till, hark! an answering shout I hear—
    The rover is found again.
Ah! mother, fond mother, your heart is light
    With Joe to your bosom bound;
But many a child is lost to-night
    Who'll never, no, never be found.

Ay! somebody's child is lost to-night,
    While the wind is high and hoarse,
And the scudding ship, like a bird a-fright
    Flies shivering on its course.
She suddenly drops in the yawning deep
    As never to return;
She leaps atop the watery steep,
    A-creaking from stem to stern.
Hold well, good bark! for a score of lives
    Comprise thy costliest freight;
Else loving mothers, and maids, and wives
    Will ever be desolate.
And well she holds, with a single sail
    Outspread to guide her way,
While all the furies of the gale
    Around her bulwarks play.
The sailor-boy, with a fearful heart,
    Sighs for his distant home,
And the hasty tears from his eyelids start,
    And drop in the briny foam.
In the months agone a father sigh'd,
    And a mother trembled with fears;
But that father's law had he defied,
    And he scorn'd that mother's tears.
The pitiless blast now mocks his grief,
    And a huge and hungry wave
Bears him away beyond relief
    To the depths of an ocean grave.

The brand is blazing upon the hearth,
  The work of the day is done,
And the father's heart runs over the earth
  In search of the wandering son.
"Oh! where is our poor boy to-night—
  This night so bleak and wild?"
The mother shuts her eyes to the light,
  And inly prays for her child.
The busy needles all cease their flight,
  While their hearts say, "Where is he?"
They dream not he has sunken from sight,
  Down, down, down in the sea.
The mother may pray, and she may weep
  Till she weep her life away,
But never more will she find the sheep
  That wilfully went astray.

Somebody's child is lost to-night!
  Oh! sorrow is on the day
When a virgin's fame is marr'd with blight
  That cannot be cleansed away.
An humbled family sit in the gloom,
  Bemoaning their hopeless shame:
Would that she were safe in the tomb
  With honour upon her name!
While deck'd in garments of satin and sin,
  The fallen daughter, I ween,
Is scorch'd with a fever of heart within,
  Though reigning as wanton-queen.
O merciful Father! is this the child
  Thy hand created so fair,
With eyes where simple innocence smiled,
  And coy and maidenly air?
Is this the promising morning-flower,
  The brightest its rivals among?

Is this the bird that sang in the bower
    With sweetest and merriest tongue?
Ah me! this child is more than lost;
    For her low-fallen form,
On sin's voluptuous surges tost,
    Will perish in passion's storm.
And the mother may sigh, and she may weep
    Till she weep her life away,
But never more will she find the sheep
    That wickedly went astray.

Somebody's child is lost to-night—
    A widow's only son,
With brow as light and eye as bright
    As you ever look'd upon.
"And he will be my staff and stay"—
    Her words were inly spoken—
"When I am old, and my hair is gray,
    And my natural strength is broken."
Her motherly soul with pride o'erran
As the lad grew up to the estate of man,
      And she said, in her joy,
      That nobody's boy
Could match her paragon by a span.
Time stole along, and her locks were gray,
    But her heart had lost its pride;
For the man had wander'd so far astray,
    'Twere better the boy had died.
A loathsome, vile, and gibbering thing,
Stung by the poisonous still-worm's sting,
Despised of man, contemning GOD,
And gnashing at the avenging rod
Wherewith his passions scourged him sore,
Till, fainting, he could feel no more,—
Ah! somebody's child was lost in him

When he took up
The wassail cup,
And sipp'd perdition from its brim.
Then his manhood died,
And the beautiful boy
Of his mother's pride
Spill'd in the sand the cup of her joy.
Instead, she quaff'd
A wormwood draught,
A sorely-smitten woman;
Yet loved she still,
Through every ill,
The child so scarcely human.
In weariness and watchings often,
Unmurmuringly her grief she bore,
Until, unwrapt in shroud or coffin,
Her son lay dead before her door.
Her sorrows had come so thick and fast
They cluster'd round her everywhere,
Till, reason utterly overcast,
The darkness hid away her care.
Yet ofttimes would she ask for one
Long gone from home, her beautiful son;
And while she chided his long delay,
She would sigh, and whimper, and pray.
That mother will sigh, and she will weep
Till she weep her life away;
But never more will she find the sheep
That wickedly went astray.

So many children are lost to-night
That I, even I, could weep
As I hear the breathings, soft and light,
From the crib where Tommy's asleep.

And I strain my vision to pierce the clouds
  That hang over years to come;
But utter darkness the future shrouds,
  And the tongue of the seer is dumb.
So I lay them down in the bosom of grace,
  The children whom GOD has given,
Trusting he'll bring them to see his face,
  The face of our LORD in heaven.

SPRINGTIME.

THE sovereign Sun unbars the icy gates
  To let the Spring with all her train come in;
But timidly the bashful maiden waits,
  Or flees affrighted from the stormy din
And elemental strife.   While she doth stand
  In hesitance, the soft, warm southern breeze
  Steals from the isles of lime and orange trees,
And blithely Spring trips o'er the smiling land.
    Hurrah! the buds grow big;
    They burst their swaddling-bands;
      The spiral sprout
      Is shooting out,
  And grass is creeping o'er the meadow-lands.
    Hurrah! ten thousand rills
    Are hurrying down the hills;
  And, sparkling as they run,
    They symbolize the boy
    So over-full of joy
His very eyes are scintillating fun.
    Hurrah! a fly, a real fly!
With legs so slim and will so strong,
    So impudent and sly,
So busily idle all day long;

Where didst thou hide the freezing winter through?
    Hadst thou a cosey cell
    Where thou didst dwell
    When the snows fell
And the north winds blew?
    Ah! have a care, gay chap!
      For many a snare,
      In earth and air,
    Is hidden in a silken trap.

      How genial is the ray
      Of this luxurious day,
That vivifies the bosom like a thought
Of other days with happy memories fraught;
      The young-life days that seem
      But a delicious dream
That flitted o'er a brain whose vision
Glimpsed upon a scene elysian,
      Too unreal for a world
      By manhood into chaos hurl'd.
    A tear! why, sure, there's still
      A living rill
Beneath the rubbish piled upon the heart,
      That bubbles up
      And yields a cup
Of healing for a bosom-smart.

Let's forth, my friend, and wander slow
    Over the fields of tender green,
      Where, as we go,
    The earlier flowers are seen,
      With bluish eyes,
      Up-peering to the skies,
    Like childhood looking up to GOD
      From bended knees.

How fragrant is the sod,
    Where no o'ershading trees
Prevent the blessing of the sun
    From coming down,
    With odorous plants to crown
The lea that erst was desolate and dun!
    Companion mine!
    Thou of the musing race!
Seest thou the beams that round us shine
    Of Heaven's premeditated grace?
Oh! speak; for thou'rt a master in the speech
That to the soul's remotest depths can reach:
    A place there is within thy poet heart
Where heavenly thoughts like holy angels bide;
Thou drawest at times the hiding veil aside,
    And from its home thou causest to depart
A living verse to go abroad, and be
A missioner of good to our humanity:
So speak thou now in this love-moving hour,
When newborn Nature wakes in mystic power.
    Ah! silent still! I see! I see!
        I find a key
        That opes to me
        The mystery
Of thy deep silence now: I see
    The cloud that hangs above thy joy;
    Thy memory rests on thine angelic boy
Who held thy hand when on thy evening walk,
    And by his little talk
    Beguiled thee so
That life without him seem'd an utter wo.
    Thy lamb is safely gather'd in the fold,
The fold eternal, in the better land;
His hand is in the gentle Shepherd's hand,
    And by His side he walks, as once of old

He walk'd with thee along this beauteous earth.
His eye, that glisten'd with a sinless mirth,
  Is brighter now: his voice,
Excelling in its sweetness any bell,
Is sweeter now in its harmonious swell,
    In that grand hymn wherewith the blest rejoice.
      He cannot come to thee; but thou,
      When GOD shalt change thy brow
      And make thy vision dim,
      Shalt go to him.
      What though we turn to clay—
      A springtime resurrection-day,
        Remember, shall be his and thine
          And mine
And every soul's that loves our LORD
        In this brief time:
        Immortal prime
Is theirs who trust the Master's word.

Let's homeward now: thy face again is bright;
The springtime shadows soon resolve in light.

MY DAUGHTER.

PALE and silent Harriet lies:
  Folded hands and veiléd eyes—
Pass'd from me up to the skies,
    My daughter—O my daughter!

If an angel hither came,
Dwelling in a mortal frame,
Thine the blessed spirit's name,
    My daughter—O my daughter!

Scarce a score of years had run,
In its number lacking one;
Time with her so early done!
  My daughter—O my daughter!

Firstling of our household band
To appear in glory's land,
Still I clasp her wonted hand,
  My daughter—O my daughter!

Mid the many cares of day,
Pressing through them as I may,
She goes with me all the way,
  My daughter—O my daughter!

Smiling from the glory cloud,
Clad in light instead of shroud,
I behold her in the crowd,
  My daughter—O my daughter!

Wakeful in my bed at night,
She is present to my sight
In her look of love and light,
  My daughter—O my daughter!

If 'twere fitting she should go,
Should I weakly answer No!
Though it were a bitter wo?
  My daughter—O my daughter!

Let Thy will be done! I say
In my sorrowful dismay:
This the daily prayer I pray:
  My daughter—O my daughter!

CRAZY NORAH.

WILD, fantastic, wayward creature,
    Lean and sharp in every feature;
Slyly shrewd and simply cunning,
Whether chiding, praying, dunning;
Earning many an honest penny,
Loving none nor fearing any;
With her box or satchel laden,
Jeer'd by boy and fear'd by maiden,
Up and down the streets a-going,
Through the alleys of the city,
Better known to all than knowing,
Moving gentle women's pity.
Did the fiends her path environ?
Arm'd for battle, with gridiron,
Frying-pan, or tongs, or other
Weapon, fell assaults to parry,
And the haunting imps to harry,
Calling saints and grandam-mother;
Prayer and benediction uttering,
Wrath and imprecation muttering:
Fain her rooted faith to foster,
Teaching urchins *Pater Noster*
And the Creed of ancient ages
Found in early Fathers' pages.

Why in pathways dark and mazy
Trod the feet of Norah crazy?
Had her heart been vilely broken
By a vow in falseness spoken?
Had the love her first love grew to,
Twining rootlets all around it,

8*

Dried to dust, and proved untrue to
Her whose soul had closely bound it,
Till with love died also reason,
Root, and stem, and bud, and flower,
Dying in the noontide hour
Of the summer's scorching season?
Was it that unholy rancour
Gnaw'd her spirit like a canker,
Till the cable from the anchor
Parted, and away she drifted,
Evermore from haven rifted?

In the times yet unforgotten,
Symbolized by learned Cotton,—
When the Quaker, neck-suspended,
Had his dream of life rough ended,—
When the witch, perchance demented,
Old and poor, yet still contented
With the lot of Heaven's frowning,
Was consign'd to murderous drowning,—
Shrift but short had been allotted
To a wretch with wit out-blotted.

In these better days prevailing
In the city of the Quaker,
Norah, 'mid her sore assailing,
Found no hand so rough to take her—
None so vile to hale to prison
One whose sun, in brightness risen,
Was eclipsed till day immortal
Burst through death's mysterious portal.
Plodding in a pathway lonely
Till her temple-locks were whiten'd,
Kindness waited on her only,
Kindness by her whimseys heighten'd,

Till her eyes were re-anointed
In the time of GOD appointed :
Then the people, if unmournful,
Said, " Poor Norah's dead !" unscornful.

BROTHER! TAKE MY ARM.

WHEN grief falls heavy on thee,
  Or boding ills alarm,
Fear not to lean upon me,—
  Then, brother! take my arm.
There's many a carking trouble
  That taketh two to bear,
And one would bend quite double
  Beneath so sore a care.

If malice, in its rancour,
  Has sought thy mortal harm,
My shoulder be thine anchor,
  Here, brother! take my arm.
Though all, in time of trial,
  May turn their look away,—
Nay, brother! no denial,—
  My arm shall be thy stay.

If grief were mine to-morrow,
  A grief but love could charm,
I'd cry, amid the sorrow,
  Good brother! give thine arm.
'Tis Christlike when another
  That sinking cry shall heed;
For man to man's a brother
  More truly when in need.

JOHN MAYNARD,

THE PILOT OF LAKE ERIE.

THE morn was fair as e'er a morn
  Of summer in her beauty born:
The rarest tint of ancient dye
Were pale beside its wondrous sky;
No fleece by fuller wrought upon
Were whiter than the clouds that hung
As if on snowy pinions swung
About the pathway of the sun.
The breeze came tripping o'er the lake
With ripples chasing in its wake,
And frolicking in open day
Like dimpled urchins at their play;
While sea to sky and sky to sea
Flash'd messages responsively,
As glimpsing glances fond and shy
Are met by passion's answering eye.

A steamer grandly rose and fell
Upon the bosom of the swell
Created by her wheels, as if,
Impatient at the hawser's check,
She'd snap the rein that, taut and stiff,
Lay on her proud imperial neck.
The bell had clang'd; the captain roar'd
In trumpet accent, "All aboard!"
The cable loosen'd, forth she sprang
Like restive racer on her course,
While landsmen's shouts, prolong'd and hoarse,
With many a GOD-speed bravely rang.
The pennant stream'd out at the fore,
The flag was gayly flapping aft,

While the pent steam with hissing roar
Whirl'd round and round the ponderous shaft,
That drove the ship impetuous o'er
The deep green waters far from shore.

Her decks are laden with a freight
Richer than gems of far Brazil
Or gold from every treasure hill
Of modern or of ancient date—
Of living souls, the grave, the gay,
The child, and sire with temples gray.
Without a thought of lurking ill
The sense of present joy to kill,
A hum of voices steals along
Like murmurs of a far-off song:
The while the pilot at the wheel,
With wary eye and nerve of steel,
In watchful silence holds his post
Serene above the chatting host.

But, lo! a cry! All lips grow dumb;
Thin wreaths of smoke from hatchways come.
Strange noises now are heard below,
A hasty rushing to and fro.
"Pass on the buckets!" Every ear
Is startled with a sudden fear:
Yet calm and stern the captain stands,
His voice sonorous as a bell:
"Be lively, men! Come, bear a hand!
Work with a will, and all is well."

They struggle hard, they labour long;
The enemy is fierce and strong,
And when the flame bursts from the hold,
The blood in many a heart runs cold.

"John! head the vessel for the shore!"
The captain to the steersman cries;
"We're safe in thirty minutes more!"—
"Ay, ay, sir!" cheerly John replies.

With many a prayer to Him who saves,
The trembling crowd press to the bow,
For aft the flame is rushing now:
And as the fire-ship cleaves the waves,
Its fury to the wheelhouse sweeps;
Down to the deck the pilot leaps,
And at the stern he takes his stand
Holding the helm with steady hand.

The boat speeds on her headlong way,
Dashing before her clouds of spray,
The while her sturdy ribs of oak
Quiver beneath the engine's stroke.
A mile away—it may be more—
Serenely smiles the verdant shore.
O grant, good LORD! that she may reach
That quiet, grass-emborder'd beach!
"John! hold on but five minutes more!"
The captain to the helmsman cries.
Ringing above the furnace roar,
"I'll try, sir!" simply John replies.
Around him fall the glowing brands,
The red heat blistering face and hands.
Lifting a prayer to GOD on high,
As one who prays when doom'd to die,
He bends him down, and firmly grasps
The tiller as with iron hasps.

Thrice-bless'd be GOD! the shore is reach'd,
Far on the sand the ship is beach'd;

All leap ashore, and wild delight
Chases away their wilder fright.
But where is he who held his post
Serene above the trembling host?
Where is the pilot? 'Neath the deep
John Maynard sleeps the martyr's sleep.

Some die in quiet on their bed,
With gentle arms beneath the head,
While prayer and promise in the ear
Disperse the final doubt and fear.
Some nobly fall in battle's strife,
For home and freedom giving life:
In the heroic front they die
Mid ringing shouts of victory!
To few 'tis given to stand alone
And die as our dear LORD hath done,
Content to perish so they save
Their brothers from a fiery grave.
The victim of that day of dread,
The pilot died as martyrs die,—
The crown of flame around his head
His crown of glory in the sky.
As long as stars their radiance give
His memory on earth shall live;
And tender eyes shall dim with tears
For him who perish'd in the flame,
And heroes born in coming years
Shall emulate John Maynard's fame.

A PEEP INTO THE PARLOUR.

L OVE, where's the poker?   I would stir the fire;
    'Tis getting low: the wind is "getting high."
  Come, draw your sewing chair and footstool nigh;
The glowing coals will cheerfulness inspire,
    And while you ply the needle, I will write
    The gentle words the muse may speak to-night.
Ah! what is that?   "You wish I'd talk," you say.
    Just as you like; but let me end my strain,
    Or I shall tangle all my fancy's skein,
And lose the thread-end of my pretty lay.
    "You wish I'd crack some nuts and eat a pippin!"
You know my hobby, dear!   You bring me low,
And conquer with a single loving blow;
    The nuts and apples cheerfully I'll dip in.

You want to know "What nonsense I am writing!"
    Ah, now, methinks you're somewhat too severe:
    The Muse, you know, is but my second dear,
And she, like you, impels me to inditing
    The rhymes you say are sometimes so inviting.
    But we'll not quarrel for such little things;
    Peace in our dwelling folds her downy wings,
And generals and roughs may do the fighting.—
    Hist! how the wind is howling round the roof!
The tempest-king is riding on the air,
And we've a turkey on a nail up there,
    Of Christmas nigh at hand a pleasant proof.
Then listen, love!—(be off, you frisky kitten,
And let my foot alone!)—I'll read you what I've writ-
        ten:—

The wind is out in his strength to-night,
  And the frost is under his wings;
Downward to earth he bendeth his flight,
  And wild is the song he sings;
Wo, wo to the wretch whose hapless head
Hath shelter none, nor fire, nor bed!

The wind is putting the trees to rout;
  He rends them in his wrath:
At his will he scatters the leaves about,
  And litters the forest path;
He splinters the den of the sleeping bear,
And the torpid brute is cast from his lair.

The wolves are howling the forest through,
  And the savage panthers growl;
The echoing woods the noises renew,
  Like the screechings of the owl.
The men are in peril, who, far from home,
On such a night in the wild woods roam.

The wind on the sea is blowing a gale;
  He rolls the waves on high;
And the quivering ships, without a sail,
  O'er the face of the ocean fly.
A tear and a prayer for the sailor be given
Whose vessel is on a lee-shore driven!

He pierces the hut of the shivering poor;
  No sigh of pity has he!
What mortal can tell the pangs they endure
  Whose portion is poverty?
Rich stewards of Heaven, to want unknown,
God's creatures starve for lack of a bone!

"Enough," you say; and so say I.   It pains
   My inmost soul while I depict the woes
That many a poor, unmurmuring man sustains
   As mournfully along life's way he goes.
The poor are with us alway.   Let us give
   To them a share of what to us good Heaven
   In brimming cups of happiness has given;
And they may learn how good it is to live.
   Good-night!   The Sabbath hour is drawing nigh;
We'll lay aside our labours, love! and rest:
Our Father sends His blessing to our breast
   While humbly we for His sweet favour cry.
We fear no evil when we sink to sleep;
For He who loveth all His loving ones will keep.

OUR SON.

A LITTLE son—an only son—have we;
   (God bless the lad, and keep him night and day,
   And lead him softly o'er this stony way!)
He is blue-eyed, and flaxen hair has he,
   (Such, long ago, mine own was wont to be;
   And people say he much resembles me.)
I've never heard a bird or runlet sing
   So sweetly as he talks.   His words are small
   Sweet words—oh! how deliciously they fall!
Much like the sound of silver bells they ring,
   And fill the house with music.   Beauty lies
As naturally upon his cheek as bloom
   Upon a peach.   Like morning vapour, flies
Before his smile my mind's infrequent gloom.

A jocund child is he, and full of fun :
  He laughs with happy heartiness, and he
  His half-closed eyelids twinkles roguishly,
Till from their lashes tears start up and run.
  The drops are bright as diamonds. When they roll
Adown his cheek, they seem to be the o'erflowing
  Of the deep well of love within his soul,
The human tendernesses of his nature showing.
  Tis pleasant to look on him while he sleeps :
His plump and chubby arms, and delicate fingers,
  The half-form'd smile that round his red lips creeps ;
The intellectual glow that faintly lingers
  Upon his countenance, as if he talks
  With some bright angel on his nightly walks.

We tremble when we think that many a storm
  May beat upon him in the time to come,—
That his now beautiful and fragile form
  May bear a burden sore and wearisome.
Yet, so the stain of guiltiness and shame
Be never placed upon his soul and name,
  So he preserve his virtue though he die,
And to his GOD, his race, his country prove
  A faithful man, whom praise nor gold can buy,
Nor threats of vile, designing men can move,—
  We ask no more. We trust that He who leads
The footsteps of the feeble lamb, will hold
This lamb of ours in mercy's pasture-fold,
  Where every inmate near the loving Shepherd feeds.

THE NEWLY-COME.

THE morning of the day that bears the name
    Of Erin's famous spiritual daddy,
 (Call'd variously St. Patrick, Pat, or Paddy,)
A tiny stranger to our dwelling came.
    Unknown, unnamed, without a mark or label,
Save those which Adam's offspring ever wore,
She came to us as five had come before,
    To make another sitter at our table.
She waited not the word of invitation,
    But crept into our hearts at once, and took
    A life-possession of a little nook
Erst fitted up for her inhabitation;
    And there will she forevermore abide,
    Let joy or sorrow, life or death betide.

'Twas on this wise.   From certain premonitions,
    There seem'd to me that, hid some otherwhere,
    There was a cherub, tiny, young, and fair:
And every day gave strength to my suspicions.
    And therefore kept I watch till past night's mid,
When suddenly I fell into a doze.
My heavy eyelids scarce had time to close,
    Before I heard a voice—I surely did!
And lo! behold, in the adjoining room—
In life and tears—a bud just come in bloom!
    Love's gentle dews long, long on her descend,
The youngest, tenderest prattler of our hearth;
    In every hour, the Highest be her friend,
And life immortal spring from mortal birth.

THE SLEEPING WIFE.

M Y wife! how calmly sleepest thou!
A perfect peace is on thy brow:
Thine eyes beneath their fringëd lid,
Like stars behind a cloud, are hid;
Thy voice is mute, and not a sound
Disturbs the tranquil air around:
I'll watch, and mark each line of grace
That GOD has drawn upon thy face.

My wife! thy breath is low and soft;
To catch its sound I listen oft;
The lightest leaf of Persian rose
Upon thy lips might find repose.
So deep thy slumber, that I press'd
My trembling hand upon thy breast,
In sudden fear that envious death
Had robb'd thee, sleeping, of thy breath.

My wife! my wife! thy face now seems
To show the tenor of thy dreams:
Methinks thy gentle spirit plays
Amid the scenes of earlier days;
Thy thoughts, perchance, now dwell on him
Whom most thou lov'st; or in the dim
And shadowy future strive to pry,
With woman's curious, earnest eye.

Sleep on! sleep on! my dreaming wife!
Thou livest now another life,
With beings fill'd, of fancy's birth;
I will not call thee back to earth:
9*

Sleep on until the car of morn
Above the eastern hills is borne;
Then thou wilt wake again, and bless
My sight with living loveliness.

OUR BOY FOR EVERMORE.

NOW lay your head close to my breast,
   My wife Elizabeth!
Our Tommy is no more distrest:—
   The neighbours say, 'Tis death:
We know the child has gone to rest,—
   A word that comforteth.

How often, wife, we deem'd the boy
   Too early wise for earth!
We felt he was no idle toy,
   To wake a transient mirth:
Our LORD had lent him as a joy
   To sanctify our hearth.

He never pain'd our hearts, you know,
   Save in this bitter grief:
'Tis well the tears a while should flow
   To give the breast relief;
But, lest we sin in doing so,
   Let sorrow's time be brief.

Why question aught the LORD's decree?
   'Twere wiser to adore
The grace hid in grief's mystery
   We knew not of before,
That Tommy in our minds shall be
   Our boy for evermore.

Let not our faith grow faint nor cold;
  GOD'S goodness claims our praise,
That makes the cup of sorrow hold
  The joy of many days,—
For Tommy, never growing old,
  The same shall be always.

The child of scarce five summers, we
  Shall see him every day:
Now skipping in his sinless glee
  Out on the lawn at play;
Now meekly bending at your knee,
  His evening prayer to pray.

He stands on tiptoe at the gate
  Before the sun goes down,
In glad expectance wont to wait
  Our coming from the town;
He runs with eager haste elate
  To catch you by the gown.

At table, on his 'customed chair,
  The while the grace is said,
He shuts his eyes with reverent air,
  And gently bows his head:
His knife, his fork, his napkin there,—
  Our Tommy is not dead!

We see the cherub in the skies
  Among the children stand
Near to the LORD whose gracious eyes
  Smile on the loving band:
His sisters dear, with glad surprise,
  Clasping his tiny hand.

Ere yet nineteen, our firstling died
  In bloom of maiden grace:
Her brother now is by her side,
  Who never saw her face
Till she became his gentle guide
  Around the heavenly place.

When on their children honours fall,
  Men give it proud report:
What glory that the King should call
  Our children to his court,
To stand before him in his hall,
  Where heavenly ones resort!

How gently with us GOD has dealt!
  So deals He with us still;
The double sorrow we have felt
  He never meant for ill:
The Finer lights the fire to melt
  The metal to his will.

'TIS FIVE-AND-TWENTY YEARS.

SITTING upon our cottage stoop,
  By autumn maples shaded,
I call the gentle visions up
  That time had nearly faded.
The evening light comes from the west,
  In streams of golden glory;
So fold your head, love, on my breast,
  And hear my olden story.

'Tis five-and-twenty years, my dear,
  Since, hearts and hands together,
We launch'd our bark, the ocean clear
  And all serene the weather.
With simple trust in Providence,
  We set the sails upon her;
My fortune, hope and common sense,
  Your dowry, love and honour.

For five-and-twenty years, my dear,
  The billows lightly skimming,
One day the skies grew murk and drear,
  Our eyes and spirits dimming.
How dark that night frown'd overhead,
  When hope foresaw no morrow,
And we beside our firstling dead
  Drank our first cup of sorrow.

'Tis five-and-twenty years, my dear,
  Yet music's in our dwelling,
The children's prattle that we hear
  About our hearthstone swelling.
GOD bless them all, the loving band
  So glad to call you mother;
With heart to heart and hand to hand
  Clinging to one another.

Through five-and-twenty years, my dear,
  Whene'er my arm was weary,
And scarce I knew the way to steer,
  Your words were ever cheery.
When mid the tempest and the night,
  With courage sorely shrinking,
Then on our way GOD gave us light
  That kept our faith from sinking.

'Tis five-and-twenty years, my dear,
    Slight change in you revealing;
But o'er my brow—you see them here—
    The silver hairs are stealing.
Yet let them come, while still thy breast
    Retains the fond emotion
That nerved my arm when first we prest
    Our way out on life's ocean.

THE DEAD WIFE.

THERE is no room for sorrow here:
    I tell my heart so every day:
Mine eyes betray no open tear,
    And yet the lesson will not stay.

My heart still goes its daily round,
    Seeking for one it misses sore;
It gives new sharpness to the wound,
    That she will come to me no more.

The 'custom'd social table-chat
    Palls on my apathetic ear:
I see the chair whereon she sat,
    But her sweet voice I cannot hear.

The wonted pillow where she lay
    Is now unpress'd throughout the night;
In wakeful longings for the day
    I watch and wait the morning light.

The motherless stand by my side,
  With many a kiss and fond caress;
And more I reach for her who died
  And left my children motherless.

Like children on their schoolward way,
  Close side by side we went along,—
I helping in her trying day,
  She helping me when she was strong.

No weakling creature of romance,
  Sighing and fainting all the day,
Wasting in sentimental trance
  The sacred trust of time away:

Her life was work in love and grace,
  Doing her Master's will in deeds,—
Good deeds of service to her race,
  Kind thoughts for others in their needs.

I hear the sobbing of the poor,
  The sisterhood of toil and care,
Who never left her honest door
  With poverty's mere stinted share:

I hear the sighs that from afar
  Come from the wanderers whom she sought:
How vain their sighs and sobbings are
  To move again her careful thought!

For her dear sake I planted flowers,
  And April brought the early bloom;
But the wise GOD had mark'd her hours,
  And weeping flowers besprent her tomb.

I pluck'd the choicest buds that grew,
　And held them to her fading eyes:
She saw them not; her soul, I knew,
　Was looking into Paradise.

I sat beside her weary bed,
　And hymns of heaven with her I sung,
Sweet words of Holy Writ I read,
　And stammering prayer dropt from my tongue.

I tried to say, Thy will be done!
　'Twas only words; the heart cried Nay!—
Father! forgive the erring son,
　So blinded that he could not pray.

She drew my face to her dear face,
　And folded me to her dear breast
In one last, loving, long embrace,—
　My lips are dumb to tell the rest!

The martyr stoned to bitter death
　Saw CHRIST in glory on His throne;
And so, before her parting breath,
　His glory in her bosom shone.

I know that all is well with her,
　That she is near the Master's side;
That neither care nor pain can stir
　The loved for whom the Loving died.

So, though my heart cries out anon
　A yearning, lonely, human cry,
I bid my selfishness begone,
　And meet the world with tearless eye.

ANNA MARIA ROSS.

WHAT is death to one that liveth
   In the love of our dear LORD,
When its summons only giveth
   Rest, and peace, and large reward?

Toiling, watching, waiting, serving,
   Blessing sad and suffering ones,—
Loving, and with faith unswerving,
   Seeking, soothing misery's sons:

Beautiful in woman's graces,
   Cheerful as the springtime birds,
Joy lit up their pallid faces
   At the music of her words.

Wheresoe'er her footsteps tended,
   Earth put on a heav'nly look :—
Weep, that here her course is ended,
   Ye that of her care partook.

Weep, ye wounded of the nation,
   Ye who bled at duty's post,—
She has fallen at her station,
   She who led sweet mercy's host.

When GOD taketh whom He loveth
   From the striving to the crown,
Love His action wisely moveth,—
   Why then let our courage down?

10

Death is naught to one that dieth
    When her work and watch are o'er:
In her LORD's dear arms she lieth,
    Who His cross so bravely bore.

Glory to the LORD of glory
    For the bright example shown!
While we tell it o'er in story,
    Help us make it, CHRIST! our own.

THE SOLDIER TO HIS MOTHER.

ON the field of battle, mother,
    All the night alone I lay,
Angels watching o'er me, mother,
    Till the breaking of the day.
I lay thinking of you, mother,
    And the loving ones at home,
Till to our dear cottage, mother,
    Boy again I seem'd to come.

He to whom you taught me, mother,
    On my infant knee to pray,
Kept my heart from fainting, mother,
    When the vision pass'd away.
In the gray of morning, mother,
    Comrades bore me to the town:
From my bosom tender fingers
    Wash'd the blood that trickled down.

I must soon be going, mother,
    Going to the home of rest:
Kiss me as of old, my mother,
    Press me nearer to your breast.

Would I could repay you, mother,
  For your faithful love and care:
GOD uphold and bless you, mother,
  In this bitter wo you bear.

Kiss for me my little brother,
  Kiss my sisters, loved so well:
When you sit together, mother,
  Tell them how their brother fell.
Tell to them the story, mother,
  When I sleep beneath the sod,
That I died to save my country
  All from love to her and GOD.

Leaning on the merit, mother,
  Of the One who died for all,
Peace is in my bosom, mother,—
  Hark! I hear the angels call!
Don't you hear them singing, mother?
  Listen to the music's swell!
Now I leave you, loving mother:
  GOD be with you—fare you well.

AN EVENING STORM AT THE SEASIDE.

THE heat is on the land and sea,
    And every breast is panting;
Still from the westward, burningly,
  The fervid rays are slanting;
When lo! a long-drawn line of cloud,
  Far in the north-east quarter,
Sends mutterings ominous and loud
  Over the land and water.

See night-black clouds, uptoppling fast,
  To heights of heaven soaring,
Whose heralds sound a startling blast
  As troops of lions roaring.
The hurrying winds rush to and fro
  Like armies struck with panic,
While streams of liquid lightning flow
  From cloudy mounts volcanic.

Over the land and over the sea
  The thunder-peals are crashing,
And merrily—oh, how merrily—
  The countless drops are plashing!
Down pours the wild fantastic rain
  On maple and the willow,
And roof and wall and window-pane,
  And meadow, beach, and billow.

The curtain rises: far away
  The cohorts stern are flitting;
The sun comes forth in grand array
  On a throne of glory sitting.
The clouds that shroud the flying storm
  With bows of promise lighting,
Majestic beauty wreathes the form
  Whose mission seem'd so blighting.

Oh, glorious is the sight to see!
  And gentle bosoms, burning
With pure and holy ecstasy,—
  Their vision upward turning,—
Bless GOD for storm as well as calm,
  Alike the theme of wonder,
And reverent voices swell the psalm
  To Him who wields the thunder.

Ho, brothers! this of mortal life
Most truly is the limning:
What joy, what wo, what peace, what strife,
The burden of our hymning!
Though dark the clouds within the breast,
Though horrors round us gather,
Our LORD will give His perfect rest
To all who love the FATHER.

LET ME KISS HIM FOR HIS MOTHER.

LET me kiss him for his mother!
Ere ye lay him with the dead:
Far away from home, another
Sure may kiss him in her stead.
How that mother's lip would kiss him
Till her heart should nearly break!
How in days to come she'll miss him!
Let me kiss him for her sake.

Let me kiss him for his mother!
Let me kiss the wandering boy:
It may be there is no other
Left behind to give her joy.
When the news of wo the morrow
Burns her bosom like a coal,
She may feel this kiss of sorrow
Fall as balm upon her soul.

Let me kiss him for his mother!
Heroes ye, who by his side
Waited on him as a brother
Till the Northern stranger died;
10*

Heeding not the foul infection,
　　Breathing in the fever-breath:—
Let me, of my own election,
　　Give the mother's kiss in death.

"Let me kiss him for his mother!"
　　Loving thought and loving deed!
Seek nor tear nor sigh to smother,
　　Gentle matrons, while ye read.
Thank the GOD who made you human,
　　Gave ye pitying tears to shed;
Honour ye the Christian woman
　　Bending o'er another's dead.

A MORNING STORM IN THE ADIRONDACKS.

THE multitude of mountains rest below
　　The overlying heavens, serene, sublime,—
Heaved from the depths in nature's earliest throe,
　　Before the annals of recorded time.
Like sleeping mammoths on this cloudy morn,
　　No sign give they save in the steamy breath
That, issuing from their nostrils, is upborne
　　To regions where the storm-king thundereth.
His tones how angry when he deigns to speak!
　　How thick the darkness looming o'er his path,
Save when his lightnings play around each peak!
　　Yet reck not they the muttering of his wrath;
For this shall harmless fall, while they shall stand
　　Unmoved until the great prophetic day
When He shall speak who form'd them by His hand;
　　And then the olden things shall pass away,
And a new earth, more glorious, pure, and bright,
Shall dawn on man's regenerated sight!

THE TAKING OF THE CHILD.

WE heard no knocking at the door,
  There was no stealthy tread
Of vagrant feet upon the floor,
  To fill our souls with dread.

We heard no voice within the room,
  Nor saw a stranger's face,
And yet a trembling and a gloom
  Crept over us apace.

Without the night was wild and drear,
  Within was woful care:
And silence magnified our fear
  Till broken by a prayer.

The dying boy wist what I said,
  For simple words were they:
He clasp'd his hands and bent his head,
  OUR FATHER heard him pray.

As on his mother's breast reclined,
  Nestling his flaxen head—
His little hands in hers entwined—
  In quick surprise he said,

"Say, mother! what is that I see?"
  He pointed to the dim:
Sure something in the vacancy
  Was beckoning to him.

Between the going-out of night
And coming-in of day
His spirit, like a meteor light,
Stole suddenly away.

A tearful company, we drew
Around the mother's chair,
And knelt in reverence, for we knew
The LORD himself was there.

ELISHA KENT KANE.

TOLL—toll—toll!
Let the great bells knoll
For the parting soul,
Envoicing a nation's wo:
Let the funeral chime
As a plaining rhyme
Ring mournfully and slow:
In the isle where the lime and the orange trees grow
A good man—a true man—in death lieth low.

Toll—toll—toll!
Let the great bells knoll
For the parted soul,
The hero wise and brave:
O'er the frozen sea
Wounded conqueror, he
Has found an early grave
In the home where he play'd ere he ventured the wave,
In the freest of lands that the wild waters lave.

Toll—toll—toll!
Let the great bells knoll
For the parted soul,
The young and daring chief:
Solemnly resound
Christendom around
The ponderous tones of grief;
For the fame of his name, though his years were so brief,
Is like the halo'd glory of old heroes of belief.

Toll—toll—toll!
Let the great bells knoll
For the parted soul,
The honour'd of the age:
Years but of a youth—
Heart of gentle ruth—
With calmness of the sage:
To the giant of the North he threw a daring gage,
And won immortal name on the world's historic page.

Toll—toll—toll!
Let the great bells knoll
For the parted soul,
Upcallèd to its GOD:
With a hopeful face
Looking for His grace—
The path of peril trod—
Now with the sandals of the better country shod,
How gratefully he rests 'neath his loved natal sod.

OLD PINE STREET CHURCH,
PHILADELPHIA.

A HUNDRED years ago
   The mason laid the stone;
Yet stately is the temple now,
   And comelier has it grown.
The people gather'd round
   With meek, uncover'd head;
They felt the spot was holy ground,
   And trod with reverent tread.

A hundred years ago
   Our fathers, moved by grace,
Toil'd long with heart and hand, and so
   They built the holy place:
Confiding in His word,
   The sturdy walls were rear'd,
And then the glory of the LORD
   Within the courts appear'd.

A hundred years ago
   The patriot Duffield came,
His soul with zeal and love aglow,
   His tongue a warming flame.
Smith, versed in holy lore—
   Milledoler, wisdom-fraught—
And Alexander, man of power—
   Ely, of crystal thought.

A hundred years ago—
   Ah, men of might were then;

Yet good Old Pine Street Church, I trow,
  Hath since its mighty men.
How late our cheeks were wet
  O'er honour'd Brainerd's pall!
Now Allen worthily is set
  The watchman on her wall.

A hundred years ago—
  How oft the Holy One
Here led the sinner's heart to bow
  Before the ETERNAL SON!
Here souls have pour'd their plaints
  And graciously were shriven;
Ay! multitudes of chosen saints
  Have here been school'd for heaven.

A hundred years ago
  There pillow'd not a head
Where lie in many a grassy row
  Her hosts of holy dead.
The spirits of her blest
  Must surely hover round
These courts, where peaceful, loving rest
  At JESUS' feet they found.

A hundred years ago
  Her songs of praise began;
Oh! let the joyful anthems flow
  To latest times of man!
Strong may her walls abide,
  A shelter and a tower,
Until her LORD, the Crucified,
  Shall come in pomp and power.

MATRIMONY.

I HOLD that every one is bound to carry
　　In full effect the duties of this life;
That is, that man in proper time should marry
　　And live in love and harmony with a wife.
If now and then a woman prove a shrew,
　　'Tis an exception to the general rule:
　　And I would deem him either knave or fool
Who says that woman is not kind and true.
　　There may be men who ne'er should marry,—such
　　As have a heart affection cannot touch;
But he who bears the impress of a man,
　　And has a bosom fill'd with yearnings human,
　　Should win the love of some pure-hearted woman,
And pop the question to her bravely as he can.

An angel always dwells beneath the roof
　　Where, in her virtue, a sweet wife fulfils
　　Her gentle duties; and unnumber'd ills
From that love-guarded precinct keep aloof.
　　And "he who finds a wife," 'twas said of old,
　　"Finds something good," and so I always hold.
The bachelor is a nondescript—(I beg
　　His pardon, but it's true;)—quite out of place,
　　He seems to me, among our loving race;
Unfinish'd, like a chair that lacks a leg,—
　　A knife without a fork—a book unbound,—
A lonely traveller on a lonesome way,
　　Who, faint and sad, looks wistfully around,
But from the sun of love receives no cheering ray.

If this be so, why don't he go and marry?
  'Tis autumn now; the birds long since have pair'd;
  And e'en the flowers their nuptial time have shared;
Then why should he still solitary tarry?
  Were I a bachelor, I'm sure I'd fall
A captive to some maiden of our land;
  I'd scarce know how to choose among them all:
Yet in our day a single heart and hand
  Are all the law allows; and this is well.
The love of one sweet heart on one bestow'd
  Is full enough to make his bosom swell,
And teach his feet to leap along life's road.—
  Ye bachelors, go—a loving helpmeet take,
  And send around your compliments and cake.

FROM MY PILLOW TO THE EDITOR OF THE SATURDAY GAZETTE.

DEAR MR. NEAL:—Say, did you ever rise
  When morning came, and feel as if you'd slept
Scarce half enough; but still your habit kept
Of early rising? Heavy were your eyes?
  Your head as light as though the brains were gone?
  Your trembling legs too weak to rest upon?
With fever'd skin, and tongue encrusted white?
  Your neck and face besieged by tender lumps?
If so, you can appreciate the plight
  Of your afflicted friend—he's got the mumps!
The doctor tells him they are much about,
  And gives him medicine and the grease of goose
  To make the malady its grip unloose;
And soon he hopes to turn the enemy out.

11

Bear with him, then, if in his hour of pain
   He drops his lighter rhyme, and in his breast
   He makes a deeper, purer, holier quest,
And brings therefrom a tenderer, gentler strain.
   He is, in truth, a sober-thoughted one,
And pensive in his ways, as other folks,
   Although at times he loves a little fun,
When pure and harmless wit the jest provokes.
   Awhile in tears we see an April day,
   Till laughing sunshine dries its tears away.
When clouds of sorrow overspread our sky
   We may be sure there still is light behind;
The heavenly gales shall sweep the vapours by,
   And purer bliss descend upon the mind.

List, gentle sir! and let my pillow rhymes
Fall on the ear like Sabbath morning chimes:

"Ah, aching head!—ah, feeble, fever'd frame!—
   Come, downy pillow, yield me kind relief!—
Sweet wife!—thy love's more dear to me than fame—
   Come, sing a hymn to soothe my heavy grief.
Oh, fan my brow—and lay thy cooling hand
   Upon my forehead:—how it throbs with pain!—
How anguish wellnigh has my soul unmann'd!—
   Ah, love! how kind and gentle!—press that vein
With thy soft finger:—there!—now wipe the sweat
   That gathers on my face. Water, sweet wife!
Another cup of cooling water yet!
   Then softly place my head again. Now kneel,
And let us pray; for in His hand is life;
   And in our time of woe His grace will He reveal."

AFTER TEA.

THE tastes of men are various as their faces;
 Some toast their friends, and some their bread
  and cheese;
 I like to toast my toes, and sit at ease
Beside my wife, in our accustom'd places.
 Day and its busier duties ended, we
Pursue the promptings of our inclination,—
 I with a pen or book in hand, and she
Intent on some maternal avocation.
 Our little ones, entranced in dreamless slumber,
Lie snugly nestled in their downy beds,
 With not a care their simple hearts to cumber,
With not a grief to bow their gentle heads,—
 Save when, in waking hour, some disappointment
Afflicts them so, they seek affection's ointment.

Our puss betimes sits cosily a purring,
 As if to imitate her musing master;
At other whiles she's all alive and stirring,
 And runs and springs, and springs and runs the faster.
No common cat is she; nor will she stand
 A rude, presuming trick, but shows her claws,
And leaves her mark upon the heedless hand
 That dares infringe her feline rights or laws.
She's commonly quite neat in her apparel,
Save when she falls into the charcoal barrel:
 And then, poor tabby! mousingly she goes
For many days, from kitchen to the attic,
 Robed in a garb of pepper-colour'd clothes,
And mews in tones pathetic and emphatic.

The north wind howls; but, shelter'd, safe, and warm,
 Howl as it may, we feel secure from danger:
The fire burns blue, "betokening a storm"—
 A brand falls down, "precursor of a stranger."
My thoughtful mind runs o'er the track of years,
 When, tongs in hand, at our old hearth I sat,
And poked the embers, till my mother's fears
 Broke in upon the usual social chat:
"You'll fire the chimney, son!" The sparks would fly
 Like imps of living lightning up the flue,
And snap and crackle as they soar'd on high,
 As if they felt some pleasure in it too!
That fire is out—that hearth is cold—and they
Who felt its pleasant warmth have mostly pass'd away.

A DAY WITH THE INFLUENZA.

IF one should ask, "What have you done to-day?"
 As brief as Cæsar, I'd reply, "I've sneezed."
 Ne'er loving swain his damsel's fingers squeezed
(To tell the tale his lips refused to say)
 More tenderly than I my stricken nose.
'Twere vain to attempt to stand upon decorum,
I had to sneeze behind folks and before 'em.
 At every sneeze, it seem'd that ringing blows
Fell on my head, that throbb'd and ached to frenzy;
 From weeping eyes my strength appear'd to ooze,
 And all my body was a general bruise:
I yielded captive to the influenza,
 And I went home at dinner-time, and there
 Sought help in medicine and my rocking-chair.

Much like the custom of the ancient cities,
  My nasal gateways closed at dusk of day,
And scarce a breath, for love's sake or for pity's,
  Got in or out by the accustom'd way;
So on my couch I lay with open lips,
  To let the air into the cells of life.
Instead of sleep, a dreamy-like eclipse
  Came over me; and vagaries were rife
Within my mind. The thread of dreaming broke
At intervals, and startled I awoke;
  I turn'd the pillow 'neath my fever'd head,
And gazed awhile upon the taper's smoke;
  And when a sigh of suffering softly sped,
A tender voice to me in tones of pity spoke.

A day thus pass'd is not a day misspent,
  If it but teach a lesson—as it may—
  That man is tenant of a house of clay,
Which he must leave whenever word is sent.
  There's nothing here to grumble at, if we
  The why and wherefore of our pains could see.
As our good pastor said, in all the year
  There are more days of sunshine than of gloom.
More joys than griefs to virtuous men appear;
  And round the path of every mortal bloom
Sweet flowers of love, and he may multiply
  The generous plant by gracious words and deeds.
  He reads amiss who never wisely reads
What heavenly mercies in our sorrows lie.

LILLY.

ROBE the beautiful for the tomb:
 We may no longer stay her;
She has pass'd away in virgin bloom,
 In vestal white array her.
A single dark-brown tress we crave
 Before her face ye cover:
Why should the cold and grasping grave
 Take all from those who love her?

Bear the beautiful to the tomb
 While yet the sun is shining,
Ere the shadows and evening gloom
 Denote the day's declining.
Bear her softly and slowly on,
 Disturb no placid feature;
Deep the sleep she's fallen upon,
 The last of a mortal creature.

Bear the beautiful to the tomb:
 A voice of rarer sweetness
Shall ne'er, till earth shall come to doom,
 Be heard in more completeness.
What liquid notes flow'd from the tips
 Of her enchanted fingers!
And the holy music of her lips
 Still in our memory lingers.

Bear the beautiful to the tomb:
 'Twas heavenly the calling
Her LORD's sweet love bade her assume
 To help the weak and falling:

Tenderly as her tender LORD
  She wrought her loving labour,
And ever had she a hopeful word
  For erring friend or neighbour.

Bear the beautiful to the tomb:
  Mark ye the smile of heaven,
Holier than the rays that illume
  The western skies at even,—
The smile that lit her lovely face
  When her footstep cross'd life's portal,
As though her Saviour, in his grace,
  Crown'd her with bliss immortal?

Give the beautiful to the tomb,
  The unselfish, guileless maiden:
Weep, children of unhappy doom!
  Her hands for you were laden
With love's rich benisons of good:
  She was so gently human,
Ye know her name most rightly stood
  For all that honours woman.

Lay the beautiful in the tomb;
  Beneath the drooping willow
Let the maiden have sleeping room,
  And softly spread her pillow.
Angels hasten from realms of bliss,
  Their watch above her keeping:
Dear to the heart of the holy is
  The place where she is sleeping.

Lay the beautiful in the tomb,
  The daughter of Heaven's sending,
To comfort, in its time of gloom,
  My heart with sweet befriending.

A shade is lying upon my way
  That earth can no more brighten;
A burden of woe is mine to-day
  That only CHRIST can lighten.

Leave the beautiful in the tomb;
  There may be others fairer;
A haughtier head may wave a plume
  With glory to the wearer;
But so beautiful and so good
  —Think we who dearly held her—
Earth in its rarest sisterhood
  May never have excell'd her.

THE HYMNS MY MOTHER SUNG.

THERE are to me no hymns more sweet
  Than those my mother sung
When joyously around her feet
  Her little children clung.

The baby in its cradle slept,
  My mother sang the while:
What wonder if there softly crept
  Across his lips a smile?

And once a silent, suffering boy,
  Bow'd with unwonted pain,
I felt my bosom thrill with joy
  To hear her soothing strain.

The stealing tear my eye bedims,
  My heart is running o'er:—
The music of a mother's hymns
  Shall comfort me no more.

THE REAPER'S RETURN.

A LONG the meadows,
    After the day
    Has pass'd away,
The twilight shadows
    Of trees and posts,
    Like gauzy ghosts,
Are falling faintly:
    The early moon,
    Uprising soon,
With aspect saintly,
    Shines on the edge
    Of the rocky ledge,
And glances and dallies
    In shimmering beams
    Upon the streams;
While deep in the valleys
    The darkness lies,
    And clouds the eyes
Of the sickly sleeper.
    His labour done
    At set of sun,
The wearied reaper,
    Stalwart and strong,
    Hastens along
To his peaceful dwelling,
    While thoughts of home
    In his bosom come,
Like a fountain welling.
    He treads the ground
    Where once, to the sound

Of the trumpet's braying,
　　Armies of men
　　On hill and glen
Were wounding and slaying;
　　Where the brave and good
　　Unflinching stood
In the hour of danger,
　　When 'gainst the cause
　　Of their land and laws
Came Hessian and stranger.

Now peacefully sleeping
　　The sod below,
　　Their mortal wo
And time of weeping
　　Have pass'd away
　　This many a day.
The life-blood creeping
　　Through gaping wound
　　Over the ground—
The verdure steeping
　　In pools of gore—
　　Is seen no more.
There winds are sweeping
　　As sweet and low
　　As when they blow
Where flowers are peeping
　　On meadow-side
　　At evening-tide,
When June is keeping
　　A festival
　　That blesses all,
And men are reaping
　　A harvest-yield
　　From nature's field,

And hearts are leaping
  With present pleasure
  Surpassing measure.

The field of battle,
  Where men have died
  On freedom's side
Amid the rattle
  And roar of shot,
  Is sure the spot
Where love will linger:
  There maids will stand
  With lifted hand,
And point the finger
  In heartiest mood
  Of gratitude
To the place where brother
  And father fell;
  And they will tell
To one another
  The bitter wrong
  That, suffer'd long,
Led wife and mother
  To buckle on
  The sire and son
The sword long rusted,
  And bid them go
  And meet the foe,
That proudly trusted
  To smite the land
  With blade and brand.

To GOD be glory!
  They hush'd the boast
  Of the hireling host:

And song and story
In future age
Shall fill the page
Till earth is hoary;
And in the breast
Of men oppress'd—
For freedom yearning—
Our name and fame
Shall light a flame
That, fierce and burning,
Shall snap the cords
Of priests and lords:
Then, meekly learning
In Bethl'em's school
The golden rule,
And wisely spurning
The bigot's control
Over the soul,
Men, Christward turning,
Shall seek and find
Their Maker's mind;
Then scenes of gladness,
And love, and mirth,
From heart and hearth
Shall banish sadness,
And earth shall see
A jubilee.

The ravage and riot
And wrath of war
Were seen no more;
And comfort and quiet
In heart and home
Of man had come:—
The elders older

And feebler grew,
Till 'neath the yew
They lay to moulder:—
The children, then,
Were grown to men,
And on their shoulder
The locks of white
Fell thin and light:—
The share of the plower
Upturn'd the stones
Mingled with bones;
And fruit and flower
Fertilely rose
Where mortal foes
Together were buried:—
The sun at morn
Shone on the corn
All tassel'd and serried:—
The tops of the trees
In the evening breeze
Were waving lightly:—
The mocking-bird
The silence stirr'd
Sportively, sprightly:—
When, after threescore
Of years, or more,
Light-hearted and cheery,
The reaper trod
Over the sod
Where groanings dreary
And cries of fear
Once met the ear
From the wounded and weary.
He lifts his eyes
To the moonlit skies,

And thoughtfully ponders
  On sacred things
  The stillness brings
To him as he wanders.
  To the land above
  Friends of his love
Long have departed,
  But faithful he bears
  His daily cares,
Strong and stout-hearted.
  A man is he,
  Though lowly be
His human condition:
  Nor will he bow
  With servile brow
In humble petition
  To scornful pride
  That turns aside
From those who are lowly;
  Yet meekly he
  Doth bend the knee
To his Maker holy.

  His children wait
  At the garden-gate,
Till the skies darken;
  And far in the dim
  They look for him,
And earnestly hearken.
  In a glad shout
  Their lips break out;
They cry to their mother,
  "See! father's here!"
  And run like deer
One after the other:

They round him stand,
And grasp his hand,
And sister and brother
Mid general din
Usher him in.

A REVERY IN AN ANCIENT
POTTER'S-FIELD.

THE sultry summer-day was past,
   I sat me down beneath
A sycamore, the cooling winds
  Of eventide to breathe.

I sat me down in silentness,
  Half-hidden in the shade:
My thoughts on wondrous mysteries ran,
The birth and life and death of man,
  And fancy freely play'd.

The lovely and the young were there,
  And voices sweet and clear
As sound of bells o'er waters heard,
The air of early evening stirr'd,
  And pleased the listening ear.

I heeded not the pleasant tones,
  My spirit turn'd away
From present scenes to scenes of old,
  When 'neath this very clay,
The poor and friendless sons of men
  In strange confusion lay.

Methought the graves again appear'd,
  Neglected, as of old;
The bones protruding here and there,
A broken tooth, a lock of hair,
  The pauper's portion told.

"This dust shall live again," I said,
  "Though 'tis but pauper flesh;
These bleaching bones the Word of GOD
  Shall clothe with life afresh."

Methought, ere to this gospel truth
  My lips bare utterance gave,
Lo! slowly every corpse arose
  And sat upon its grave.

My hair stood up in utter dread,
  And horror fill'd my breast;
I closed mine eyes, but still the sight
Was clear to me as noonday light,
  And to my side there press'd
A meek-eyed being, pure and bright,
  Who thus mine ear address'd:—

"Fear not, O lover of the poor;
  Mine errand is to thee:
Arise and walk, and wisely mark
  This wondrous mystery."

I gazed within his eye of peace:
  I loved him, and my fears
Departed like the morning mist
When, by the morning sunbeam kiss'd,
  Unseen it disappears.

We walk'd together, he and I,
　Among that silent throng:
The corpses lifted up their eyes,
And gazed on us without surprise,
　While slow we paced along.

Each corpse upon its forehead bore
　The method of its death;
A few had died in peaceful hour,
When nature, failing in her power,
　Gave mildly up her breath.

The pestilence had garner'd here
　A multitude of slain,
When winds of doom pass'd o'er the land,
　And men, like drops of rain,
Fell in the swollen stream of death
　That swept the human plain.

The hand of hate had hurried some
　To judgment and the dust;
And some had perish'd 'neath the smart
Of cruel words, that eat the heart
　Like canker and the rust.

The meek-eyed angel still my guide,
　We wander'd round and round,
And ever and anon we stood
　Before a broken mound
Whereon a corpse was sitting, who
　Had risen through the ground.

Among the congregated throng
　Nor voice nor sound was heard;
What things the angel said to me
12*

I understood, yet audibly
   He never spake a word.

We halted at an humble spot
   Where sat a wasted form;
Her eyes were like the evening light
   Of Venus after storm.

"A daughter of the King is she;
   Unknown she lived on earth:
Of lowly name and low degree,
   She had a royal birth.

"They laid her in the potter's-field:
   But little boots it where
The loving and the loved of CHRIST
   Their dying portion share;
They safely rest in earth or sea,
   If He be with them there."

Three children sported on a grave,
   Two sisters and a brother;
An old man and his daughter sat
   Together on another;
A little child lay also on
   The bosom of its mother.

The suicide was there: he bore
   Upon his forehead plain
A deeper furrow, dug by guilt,
   Than mark'd the brow of Cain:
The harden'd gore was still unwash'd
   That issued from the vein
His hand had sever'd; and his breast
   Was crimson with the stain.

The drunkard trembled on his grave,
  The travesty of man:
Two of his sons had drunkards died;
Another for his life was tried—
  A halter was its span.

The wife and mother meekly sat,
  Her eye undimm'd by tear,
Though bitter was the weary life
  That found its quiet here,—
A-resting till the day of days
  Shall welcomely appear,
And bliss shall quench the memories
  Of early woe and fear.

A rover of the deep was there,
  His comrades by his side:
They'd sped their way to India's shore,
  And gladly homeward hied:·
They saw again their native land
  With arms outstretching wide,
When fiercely tempest-winds did sweep
Across their path, and in the deep
  A score of sailors died;
And in this field were laid the few
  Relinquish'd by the tide.

The living dead!—the living dead!—
  I shut my tearful eyes,
And seekingly I turn'd my face
  Unto the placid skies.

The midnight hour toll'd solemnly,
  And lo! I wept alone;

The moonlight crept along the ground,
And katydids were chirping round
    With shrill and lively tone;
And o'er my head the sweet, cool breeze
Stole in and out among the trees,
    As if some sprites had come
Upon the boughs, and lightly swung,
And holy hymns together sung
    Of their immortal home.

THE DESECRATED CHURCHYARD.

DOWN among the dead men's bones
    Lay the deep foundation-stones:
Mingle with the sand and lime
Dust of folk of bygone time:
    Set the brick in order fair;
Be the timber sound and tough;
Make the plaster strong enough—
    Intermix'd with human hair.
Let the rafters crown the walls,
    Let the parapets be set;
Now the useless scaffold falls,
    But the toiling ends not yet.
Crowd in many a rough-hewn box
    All the surplus bones ye may;
Shake them down with sudden shocks,
    They are but insensate clay.
Still the sleepers shall remain
    Mid the haunts so long their own,
Shelter'd from the snow and rain,
    Hedgèd in with beam and stone.

In the shops of gainful wares,
  Ghosts among the buyers stray:
Viewless up and down the stairs
  They shall glide by night and day.
When the songs of maidens gush,
  Spectral hands the time shall beat:
In the mazy waltzing rush
  There shall whirl the silent feet:
When the lovers whisper low,
  Dreamless of a listener near,
Shadowy ears shall eager bow
  Pretty words of love to hear:
When the babe first wakes a cry,
  Spirit-fingers press its hand;
When the aged fail and die,
  Sprites beside the pillow stand.
Never till the judgment-day
May ye drive the sprites away.

Man in olden day this spot
  Set apart as sacred ground,
Where, in his appointed lot,
  He should wait the trumpet's sound:
He was comforted and blest,
  Toiling till the day was done,
So he'd have a place of rest
  At the setting of the sun,
Wife and children spreading flowers
Over him in summer hours.
Tiny breathers of a day,
  Falling in the skirmish strife—
Youth cut down in morning gray—
  Matrons ripe for heavenly life—
Here were laid, in hopeful trust,
Till the rising of the just.

Much I wonder if the bones
Rattled underneath the stones,
When the mattock, pick, and spade
Horrid noises o'er them made;
Ribald jests and wrangling riot
Breaking on the spirits' quiet!
As a swarm of angry bees
   Sting the robbers of their hoard,
When the woodmen fell the trees
   Where the hivèd honey's stored,
Did the uneasy ghosts arise,
   Clustering round the diggers there—
Spirit tear-drops in their eyes,
   Terror bristling up their hair—
Striking with their hidden hands
At the rough-shod working bands
Who so rudely rent away
Shelter from their coffin'd clay?

'Twas an ancient phrase,—to make
   Honest hearts the wretch despise,—
Curst the caitiff who would take
   Pennies from a corpse's eyes:
'Twas for man of modern day,
   Slave of gold, to do the sin,
And invade the house of clay
   That the dead were sleeping in.
O ye living, lay your dead
   Far beyond the haunts of men;
Sink them in the ocean's bed,
   Hide them in the desert fen:
Bury them, like Moses, where—
   By the covetous unknown—
They may rest till in the air
   CHRIST shall sit on doomday throne.

OUR AUTUMN WEATHER.

THE peerless bird is yet unfledged whose quill
 Shall form a pen to write in numbers fit
Of our sweet Indian summer. He is still
 Unborn who has been gifted with the wit
To sing its glory, loveliness, and worth.
Our land becomes the paradise of earth,
 And angels cannot then be far away.
The wind like love's low breathing moves along,
And sighs in tones surpassing mortal song.
 Such spiritualness gets in our heavy clay,
Our earth-born souls uplift themselves : we see,
 · We hear, we feel, we breathe the beauty in ;
 A holier sense comes o'er the breast of sin,
And man in humbleness adores the Deity.

Autumn is life in sober quietness ;
 'Tis manhood full of strength slow growing old ;
 'Tis womanhood mature, within whose fold
Are gather'd stores that man and nature bless.
 The autumn 'minds me of a sire whose hair
Is beautifully silvering o'er—whose eye
 Is mild with love : there stand around his chair
Right noble sons and daughters fair ; and by
 His side the wife—the mother—sits, beloved
 And loving all. By lapse of time well proved,
Their virtues bide rock-founded. Holy sight !
 The Indian summer-time of human life,—
 The resting-hour from turmoil and from strife,
Before the spirit takes its heaven-directed flight.

WHERE IS THE APPLE-MAN?

THE whereabouts—the present whereabouts—
   Of that old man, can any person tell?
The tall, spare, gray old man, who used to sell
Nuts, cakes, and apples near the park?—Some doubts
   Have I if he be still alive; but if he be,
   His kindly face I'm fain again to see.
A pleasant thing to me it was to meet,
   As day by day I pass'd, his smiling look:
   (The human face is my delightful book,
Wherein I read while walking in the street.)
   Some kindliness, methought, was garner'd up
Within his heart: though he was poor and old,
   Yet sure am I his hand would ne'er withhold
From misery's lip love's rich, refreshing cup.

There patiently he stood, from early morn
   Till watchman's call at night, beside the corner
Of Sixth and Walnut—(keep your little scorn
   And pitying laugh within your bosom, scorner—
I write of things beyond your heart and head:)
   There, doling out for pence his sugar'd ware,
   His little gains from children in the Square
Sufficed to find him in his daily bread.
   I never learn'd the old man's history,
Nor whence he came, nor whither he has gone:
   'Tis my belief no living kin had he,
But lonely in this world he plodded on.
   Well! if from earth he in GOD's time has pass'd,
   This stone on his memorial heap I cast.

THE DEAF.

THE deaf do live alone.   In all the earth
 There is no helpmeet found for them ; within
One circle is their empire bound.   No din
Invades the temple of their mind : the mirth
 And sighs of 'men are sounds to them unknown,
 Though well they know the spirit's inward groan ;
And mortal agonies belong to them
 As well as to their fellow men ; for death
 Hath pass'd on all who draw the vital breath,
And where sin is, there doth the law condemn.
Ah, hapless men ! relentless silence keeps
 Her watchpost at the portals of the ear ;
 No heavenly word or sound approacheth near,
And music's magic harmony in lasting stillness sleeps.

To them, the tongue of Nature speaketh not
 When on the earth her holy voice is heard ;
The sighing winds that haunt the shady grot,
 The murmuring brook, the merry singing-bird,
Are mute to them.   They have not learn'd how sweet
 Are human tones when kindness tunes the voice,
 Nor how a word may make the heart rejoice,
And change its sadness into bliss complete.
 From all things audible debarr'd, they live
In lonely isolation, each apart :
 Yet not for ever !   CHRIST in heaven shall give
The hearing ear to *all* the pure in heart.
 With what delight the music of the spheres
 Shall fill their rapt and newly-gifted ears !

THE DINNER HOUR.

AT one o'clock I set aside my work,
 And go to dinner.   One whole hour is mine
 To frolic with the children and to dine.
I walk the pave as gravely as a Turk,
 And muse in quietness along the way.
My dwelling is, perhaps, about a mile,
And yet, so busy is my mind the while,
 The road seems short, e'en on a summer-day.
My children oft are peeping out the door
 To see me turn the corner of the street,
And their bright eyes with joy are brimming o'er.—
 As my good father did, before we eat
We seek the grace of Heaven, and then partake
The food that GOD provides for our Redeemer's sake.

" Did" is a word of past signification,
 A sad and touching word when used to tell
Of those who've pass'd through toil and tribulation
 To reach the land where saints and angels dwell.
A score of years have nearly pass'd away
 Since I was seated at my father's table,—
Since, pallid, cold, and still, that father lay,
 And our sad hearts were robed in funeral sable.
The shaft of sorrow pierced our mother's bosom.
She pined and sigh'd.   The summer's fragrant blossom
 Soon also bloom'd upon the mother's grave;
And forth into the world the children went,
And GOD watch'd o'er those little ones, and sent
 An angel with them charged to guide and save.

(How strangely memory leads me from my theme !
  Thus frequently my retrospective mind
  Doth cast a fond and "lingering look behind,"
Till rude reality disturbs the dream.
  But life is strange, and often wide extremes
  Are nearer kin than many a witling deems.)
The school-bell rings.   The children rise to go ;
  They say " Good by !" and gayly trip along.
My hour is past ; (oh, Time ! why not more slow ?)
  The risen tide of sonnet and of song
Begins to ebb, and all is calm again.
  I haste once more to business and to care,
  And my accustom'd countenance I wear,
And I become a man like most of other men.

HENRY REED.

FOR many days our eyes have seaward wander'd,
    As if to search the Ocean o'er and o'er,
And tender hearts have sorrowfully ponder'd.
  " Shall we behold his gentle face no more ?"
The silent sea no glad response returning,
  We cry, " O sun ! that lightest nature's face,
  Dost thou not shine upon some favour'd place
Where he is cast for whom our souls are yearning ?"
  No answering voice allays our trembling fears,
  And long anxiety gives way to tears.
Beneath the waves o'er which great ships go flitting,
  He waits the day when Ocean yields her dead ;
  And sighs are breathed and bitter tears are shed
By desolate ones around his hearthstone sitting ;
  And, while they mourn the gifted and the good,
  The general grief shows holy brotherhood.

TO THE COMET.

WHENCE thou, and whither bound, celestial
    ranger?
And what's thy mission in these lower skies?
Com'st thou from spheres beyond our mortal eyes,
Prognosticating some impending danger?
    Or art thou on a tour of observation,
    Before thou tak'st a permanent location?
In olden time, the world had gone demented
    To see thy tail long trailing 'neath the stars,
    The sign of woes, of famines, and of jars
Among the nations, not to be prevented.
    To them thou wert a spectacle of doom,
They fear'd thy train the earth would overwhelm;
    To us it seemeth merely as a broom,
Wherewith the angels sweep their starry realm.

But why so hasty in thy northern flight?
    And where's thy head? why hide it, like a maiden,
Behind a veil knit of fine threads of light
    Abstracted from the sun, and richly laden
With gems and dyes of a celestial hue?
    Say, art thou journeying to the far-off place
    Where Uranus runs his chilly, lonely race,
To learn how all thy brother comets do?
    Ethereal stranger! when wilt thou return
    In silvery splendour in our skies to burn?
Methinks the light of many eyes shall pale,
    And sorrowing spirits find a welcome rest,
Ere thou again thy glittering form shall trail
    Athwart the heavens, fleet Meteor of the West!

TO A TROUBLESOME FLY.

WHAT! here again, indomitable pest!
Thou plagu'st me like a pepper-temper'd sprite;
Thou makest me the butt of all thy spite,
And bitest me, and buzzest as in jest.
Ten times I've closed my heavy lids in vain
This early morn to court an hour of sleep;
For thou—tormentor!—constantly dost keep
Thy whizzing tones resounding through my brain,
Or lightest on my sensitive nose, and there
Thou trimm'st thy wings and shak'st thy legs of hair:
Ten times I've raised my hand in haste to smite,
But thou art off; and ere I lay my head
And fold mine arms in quiet on my bed,
Thou com'st again—and tak'st another bite.

As Uncle Toby says, "The world is wide
Enough for thee and me." Then go, I pray,
And through this world do take some other way,
And let us travel no more side by side.
Go, live among the flowers; go anywhere;
Or to the empty sugar-hogshead go,
That standeth at the grocer's store below;
Go suit thy taste with any thing that's there.
There's his molasses-measure; there's his cheese,
And ham and herring:—What! will nothing please?
Presumptuous imp! then die!—But no! I'll smite
Thee not; for thou, perchance, art young in days,
And rather green as yet in this world's ways;
So live and suffer—age may set thee right.

A COLLOQUY WITH MY PEN.

O SILENT solace of my lonely time,
   Beloved pen! why so reserved of late?
Hast thou renounced all fellowship with rhyme,
   And grown at once both rusty and sedate?
Art thou a-weary with thy journeyings o'er
The paper plain, and wilt thou go no more?
Or is thy jetty fluid all expended;
   The standish dry?—or hast thou lost the art
   Of limning well the passions of the heart?
Or art thou, like a touchy thing, offended
Because thou hast so long time been untended?
   Do tell what is the matter; let me know
   Why is't, my friend, that thou behavest so,
And all thy grievances shall soon be ended.

Stoutly the pen replied: "Good master mine!
   Thy willing servant 'tis my pride to be:
Why chide me when the blame is only thine?
   But seldom lately dost thou fondle me;
Seldom dost thou, with mild and musing air,
Doze dreamingly on thy accustom'd chair;
   To spread the sheet but seldom dost thou come,
And in thy former firm, affectionate way,
   Embrace me 'tween thy finger and thy thumb,
To note thy flitting thought. Wo worth the day
   When I no more may share thy fond regard!
Who'd wish to live when he no more is prized?
My throat is dry—my frame is oxidized;
   Indeed, good sir, you use me very hard!"

Nay, faithful pen! somewhat have I to say
   In my behalf.   Mine is a busy life;
And man, remember, is a pipe of clay,
   And often breaks while hardening in the strife
And fiery fury of this world's red oven,
   And needs a time for soldering and cooling—
An idling-time, though he be not a sloven,
   To mend his ways, and cease from self-befooling.
Then too remember, pen! the summer weather,
When every thing seem'd doom'd to melt together.
   The mind, besides, may have its wintry season,
When feeling flags, and all the mental sap
   Runs down into the root, and rhyme and reason
And thought and fancy take a quiet nap.

Remember further, pen! I'm growing older,
   And lazier too, perchance, in my estate;
Or it may be, too much is on my shoulder,
   And I bow down a little 'neath the weight;
Or I may think my wit has lost its salt,
   If ever truly thus 'twas impregnate;
   Or I may murmur at the poet's fate,
E'en though he be the sinner chief in fault.
Be what the cause, say not I love thee less,
   Nor chide me that I love thee not the more;
Some days like early ones may be in store,
When I again thy polish'd form shall press,
   And I create, and thou daguerreotype
The thinkings of my mind in every shade and stripe.

LINES TO MY SPECS.

MÆONIDES rehearsed a tale of arms,
And NASO told of curious metamorphoses;
Unnumber'd pens have pictured woman's charms,
While crazy LEE made poetry on porpoises:
But mine the glory to recount thy worth,
O crystal SPECS! that stand'st invisibly
Before mine eyes, and giv'st them power to see
What else they had not seen in heaven or earth.
Thou second-sight that sham'st old Scotia's seers!
Thou vision-giver of the scenes that lie
Beyond the reach of unanointed eye,
Far, far away in sight-confounding spheres!
Thou scal'st the very fortress of the stars,
And climb'st its gate for me, and lettest down the bars.

Without thee, what were life? A misty vision,
A murky morn, ne'er breaking from its gloom;
A barren world, without a field elysian;
A weary waste, with not a flower in bloom.
When, in time past, thou gottest first a-straddle
This nose of mine, a sort of nasal saddle,
Mine optics caper'd in the field of sight,
Like a young horse let loose among the clover,
That kicks his heels, and flies the meadow over,
And loudly whinnies in his fond delight:
Now, soberer grown, I sit like reverend sage
Beside the hearthstone while old Winter blows;
I place thee on my patriarchal nose,
And ponder gravely Wisdom's pregnant page.

Art's wondrous world thou layest bare to me;
  The painter's skill, the sculptor's graceful line:
  Thou openest the entrance to the mine
Of hidden treasures of philosophy;
Or, by thy magic power, I plume the wing,
  And fly to realms where deathless poets dwell:
I hear the lays their lips immortal sing,
  And list the tales their tongues were wont to tell.
By thee I scan the "human face divine,"
  The pleasing study loved so long and well;
I mark the graces that within it shine
  When in the breast the deep emotions swell,
Till mine own heart impulsively gives vent
To streams of gladness and affection blent.

THE OX AND THE GNAT.

A PEACEFUL ox, in ruminating mood,
  Beneath a tree one summer evening stood.
A hungry gnat, emerged from stagnant pool,
Cried angrily, "I'll kill that plodding fool!"
Its ire grew hot against the useful beast,
And straight got ready for a fight and feast.
"My blade I've drawn to take away thy life:
Thou booby brute, prepare thee for the strife!"
The ox disdain'd to give the gnat reply,
Nor turn'd his head, nor even wink'd his eye.
"Have at thee, then!" the fiery insect said;
The ox but whisk'd his tail—the gnat was dead.

VISITERS' WELCOME.

RIGHT welcome, good friends! but madam
    would know
Do ye come as the rain or come as the snow?
If ye come as the rain, it passeth away:
If ye come as the snow, it maketh a stay.
So come ye as rain or come ye as snow,
Ye're welcome to stay and ye're welcome to go.

WINTER'S PHASES.

ALL day long the clouds have hover'd,
    Drizzling on the earth below:
Tree and shrub with ice are cover'd,
    And like gems the branches glow,
        And twisted twig and slender stem
        Outglory any diadem.
Were the dull clouds to break away,
    Were the mid-heaven sun to shine,
The jewell'd world would flash to-day
    As if it were a diamond mine:
The dwellers on the orbs afar
    Might gaze in rapturous surprise,
And shout "A new-created star
    Is rising in the distant skies!"
But drearily the day runs down,
And night comes with a sullen frown.

Gather near the crackling embers,
Toast the slipper'd nether members,

While the wind among the willows
  Sweeps with deep re-echoing roar,
Till we seem to hear the billows
  Breaking on the sandy shore.

What rattles so against the pane,
Unlike the pattering of the rain?
'Tis hail! 'tis hail!   The rushing blast
Impels it furiously and fast:
Like pebbles pelted at a pillory,
Cracks the storm-cloud's small artillery.
    It ceases now;
    The noiseless snow
Coquettishly comes sidling down,
    And here and there
    And everywhere
It lies all o'er the dingy town,
  Like a pure mantle thrown above
  A sinful soul by pitying love.

The wind exults in sportive power;
Look out, and mark the frosty shower
It whirls from housetop and from tree
Till they are bare as poverty,
    And many a heap,
    Half fathom deep,
Is piled away in quiet nooks;
    And the plastic
    Snow, fantastic,
Whirls and twirls in curious crooks,
    Until we gaze,
    In feign'd amaze,
As if it were the work of spooks.

How beautiful the morning scene!
    A single peep

Reveals what pranks the wind has been
  About throughout
The hours when we were sound asleep.
And it has blown against the door
A heap so high 'twill make us sore
   To bear it hence away;
And, buried inches deep below
The surface of the untrodden snow,
   The spade is gone astray!

Who needs must work, and cannot play,
Alone go forth this snowy day
Till the path-finders clear the way;
And then hurrah for the gliding sleigh!
Cheerily, cheerily now they go,
Skippingly, trippingly over the snow;
      Ears a-tingling,
      Bells a-jingling,
And every belle beside a beau,
With eyes a-light and cheeks a-glow.
Skip it and trip it while ye may,
For a melting change is coming to-day.
There's a gentle breeze—it comes from the South–
As sweet as breath from the milch-kine's mouth;
   And the rays of the sun bend down to kiss
      The ice and the snow,
      And away they go
As if they perish'd beneath the bliss,
   Like simple souls in human clay
   Whose love has stolen their life away.

The cold, hard coat earth lately wore
   Grows soft and sleek as muddy ooze;
And happy they who have good store
   Of patience and impervious shoes.

It drips from the cornice,
  It drips from the eaves,
It drips from the boughs
  That are barren of leaves.
It thaws in the garden,
  It thaws in the street;
Alas for the bonnet
  And slight-cover'd feet!

The smoke from our chimney's too lazy to rise,
And like a sad story brings tears in our eyes;
  While, aching and sneezing
  And shaking and wheezing,
For weather that's freezing the invalid sighs.

  Lo! the king of the North
  Again rushes forth,
A ravenous beast from his lair,
  And, howling and growling,
  Around he goes prowling,
  As fierce as his own polar bear.
He touches the brooks, and the frighten'd elves
'Neath roofs of crystal conceal themselves;
And the earth grows hard as a selfish heart
That lives from its human-kind apart.

The frosty king has ceased his din,
And cold and quiet night sets in;
The stars, incomparably bright,
Swing near the earth their lamps of light,
As if to cast a cheering glow
O'er the dark and frozen world below.
There is a hearth—I know it well—
Where love and peace and plenty dwell;

And thankful hearts are biding there,
Who praise the Giver in their prayer:
And many such are in our land
Where love and hope link hand in hand;
Yet are there not GOD'S poor who shrink,
On night like this, from every chink,
And crouch like beasts that have no soul
Before a dim and dying coal?
Oh, *Thou* whose pity, love, and power
Around us hover every hour,
Awaken in our breasts the zeal
To toil for man as well as feel,
And for the love we bear to Thee
To comfort poor humanity.

ELLEN.

I.

NEAR where the crested billows kiss
    The Hudson's crystal water,
In years agone there lived in love
    A widow and her daughter.

Dear Ellen was a gentle girl,
    With sister none, nor brother:
Her sire had perish'd in the sea,
And other kindred none had she,
    None but her GOD and mother.

I've wander'd in a summer wood
    When all around was stilly,
And in a wayside nook I've seen
    A solitary lily.

Like such a lily, Ellen bloom'd
  In modesty and sweetness,
And, nurtured by a heavenly care,
  She grew in heavenly meetness.

I've wandered on the mountain side
  With gladness reigning o'er me,
And suddenly a wily snake
  Uncoil'd its form before me.

So in her peaceful path there came
  A man with aspect smiling;
He came as Satan came to Eve,
  In look and word beguiling.

"Beware of him whose speech is smooth,"
  The mother spake her daughter;
"The deepest depths are ever found
  Where flows the smoothest water."

"His heart is like an angel's heart,"
  The daughter spake her mother;
"He seeks to be to thee and me
  A loving son and brother."

For Robin laid his cunning game
  With art so deep and skilful,
That gentle Ellen's mind was turn'd
  To disobedience wilful.

And secretly at eventide
  . She left her home and mother:
The reverence to her parent due
  She gave unto another.

They stood before the man of God,
  Without a mother's blessing;

Then came again, and knelt to her,
  The hasty act confessing.

II.

The days of honeymoon were few—
  The days of joy were fewer;
For ere had pass'd the pleasant moon
That shineth in the month of June,
  The bride began to rue her.

Her sun of hope had set ere noon:
  Ah me! how sad the story,
That sudden night should follow morn
  Which woke in peace and glory.

The evening meal was set: the wife
  Was sitting by her mother:
The cloth was spread for three,—but where
  Was lingering now the other?

They sat in troubled silence there;
  The mother sadly eyeing
The speechless wife, whose eyes betray'd
  Her secret tears and sighing.

When secret tears are shed, the heart
  Has cause to be a weeper:
For hidden grief is mortal grief,
  And surely slays its keeper.

The evening time wore slowly on—
  The clock did chime eleven,
And Ellen and her mother bow'd
  And sought the grace of Heaven.

Another hour has pass'd, and, lo!
  The mid of night is over;
And where is Robin loitering still?
  Why cometh not the rover?

The dog is barking down the lane,
  A traveller's foot is coming:
And Ellen lifts her swollen eyes,
And staggering Robin she descries,
  A drinking-carol humming.

He falls upon the floor, and sleeps—
  More brutal he than human;
Oh cruel thought, that wretch so great
Should e'er become the bosom-mate
  Of meek and gentle woman!

The hours of early day approach;
  And as the morn is breaking,
Sad Ellen at the cooling spring
  Her fever'd heat is slaking,
And fearfully she waits the hour
  Of wretched Robin's waking.

Farewell to hope—the seed she cast
  Had blossom'd to be blighted!
Farewell to love—its purest gifts
  Were offer'd and were slighted!

III.

A piteous thing it is to see
  A child who has no mother,
Her father dead, her sisters dead,
  And dead her only brother.

That child is still a happy child,
  If only rest upon her
The memory of a father's name
  Crown'd with the humblest honour.

More touching is the sight to see—
  And to be pitied rather—
A hapless child whose portion is
  A drunkard for a father.

Four summers pass'd o'er Robin's son;
  His cheek was fair and glowing;
Behold him to the infant-school
  With eager footsteps going.

He walks alone; and when the school
  Is o'er, behind he lingers:
The merry children stand aside,
  And point at him their fingers.

"His father is a drunkard!" cry
  The heedless infant voices;
And Robin's boy sits down and weeps,
  While every child rejoices.

He hasten'd to his home—his cheek
  Without a smile or dimple:
"Father! am I a drunkard's child?"
  He said in accents simple.

Then Robin smote him; and he fell,
  His forehead sorely bruising,
And from his mouth a little stream
  Of blood came darkly oozing.

The boy awoke to pain and life,
  And Ellen sought to still him:
Yet reck'd he not the hand that nursed,
  Or his that fail'd to kill him.

Through many days, unmeaning words
  The hapless martyr mutter'd;
Then holy things of heaven and earth,
  By angels taught, he utter'd.

And GOD had mercy; and again
  He gave the child his reason:
And strange and wondrous things he said,—
Man's thoughts came from an infant's head,
  Like fruits before their season.

He never play'd again; but on
  Sad Ellen's bosom lying,
"Dear mother, sing!" to her he'd say,
And he would fold his hands and pray,
  And talk of heaven and dying.

'Twas on the holy morn that tells
  The resurrection-story,
He kissed her lips, and in her arms
  He pass'd to heavenly glory.

IV.

'Tis night. The spirit of the frost
  Upon the tempest rideth;
And wilder'd travellers o'er the waste
  A doom of death betideth.

Yet madden'd Robin wanders forth,
  Unearthly noises ringing
Within his ears, and in his breast
  Remorse, the scorpion, stinging.

The evil demon of the still
  A war with him is waging,
And reason topples from her throne,
  And Robin's wild and raging.

He wanders to the mountain's brink,
  Nor knows his fatal error;
He falls upon the jagged rocks,
  And cries in pain and terror.

The winds shriek hoarsely round his head,
  Like hungry tigers growling;
And through the night the tempest's voice
  Makes mockery of his howling.

No human ear is nigh to hear,
  And in his woe he dieth;
Upon the rocks at morning dawn
  A mangled body lieth.

v.

'Twas autumn eve. The tender flowers
  On every side were blighted;
The setting sun upon the hills
  The crimson maples lighted.

A breeze as soft as angel's breath
  Round Ellen's couch was stealing,
Where, praying fervently in faith,
  A man of GOD was kneeling.

The neighbours stood within the room
In silence all unbroken:
"The peace of GOD!" These only words
Were by the dying spoken.

The quietness of death was there
When her true soul departed;
For grace and mercy crown'd her end
Who lived the broken-hearted.

MY FATHER BLESSED ME.

MY father raised his trembling hand,
And placed it on my head:
"GOD's blessing be on thee, my son!"
Most tenderly he said.

He died, and left no gems nor gold,
But still was I his heir,
For that rich blessing which he gave
Became a fortune rare.

And in my day of weary toil
To earn my daily bread,
It gladdens me in thought to feel
His hand upon my head.

Though infant tongues to me have said
"Dear father!" oft since then,
Yet when I bring that scene to mind,
I'm as a child again.

WHISTLING.

NEGROES and boys may whistle in the street,—
      The boys because they're void of better sense,
   And Afric's sons because kind Providence
Has gifted them with whistling pipes complete,
      For oft they make a music rather sweet.
      Indeed, I listen with a sort of pleasure
      When they perform in harmony and measure,
And beat the time with swiftly-moving feet.
      And even men may whistle when they hear
   A tale that's somewhat marvellous and tough:
In case like this it may be well enough
      To make their incredulity appear;
Yet still I think most sensible men with me
That whistling is a bore will heartily agree.

At times when I have languidly reclined
      In musing silence, waiting for the birds
Of fancy to descend upon the mind,
      And sing to me the sweet poetic words
That people love,—when all the town was still
      Save the low, murmuring, human hum that rose
      Like mutter'd moanings from the lips of those
Who form the grist of death's e'er-going mill,—
Some glib performer with his music shrill
      Has made my fancies take a hasty flight,
      And, like the north wind of a winter night,
Has through my bosom sent a sudden chill.
      Despairingly, I've put my pen aside,
      And to my pillow pensively have hied.

SEPTEMBER RAIN.

PATTER! patter!
  Listen how the rain-drops clatter,
Falling on the shingle roof;
  How they rattle,
Like the rifle's click in battle,
  Or the charger's iron hoof!

  Cool and pleasant
Is the evening air at present,
  Gathering freshness from the rain;
  Languor chasing,
Muscle, thew, and sinew bracing,
  And enlivening the brain.

  Close together
Draw the bands of love in weather
  When the sky is overcast;
  Eyes all glisten,
Thankfully we sit and listen
  To the rain that's coming fast.

  Dropping—dropping
Like dissolving diamonds,—popping
  'Gainst the crystal window-pane,
  As if seeking
Entrance-welcome, and bespeaking
  Our affection for the rain.

  Quick, and quicker
Come the droppings,—thick, and thicker
  Pour the hasty torrents down:

Rushing—rushing—
From the leaden spouts a-gushing,
  Cleansing all the streets in town.

    Darkness utter
Gathers round: we close the shutter;
  Snugly shelter'd let us keep.
    Still unceasing
Falls the rain; but oh! 'tis pleasing
  'Neath such lullaby to sleep.

    How I love it!
Let the miser money covet,
  Let the soldier seek the fight;
    Give me only,
When I lie awake and lonely,
  Music made by rain at night.

LOST AND SAVED.

IT was a gallant ship
  And a goodly company
That left a peaceful port, and went
  A voyage o'er the sea.

The winds blew soft and fair,
  And sweet as a holy hymn
When chanted by the tuneful tongues
  Of heavenly cherubim.

The mariner's hearts were glad,
  And they slept without a fear;
And day and night the ship sped on,
  Till the wish'd-for land was near.

A little cloud arose,
  And a fire-ball suddenly came
With a thunder-clap from the little cloud,
  And set the ship on flame.

A circle was round the moon,
  And the North-Star hid his light;
And sorrow and fear fell on the hearts
  Of the mariners that night.

The burning ship appear'd
  Like a torch in a world of gloom;
And they knelt and pray'd to CHRIST to save
  Their souls from a fiery doom.

They launch'd their boats, and lay
  In silence on the sea;
And there they seem'd alone with GOD
  In his infinity.

With a hiss and a sudden plunge,
  The ship sunk in the wave,
And their fragile boats alone were 'tween
  The voyagers and the grave.

The morning slowly broke,
  "Ho, a sail! ho, a sail!" they cried,
And a lofty vessel, sent of Heaven,
  Came dashing o'er the tide.

Soon safe upon her deck,
  Their terrors were allay'd,
The mother was not left childless, nor
  The wife a widow made.

In many an after year,
  His children round his knee,
The father at his hearthstone told
  The dangers of the sea.

THE TWO PROCESSIONS.

ALONG the city's proudest street
  I heard the tread of many feet:
'Neath velvet pall and waving plume,
They bore a mortal to the tomb.

Ay, 'twas a grand and proud array,
And haughty mourners led the way:
Their scarfs in fashion's style were trimm'd,
Their eyes with sorrow all undimm'd.

I sigh'd, and o'er my bosom came
An utter sickening pang of shame;
And I had wept, had not mine eye
Found cause for worthier sympathy.

For as I turn'd my feet aside,
And through a nameless alley hied,
Slow issuing from an humble shed,
I saw the poor bring forth their dead.

The widow and her orphans twain
Outpour'd a sad and piteous strain:
Of husband and of father 'reft,
What had such hapless mourners left?

A moment, and the hearse was gone,
They feebly, faintly following on;

With silent tears and aching breast,
They bore him to his place of rest.

There in the potter's-field he lay
As soft as if in holier clay:
It matters little where they sleep
Whom CHRIST hath promised he will keep.

The harder toil, the sweeter rest;
More deeply cross'd, more richly blest;
And heaven a welcome boon must be
To such a weary man as he.

No holy man of GOD was there
To utter slow and solemn prayer,
Or bid them lift their weeping eyes
To homes and hopes beyond the skies.

But GOD was there; with healing balm,
He made the mourners' hearts grow calm:
They knelt and pray'd, and wondrous grace
Abounded in that lonely place.

THE BELL IN THE STEEPLE.

THE bell is hung
  In the new church steeple;
  Let it be rung
In the ears of the people;
    Ding-dong! ding-dong!
    Is the pleasant song,
    Sonorous and strong,
    It rolleth along

Over the ancient borough;
   For the founder's art
   Hath wrought its part
In a manner cunning and thorough;
   And over the rills,
   And up the hills,
And down in the verdant hollows,
   Note after note
   From its silver throat
In gambolling cadences follows.
   While the quick ear
   Of the kine and steer
Prick up in a sudden wonder,
   And skittish lambs
   Beside their dams
Frisk on the hillside yonder.
   When the birds shall come
   To their summer home,
To prey on the insect and berry
   Its musical ring
   Will charm them to sing
In choruses lively and merry.

   O comforting bell,
   Of ravishing swell,
   That steals like a spell
Over the soul of the sighing;
   And chases the gloom
   From the dim-lighted room
   Where, boding his doom,
A dim-eyed mortal is lying.
   The night creepeth on:
   "Will it ever be gone?"
The watchers inaudibly mutter.

The bell tolleth one—
The morn is begun;
And, mid a silence most utter,
The eyelids close
In a deep repose,
And, pain the breast forsaking,
GOD maketh whole
The smitten soul,
And joy salutes its waking.

O warning bell!
Its morning knell
Calleth to prayer and duty;
For the early hour.
Strengthens the power
Of outer and inner beauty.
O sleeper! rise,
And lift thine eyes
To Heaven as dawn is breaking,
And GOD shall bless
With good success
Thy righteous undertaking.

O honour'd bell!
Hung high to tell
The day of consecration—
The week's best prime,
The holy time
Of Sabbath and salvation.
A silent psalm,
Devout and calm,
Is felt within the spirit;
Though all unsung
By audible tongue,
Yet GOD's redeem'd may hear it;

And Peace comes down
And drops a crown
Of blessing on His people,
Who seek the place
Of promised grace,
When, from the sunlit steeple,
The musical din
That filleth the air
Shall welcome them in
To worship and prayer.
Let the bell still ring
To the glory of GOD,
When they who now sing
Sleep low in the sod:
When the high and the lowly
Born in all time
Shall bless the Most Holy
In chantings sublime.

INDIAN SUMMER.

THESE days of balmy breathings say
 The spirit of the south
Is lingering on her homeward way,
 Sweets dropping from her mouth:
Her presence field and forest fills,
And tunes to music all the rills.

The brilliant leaves adorn the trees,
 Within whose cooling shade
The aged men inhaled the breeze,
 And many an urchin play'd;
The trees whose dying loveliness
Is brighter than their summer dress.

The boughs are tenantless of birds;
  The squirrel's chirp is heard
Where concerts of melodious words
  The woods and orchards stirr'd:
Light-hearted warblers! wise betimes,
They've hied away to sunnier climes.

The sun, emitting modest rays,
  Hastes early to the west,
And bursts into a golden blaze
  Just as he dips his crest,
And bids our land a long good-bye
And speeds to light the western sky.

As one beloved expiring lies,
  And lifts her eye awhile
To give love's token ere she dies,
  And smiles a last sweet smile,
That e'er shall bide within the cell
Where memory's holiest treasures dwell,—

Thus Summer, as she dies away,
  Looks on the earth again,
And bids her shadows softly stray
  Amid the homes of men—
To bless them with her parting breath,
And reconcile them to her death.

THE GIRL AND WOMAN.

A CHEERY-MINDED maiden,
　　Just stepping o'er the line
Where womanhood and girlhood
　　Their boundaries combine;

The joyousness of girlhood,
　　The woman's conscious pride,
Commingled like the sunlight
　　In dalliance with the tide.

Her lips emitted music
　　That thrills my bosom yet;
Her eyes were bright as dew-drops
　　Upon a violet.

I say not she was handsome—
　　That may or may not be;
But she, in every feature,
　　Was beautiful to me.

I saw her, and I loved her—
　　I sought her, and I won;
A dozen pleasant summers,
　　And more, since then have run;

And half as many voices,
　　Now prattling by her side,
Remind me of the autumn
　　When she became my bride.

I'VE NOT THE HEART TO CUT THEM DOWN!

I'VE not the heart to cut them down!
　　These dry and dusty flowers,
That spring and summer smiled upon,
　　And fed with dews and showers:
I know they're dead; their leaves have flown,
　　Their stalks are crisp and brown;
Yet they may stand till winter's gone—
　　I cannot cut them down.

I've not the heart to cut them down!
　　For during summer's heat,
While pent within the sultry town,
　　They sprang up round my feet:
They look'd up in my face and smiled,
　　And comforted my soul,
So that I, like a chasten'd child,
　　Endured my daily dole.

I've not the heart to cut them down!
　　They were my garden's pride,
And when the buds were fully blown
　　Their fragrance wander'd wide,
And freely enter'd at my door
　　Below, around, above,
Till from the ceiling to the floor
　　The house was sweet with love.

I've not the heart to cut them down!
　　It may be they will fall
When Winter casts his heavy crown
　　Of snow upon them all:

Yet if they stand till Spring shall lay
　　Her blessing on the earth,
I'll gently bear the dead away,
　　While kindred flowers have birth.

GENTLE HUMANITIES.

SHOE the horse and shoe the mare;
　　Never let the hoof go bare:
Trotting over flinty stones
Wears away the hardest bones.

Life has many a stony street
Even to the toughest feet:
Men the sturdiest find it so
Ere through half of life they go.

Streaks of blood are in the way
Trod by humans every day,
Seen by love's anointed eye
While the blinded world goes by.

Yea, if all the sighs were caught
Wherewithal the air is fraught,
What a gale would sweep the skies
Laden with man's miseries.

Gently, then, O brother man!
Do the utmost good you can:
GOD approveth e'en the least
Deed of ruth to man or beast.

TO MY BOOT.

MINE ancient pedal friend, a last farewell!
  So many days we've footed it together
The lane of life, in fair and stormy weather,
Mine eyes wellnigh their lid-dikes overswell.
  I well remember when thou didst encase
My nether limbs with pressure warm and tight;
And many a corny twinge from morn till night
  Evinced the ardency of thine embrace.
Soon, like the love of some long-married wife,
  Thy grasp, if not so strong, was still as true,
And pleasanter; and as we grew in life,
  Thou wert as gentle as a pliant shoe;
And while on thee I trampled every day,
To shield me thou didst wear thy very sole away.

Though I despise the scandal-monger's art,
  And scorn the wretch who blackens the fair fame
Of one whose richest fortune is his name,
  (The wretch whose steel goes deeper than the
      heart,)
Yet it has been my daily wont, I own,
To black thy face until its skin has shone
  With ebon glow, as lustrous as the hue
That forms the charm of Guinea's native breed.
But 'twas not that I hated thee: indeed,
  I prized thee so, that when thy sole broke through
And let in water, 'twas my special heed
  A man of awls thy gaping wounds should sew;
And sundry pangs athwart my pocket shoot
To part with thee at last, O worn and faithful boot!

THE PRESENCE IN THE DWELLING.

AN awful Presence fills the silent dwelling—
    The dread Unseen unwelcomely is there;
And stricken bosoms piteously are swelling,
    And pallid lips are quivering in prayer.

The household band, from the young, timid lisper
    To hoary grandam, sit in sad dismay:
Their words are few, and spoken in a whisper,
    While wofully they wait the coming day.

Meek as a lamb, a victim there is lying,
    A deathly paleness covering all his face:
His mortal frame is slowly, surely dying—
    His soul is strong, and comforted by grace.

So loving is he in his last behaviour,
    His heart is touch'd by sorrowing friends' distress:
"Be thou this widow's GOD, O LORD my Saviour,
    And Father be to these my fatherless."

Before the Presence, mute is the physician;
    No drug can heal the fatal wound of Death;
And deaf alike to threatening or petition,
    He seals his victory with the parting breath.

The shadowy night, while all the earth is sleeping,
    Moves slowly on, and morning brings its cares;
The dead is here, but in the world unweeping
    Another brow a crown of glory wears.

TO BOB.

I BEAR you malice, Bob?—not I, indeed.
　　I can't afford it, Bob.　It costs too dear
To hate a human soul.　I'd rather bleed
　　Than thrust the point of hate's envenom'd spear
In any mortal's breast.　No, no! I say.
　　How could I seek a pardon at His hand
　　Who in The Book has left His stern command
That we must pardon others ere we pray?
　　There's far too much of selfishness in me
To sell my comfort for hate's paltry pay:
　　Of other's love I've grown too miserly
To cast it rashly, wickedly away.
　　Love is the all we have of heaven here;
　　If that were gone, this life were desolate and drear.

There is a bias, Bob, in every man
　　To go astray.　So was I taught in youth,
　　And later years have shown to me its truth.
Has there been one who without halting ran
　　The course of life?　If any such there be,
　　He's clad in more than our humanity:
And I am not the man, for I am frail,
　　As all earth's children are.　One—only One—
　　Once lived on earth by whom no wrong was done.
Though through infirmity I oft may fail,
　　Yet if, friend Bob! when suddenly assail'd,
I answer'd sharply when I should have smiled
　　And own'd that you had but jocosely rail'd,
Think not my mind by malice was beguiled.

16

THE STING OF THE TONGUE.

THE slanderer mingles falsehood with the truth,
    And serves the devil in his viler work.
Within his lips there may be found to lurk
A fang more deadly than the cobra's tooth.
    With keen, insane, insatiable delight,
He marks the accents of a victim's tongue;
    On idle words he sates his appetite,
And forth he goes, disgorging them among
    A world of slander-lovers.   Magnifying
The more they're spead, they tingle on the ear:
And those who tell the tale, and those who hear,
    Are apt confederates in the work of lying:
Thus a fair fame among the slanderers thrown
Is gnaw'd as hungry dogs delight to gnaw a bone.

More cruel is the slanderer than the snake;
    He spits his venom on a man's good name,
    Until the guiltless bows his head in shame,
And the fine fibres of his spirit break.
    The world avers, because his countenance changes
When some vile charge is made, that "'Tis a sign
    The man is guilty;" "That it very strange is;"
"And he deserves a punishment condign."
    But innocence is like the sensitive leaf;
Whene'er 'tis touch'd by breathings of suspicion,
    It trembles in an agony of grief,
And men misjudge its sorrowful condition:
    While brazen guilt confronts a righteous charge,
And blustering like a braggart, walks the earth at
        large.

PITY, GOOD GENTLEFOLKS.

HAVE pity on the poor, good gentlefolks;
  For they are cold and hungry. Starving pain
Is hard to bear, and oftentimes provokes
  The deed of infamy and crime, t'obtain
The bread that honest labour fails to earn.
Have pity on the poor; nor coldly turn
  The ear away from their distressful sighs.
Spurn not too rudely e'en the beggar: he
Has fallen far, yet let his misery
  Plead with your heart and dew your tender eyes.
Oh pity him! Perchance 'twas strong temptation
  That drew him to this fate: perchance 'twas grief
For loss of all. Deep is the desolation
  Of an unfriended heart. Vouchsafe him some relief.

Have pity on the poor—the hidden ones,
  Who shut their sorrows in their hearts,—the worn
And weary man,—the widow, and her sons
  And daughters fatherless,—the overborne.
Have pity on the hapless slave of toil,
  The patient, gentle, fragile sewing-girl,
  Whose thin and sunken cheek is pale as pearl,
Whose slender fingers constantly must moil,
  To wring from masters the small weekly dole
  That barely binds the body and the soul.
And ye fine ladies, beautiful and proud,
  Whose delicate forms are clad in rich array,
Remember those whose sister-heads are bow'd
  With toil for you, endured by night and day.

Ye strutters in the gilded halls of fashion,
  Who idly brush the humble man aside,—
Ye exquisites, too dainty for compassion,—
  Ye pinching, hard, unfeeling sons of pride,—
Ye who increase upon the poor man's labour—
  Who reap the harvest ye have never sown—
  Who eat the fruit that other men have grown,—
The LORD has said: "The wretched is your neighbour."
  Your brother too.   And in the Father's heart
(Who holds the world within His love, and gives
Its daily food to every thing that lives)
  Perchance he has a large and loving part.
Be kind and pitiful while yet ye may,
And sweep somewhat of human wo away.

The world is dark; and who for JESUS' sake
  Do good to man, are like the wayside lamps:
Their genial rays through yielding darkness break,
  And cheer the wanderer in the midnight damps.
They pale at breaking of the morn; but soon
  The sun majestic shall arise, and pour
A flood of radiance from the skies' mid-noon:
  Their little lamps are needed then no more,
But all enwrapt in heaven's own light and glory,
  These sons of mercy hear the Saviour say,
  "Ye did it to the suffering sons of clay,
And so 'twas done to Me."   The immortal story
  O'er the wide plains of Paradise shall fly,
  And crowds descend to welcome them on high.

THE DEAR ONE AT HOME.

OFT as I wander in fashion's crowded way,
Multitudes I see of the beautiful and gay:
With gold and with diamonds resplendent though
they be,
There's a dear one at home more beautiful to me.

Graceful as antelopes, and rouged with cunning skill,
A glance from their eyelids has potency to kill;
Their tones are as soft as the buzzing of a bee,
Yet a dear one at home is more beautiful to me.

Proudly their carriages roll along the street,
With coachman and footman and livery complete;
The fair ones within them may frown disdainfully,
The dear one at home is more beautiful to me.

They dwell in palaces, and mine's a lowlier lot;
But grandeur and palaces my soul will covet not,
If only at eventide I hear the melody
Of the dear one at home, so beautiful to me.

Our fireside has prattlers, whose laughing eyes are set
As brightly as diamonds within a violet;
And when, light as fairies, they spring upon my knee,
I love more the dear one so beautiful to me.

When I am weary and faint and overfraught,
I think of my home, and am happy in my thought;
The weight of my burden reminds me lovingly,
There's a dear one at home to lighten it to me.

WHY DELAY THE VIOLETS?

O WHY delay the violets?
   'Tis time they were
     Again astir,
My pretty, modest, blue-eyed pets!

I look'd for them but yestermorn—
   For every day
     I pass that way—
To see if they had yet been born.

I'll seek again to-morrow noon:
   The ice and snow
     Went long ago,
So I expect my darlings soon.

Then I will take my children there,
   And bid them see
     How modesty
May make the lowliest more than fair.

THE CITY-BOUND.

WHAT a pity—
   Biding in the parchèd city
All the fiery summer through!
   Dry and dusty,
Soul and body getting rusty,
   Lacking will to think or do.

Ever growing
Hot and hotter—fiercely glowing
  From the morning till the noon;
    Hot and hotter,
Like the furnace of the potter
  When it sings its 'custom'd tune.

    Not a pitcher
Full of water, to make rich, or
  Mollify the baken ground,
    Falls from heaven
From the sunrise till the even;
  All is dustiness profound.

    Of the ices,
Hundred hundred-weight suffices
  Not to cool the city's heat;
    Drinking, drinking
Is in vogue instead of thinking;
  Frozen water is our meat.

    Oh for fountains
Running down from icy mountains!
  Oh for palaces of cream!
    Oh for shadows
Cast by trees o'er pleasant meadows
  Dreamt of in a poet's dream!

    Oh to wander
Where the tinkling rills meander
  Down the hill-side to the strand;
    Often stooping,
Draughts of cooling water scooping
  With the hollow of my hand.

Oh what pity
In the hot and parchèd city
    To abide the summer through!
Dry and dusty,
Soul and body growing musty,
    Lacking strength to will or do.

THE ANGEL IN A MAIDEN'S EYES.

ONCE methought I saw an angel
    Peeping from a maiden's eyes,
And my heart was captive taken,
    Like a city by surprise.

Then it seem'd another angel,
    Springing upward from my heart,
From mine eyes look'd on the other,
    And beheld its counterpart.

At the moment of the greeting,
    From her lips no whisper fell;
And before her I was silent,
    Rapt in a delicious spell.

Love, awaking in my bosom—
    Love of pure impulses born—
Lighted up my happy pathway,
    Like a sun of summer morn.

Mark'd for mine the gentle maiden
    With the angel in her eyes,
Years agone we link'd our fortunes
    By indissoluble ties.

"HE WILL NOT AGAIN FORGET US."

THAT phrase I cannot help but feel,
 Unless my heart be made of steel:
Forget mine ancient friend—my Neal!
  "Nevermore!"
  As said the raven
 To the trembling, timid craven
 Lover of the maid Lenore,—
  "Nevermore!"

How many pleasant memories—
 And mournful ones as well—
(These to sadden—those to please)—
 Are treasured in the cell
Within my mind wherein I store
Memorials of the days of yore,—
  How many such
  But need a touch
To break their gentle slumber;
  And up they start
  Around the heart
A host without a number.

  Forget! forget!
  Nay, never yet
Have Lethe's waves my memory met;
  And far away
  May be the day
When, to "forgetfulness a prey,"
  My mental ear
  No more shall hear
Dead voices speak that once were dear.

Some days of darkness have been mine,
When hope had nearly ceased to shine;
  And I have lain
  In utter pain
Amid the blackness round me.
  Yet even then
  Light came again,
And GOD'S own mercy found me.
  No! I would not
  Consent to blot
Such times from recollection,
  For now they bring
  No barbèd sting,
But quicken my affection;
  And they fill up
  Anew the cup
That cures the soul's dejection.

Nor is it needful to forget
The sins and follies we regret:
  They well may stand,
  And mark the shoal
  Where once the soul
  Was like to strand.

The memory of our errors past
A shade upon our path may cast;
But if it lead us to abhor
The thing that grimed our soul before,—
  And turn our face
  To Heaven for grace
To do the evil deed no more,—
Then it were fitting that the sprite
Anon should dimly meet our sight;
And wiser, better beings we
Perchance were for his company.

Forget a friend whose hand I've held,
   Who sleepeth still and low,
The tumult of life's battle quell'd?—
   No! never—never! no!

OBESE HUMANITY.

'TIS a distressing sight to see
   A man of vast obesity,
Who needs but handle and a spout
To seem a pitcher out and out;
Whose dumpling cheek and double chin
Show clearly how he does within;
Whose waddling walk and portly paunch,
And shoulder-width, and breadth of haunch,
Are proof he knows the worth of steak,
And that he eats for eating's sake.

   His running days are overpast:
No fear can make him hurry fast;
If bull or dog be at his heel,
The teeth or horns he's like to feel;
If sudden showers arise and fall,
He patiently must bide them all;
While others "trip it as they go
On the light fantastic toe,"
By law of gravity he's bound
To slip along the solid ground;
When Summer dons her melting guise,
And fills with heat the earth and skies,
The hapless victim fain would be
Diminishing diurnally;

And yet but little less he grows
From crown of head to tip of toes,—
And Winter comes, soon filling him
With spermaceti to the brim.

Good-humour, cheerfulness and fun
In oily channels love to run;
And all along the way he goes
The milk of human-kindness flows;
And in the corner of his eye
A nest of smiles a child might spy,
And when he gives them wings to fly,
They flit to every bosom nigh.

I'd not be fat—I'd not be lean,
But in the middle state between.
'Tis very troublesome, no doubt,
To bear a load of flesh about;
And yet 'twere better so to do
Than be as crooked as a screw,
And lean as Cassius was, who drew
A dagger—lean and hungry too—
And with a mean and traitorous crew
The unsuspecting Cæsar slew.

But be a person fat or lean,
If he but have the grace within
To be at peace with Heaven and man,
And does his duty as he can,
With hearty will his hand I'll take,
And love him for his goodness' sake.

AUTUMN RHYMES.

I'VE several times in vain essay'd to sing
  A simple song of Autumn. Other fingers
Have oft and sweetly touch'd the tuneful string,
  And waked the pensiveness that lifelong lingers
In hearts of men, like some long-hallow'd story.
  I've seen the tender flowers grow pale and die,—
  The dry and wither'd leaves around me lie,—
The sun go down in his peculiar glory,—
The thrice-expanded moon come slowly up,
  And break a passage through the eastern vapours,—
  The clear-eyed stars light up their little tapers
And swing them out, each in a crystal cup,
  As if to lure the feet of mortals thither,
  The land of love, where hopes nor flowers wither.

And I have had within some partial movings
  Of spiritualness; some quickening of the feelings;
Yet careless heed I've given to the reprovings
  Of nature in her many-voiced revealings.
The Autumn is a solemn missioner;
  A preacher to the sons of men is she:
And happy he who learns betimes of her
  The wholesome truth of his mortality,
And ponders well the fleetness of his days,
And meekly walks in heavenly wisdom's ways.
  The fading leaf's an eloquent text to man:
" We all do fade, and wither as a leaf;"
  And he who reaches life's extremest span
Exclaims in sadness, "Ah! my days are brief!"

THE DECAYING HOMESTEAD.

A PENSIVENESS of feeling
 Unbidden comes a-stealing
  Over me
  When I see
An old house going
  To decay,—
The wild grass growing
  In the way—
The window-shutters hanging
  Half awry,
Now creaking and now banging
When the gale sweeps by,—
  The shatter'd panes
Bespatter'd by the rains—
  The empty rooms
As silent as the tombs—
  The dusty floor—
The spider weaving in the door—
The awfulness of desolation
Pervading the habitation,
  While all things wear
A comfortless, unwelcome air.

The family gathering no more is there,
  Cheerful and calm;
  No morning prayer
  Nor evening psalm:
No joyous maiden's voice is heard
Outcarolling the mocking-bird;
  No children's laugh;
No old man leaning on his staff,

Nor matron there is seen
Before the door at eventide serene.
No neighbours come to chat
    Of this and that,
And for old friendship's sake,
The Souchong cup partake;
But silence and desolation
Pervade the habitation,
    And all things wear
A comfortless, unfriendly air.

Where is the human band
    That here abode?
Have all departed to the land
    Whose only road
Is through death's dim domain?
Vain the inquiry—vain!
There is not one to tell
How the old family fell:
Pass'd out of mind,
    Forgotten quite,
The record left behind
    Is blank as night.
Gone to a world afar,
    Perchance on high
From some resplendent star
    They turn a wondering eye
To their old home below,
    And love Him with intenser **love**
Who beckon'd them from wo
    To an immortal home above,
Where holy exultation
Pervades their habitation,
And all things wear
A heavenly and glorious air.

THE BEAUTIFUL DAYS OF SPRING.

THE cold and rugged weather stripp'd the trees,
    And made them very desolate.   'Twas not
A single frosty, biting autumn-breeze
    That tore the leaves from their first nestling-spot.
The winds unkindly came day after day,
    And smote the gentle things.   They bore the blast
    Awhile, and then began to shrivel fast,
And wild December swept them all away.
The rage of winter having pass'd, the year
    Put on a milder face.   The sun broke forth
And dallied with the balmy atmosphere,
    And shone so smilingly, the frigid north
Call'd back its murky clouds, and all around
The timorous plants came peeping through the ground.

The melancholy trees revived again;
    On every bough the budding leaves appear'd;
And earth grew lovelier in the sight of men,
    And many a heart with hopeful thought was cheer'd:
For sadness with the winter pass'd away,
And spring gave promise of a better day.
    The birds came trustingly and lived among us,
And sweet-lipp'd flowers on morning breezes flung us
    A perfume delicate; and every field,
Though simply clad in garniture of green,
    The beauteous handiwork of GOD reveal'd.
How great the lesson taught by such a scene,—
    That sunny looks and kindly actions e'er
    Cause flowers of love to flourish fragrantly and fair.

THE HOME OF THE HAPLESS.

HUMANITY in its despised conditions,
   Ye tender ones whose hands are soft as down,
Is oft too touching in its exhibitions
   To wake a dainty or unpitying frown.

For here, apart from all the self-relying,
   The spirit-broken desolate abide:
Dead souls, ambitionless and unreplying,
   Their hopes long buried in the grave with pride.

And here are those by food and shelter cherish'd,
   And clad in clothing that is not their own,
Who on life's highway else outright had perish'd,
   Or stagger'd on with many an inward groan.

Here, too, are those whose minds are gone demented,
   Served tenderly and nursed with healing care;
Their shrewdest cunning wisely circumvented
   Till reason sits in her accustom'd chair.

Small children, on the shore of life's deep ocean,
   Like waifs pick'd up by charitable hands,
Are nurtured here with woman's own devotion,
   And bound in virtue's time-enduring bands.

A refuge-place for Penury's sons and daughters,
   Where they may ease its bitterness and smart;
Bethesda's pool, where angels stir the waters,
   And proffer healing for the bleeding heart.

17*

Thanks be to GOD, the wretched may be tended,
  Although his kinsmen all be far away:
Thanks to His name, the orphan is befriended
  When father, mother sleep beneath the clay.

Thanks be to GOD, that Christian love prevaileth
  Against the sin and selfishness of earth:
Thanks to His name that charity ne'er faileth,
  But now, as ever, shows its heavenly birth.

A COUNTRY SABBATH.

MORNING SCENE.

THE frost in its beauty lies over the meadows,
  Like down newly shaken from winter's young
    wing;
The sun is ascending, and skeleton shadows
  The trees in their nakedness pensively fling.

The morning is silent, save when the brook's flowing
  Awakens a music like silvery bells,
Or where the cock's crowing, or gentle kine's lowing,
  Of home and its treasures of charity tells.

The smoke from the homestead, one wreath on
    another,
  Like incense arises from piety's hearth,
Where father and mother, and sister and brother
  In harmony worship the LORD of the earth.

The sun lights the vane of a far-away steeple,
  The sound of a bell is borne faintly along,
And staidly and peacefully gather the people,
  To join in the prayer and awaken the song.

The calm of devotion refreshes the spirit,
  The soul is set down to a banquet of bliss;
The ministering angel must surely be near it,
  For earth can provide no enjoyment like this.

EVENING SCENE.

THE day is departing—the shadows are denser;
  The shrilly-voiced cock and the cattle are still;
The cold of the north becomes keen and intenser,
  And freezes to silence the tongue of the rill.

The arch of the heavens is glowing with glory,
  For diamond-lit lanterns, by angels outhung,
Swing over the earth, and a marvellous story,
  While man is unconscious, by seraphs is sung.

The darkness of night like a mantle is lying
  On the children of joy and the children of sorrow,
Who, while the still moments unheeded are flying,
  Lie down in the hope of a better to-morrow.

When the locks of old age shall fall down on my
    shoulder,
  If the wisdom of Heaven so lengthen my time,
Oh may I present to the youthful beholder
  A vision as peaceful—an end as sublime!

ASCENT OF ST. ANTHONY'S NOSE.

WE climb'd St. Anthony's Nose;
    Its sides were powder'd with snows,
Yet up to the summit we rose
By favour of fingers and toes.

The labour was toilsome and long,
Our wills were sturdy and strong,
Each sinew was tough as a thong,
And our spirits were light as a song.

The track of the rabbit was there,
And the path of the fox to his lair;
And prints—perhaps of a bear—
Admonish'd us "Boys, have a care!"

The partridges rose with a whirr,
And many a quail did we stir;
We harmless and weaponless were,
And harm'd not their feathers and fur.

As cliff after cliff we attain'd,
A cliff still higher remain'd;
Our strength more sternly we strain'd,
For a failure we proudly disdain'd.

So upward and onward we went,
And—ere we were totally spent—
Accomplish'd our purposed intent,
And stood on the topmost ascent.

We witness'd the Hudson below
Roll on with its glorious flow,
While Lilliput vessels did go
With Lilliput men to and fro.

To see what more we might spy,
We climb'd an oaken tree nigh;
But mountains and river and sky
Outran the reach of the eye.

We roll'd some rocks down the hill
Along the bed of a rill;
They went with a rush and a will—
I hear them, I fancy me, still.

Majestic each awful rebound,
As the rocks whirl'd madly around,
And frequent their clattering sound
Came up from the solemn profound.

The days of boyhood and youth—
Ere we'd an aching eye-tooth,
When fun was mingled with ruth—
Seem'd present in primitive truth.

So much delight did we sip,
Our joy ran over the lip,
As drops from a bucket will drip
That late in the well had a dip.

But feeding on ideal food
Can do the stomach no good;
We soon got over that mood,
And a course descending pursued.

A bright lookout did we keep
As we slid each threatening steep;
And now did we warily creep,
And then took a slide and a leap.

We'd done all we had design'd
The day before in our mind,
And now, as our hunger inclined,
We went to the village and dined.

If, at some notable time,
The Swiss Jungfrau we should climb,
I'll tell it in verse more sublime,
Though not in a livelier rhyme.

NEW YEAR'S EVE IN A FOG ON THE HUDSON.

WE pass'd the night at Yonkers;
 The fog above, the fog below
 Had made it quite unsafe to go
A-steaming down the river.
 The captain wouldn't—
 Couldn't—shouldn't
 Peril lives
 Of maidens, wives
 And husbands, brothers,
 Fathers, mothers—
No wonder he did shiver.
 So there we lay
 Half on our way,
Yet not a soul was fain to stay.

The darkness horrid
Deeply loom'd;
And aft and for'ard
Were entomb'd.
The drizzly drops around us fell,
The essence of the fog distill'd;
Our bosom's anguish who can tell,
With hope of home so rudely chill'd?
And there we sate
In silent state,
And like the kine did ruminate.
Without debate
The joy was great—
When tea-time came—to masticate.
It hath been never
That a man could eat forever;
And soon the tea
Was no more 'mong the things that be.
Some did this, and some did that;
Some were silent, some did chat;
Some frown'd, and others loudly laugh'd
As if a cup of fun they'd quaff'd;
When, lo! a silent gathering—
A preacher rose to pray:
And when he'd said his solemn say,
Then we began to sing,
To "Auld Lang Syne,"
"When I can read my title clear."
And oh! it made this heart of mine
Dance lightly as a mountain deer
When summer mornings shine.
Though we were met as strangers there,
We own'd our brotherhood;
And joining in the social prayer,
Before our Father stood.

I felt assured the Father's eye
Look'd kindly on that company.

The Old Year now was wellnigh gone;
  The remnant sands were falling,
When suddenly there broke upon
  Our ears the din of brawling.
Some rowdies bound for Gotham city,
  Thus prison'd on their route,
Obtuse to gentleness or pity,
  Got huge horse-fiddles out:
    They rang a bell,
    And sprang a rattle
    With many a yell
    As if of battle:
And though no human lost his life,
Yet "sleep was murder'd" in the strife.
    Quietly, quietly,
    Snug in a corner,
    Sat a small company,
Fearing no evil and heeding no scorner.
    Tired of singing,
Sleep her sweet poppies upon them was flinging;
    But scarce had an eyelid
    Reposed on its fellow,
    Ere sleep ran off frighten'd
    As the wild bellow
    And shout of the b'hoys
Astounded the Highlands with thundering noise.
    No rest was there to be found
    For the drowsy head;
    The noise of the riotous drown'd
    (It truly was said)
The snore of the sleeper, and woke him outright,
As mad as a bull and ready for fight.

So, groaning, aching,
   Chilly, shaking,
Stretching, yawning,
We awaited morning's dawning.
   Wo-begone and vigil-worn,
     Every human
     Man and woman
Grew dishearten'd and forlorn.
   Oh, how dreary,
     Sad, and weary
Was that night at Yonkers!

CELESTIAL FROLICS.

THE sun had put his night-cap on,
   And cover'd o'er his head,
When troops of stars appear'd amid
   The curtains round his bed.

The moon arose, most motherly,
   To take a quiet peep
How all the stars behaved while he
   Her sovereign was asleep.

She saw them wink their silvery eyes,
   As if in roguish play;
Though silent all, to her they seem'd
   As if they'd much to say.

So, lest their winking should disturb
   The sleeping king of light,

She rose so high that her mild eye
  Could keep them all in sight.

The stars, abash'd, stole softly back,
  And look'd demure and prim;
Until the moon began to nod,
  Her eyes becoming dim.

Then sleepily she sought her home,
  That's somewhere in the west;
And as she went, the playful stars
  Wink'd at the dame in jest.

And when the moon was fairly gone,
  The imps with silvery eyes
Had so much fun it woke the sun,
  And he began to rise!

He rose in glory!—from his eyes
  Sprang forth a new-born day,
Before whose brightness all the stars
  Ran hastily away.

THE HOUSE LOVE-HAUNTED.

GIVE me a house that's haunted,
    With Love the only sprite;
I'll dwell in it undaunted,
  Nor fear its utmost spite.

Though witching tones are swelling
  Above me and beside,
Where Love is in the dwelling
  I am content to bide.

If every beam and rafter
  And every stone and tile
Re-echo with its laughter,
  My heart shall laugh the while.

The favour'd room or chamber
  Frequented by the ghost,
I'll gladliest remember,
  And I will prize it most.

When in the midnight lonely
  Day's brighter scenes are hid,
I'll sweetly sleep if only
  Love stirs the coverlid.

When morn is stilly breaking,
  And earth is growing light,
I'll tremble not if, waking,
  Mine eyes behold the sprite.

If, as the day grows older,
  The heavenly-temper'd thing
Taps tenderly my shoulder,
  Rejoicingly I'll sing.

I'd ever be enchanted
  By Love's bewitching spell,
And in a house love-haunted
  I would my lifelong dwell.

And when my time is ending,
  And heaven is coming nigh,
Let Love, my soul attending,
  Go with me to the sky.

THE PEOPLE'S PRAYER.

HOW long, O LORD, shall this dear land be rent?
 How long must she the cup of anguish drink?
How long her children's souls, unshriven, be sent
 To nameless graves of horror-clouded brink?
Trembling with woe, she like a mother stands,
 The tears thick dripping from her cheek of clay,
Her garments stain'd with blood that brothers' hands
 Have spill'd from brothers' hearts in mortal fray.
Her sons in thousands, fever'd, maim'd, and pale,
 The wreck of men, are moaning at her feet,
While widow'd and fatherless lift up the wail
 O'er sires and husbands in their winding-sheet.
O holy GOD! let thy sweet mercy shine
To thy great glory on this land of Thine.

Let not ambition and the thirst for power
 Still rule the spirits of rebellious men:
Not lust for gold put off the lingering hour
 When CHRIST-like peace shall bless our homes again.
Purge us of sin, and let thy wrath go by,
 Lest all the people perish from the land.
For His dear sake whom Thou didst give to die
 For all the world, O turn away thy hand.
May holy men on holy days recount
The words of peace of JESUS on the mount,
 Till love shall conquer hate, and kindred foes,
Forgiving as they hope for grace from Thee,
 And turning from the sins that brought our woes,
Shall evermore abide in strengthful unity.

FANCIES BY THE SEA.

LONELY by the sea,
On the reaches
Of the beaches
Wandering dreamily,
Gazing o'er its dim expanse into infinity:
Listing to the moaning of the multitude of sprites
That skim along the waters in the dark of moonless
nights:
Listing to the groaning as of voices of the lost,
The spectral forms invisible on restless billows tost:
The tumbling and the rumbling
Of the sea, of the sea,
The shrieking and the howling and the grumbling
Of the sea,
As it rushes to the shore
With a wild and hungry roar,
While the whirling and the twirling and the curling
Of the breakers on the sand
Foreshow the wilful madness
Of passion in its badness
Dashing into ruin on vice's fatal strand.
Oh, the moaning and the groaning,
The monotonous intoning
Of the sea,
The moaning sea,
The groaning sea,
So like to humankind, so like perchance to me.
Yet the bland old sea,
The giver of our health;
The grand old sea,
The bringer of our wealth,

18*

Creator of the clouds of blessing over all the land,
    Replenishing the rills
    That, sliding down the hills,
Fructify the valleys where the growing harvests stand;
    The great wide sea,
    The sea whose majesty
Proclaims the love as well as might
    Of our most holy LORD,
Who call'd the sea and land out of realms of chaos-
    night
    At His word.

DAVID MYERLE.

WE lay him here. 'Tis but the dust
    We hide beneath the sod;
The soul is dwelling with the just,
    The saint is with his GOD:
And while our eyes bedew the clay,
From his all tears are wiped away.

Not many lines by him were writ
    In life's unfading scroll;
But they were beautiful, and fit
    For such a saintly soul,
And they will stand in living light
Before his heaven-anointed sight.

Life's more than years. He who begins
    His work at early day
The crown of glory often wins
    Ere morn has pass'd away;
And enters in his budding prime
The rest of an eternal time.

GOD'S ADOPTED.

THE sun may wrap his face in cloud,
  The midnight winds may scream aloud,
The snow may sweep o'er hill and plain,
Or vales be flooded by the rain ;
The thunder follow lightning's flash
Till earth shall tremble at the crash,
And waves may leap aloft in foam,
Yet God provides a sheltering home
Where his adopted ones may rest
Like birds safe-hidden in their nest,
Where, in the dim and silent night,
When every shadow seems a sprite,
The lambs of Jesus sweetly sleep,
While watch and ward his angels keep,
Bend gently o'er the unconscious heads
And hover round about their beds :
And in the day, when evil men
Would lure the hapless to their den,
And many a trap is laid to snare
The young and friendless unaware,
Then angel footsteps with them go
In pleasant rambles to and fro,
Their wants supply, and lessons give
How the good Lord would have them live,
And teach them in the heavenly lore
That makes them wise forevermore.
The angel-hands the child caress,
The child whose name is fatherless,
The angel kisses warm the brow
That shares no mother's kisses now.
No wings have they, these angels fair,
To soar afar in upper air ;

No strange, fantastic robes have they ;
No bands across their brows they lay ;
A holier garb they wear instead,—
A spirit meek and quieted.
The mothers of the motherless
    And fatherless, they pass along ;
So God their loving work shall bless,—
    They seek no plaudits from the throng.
This busy world is vast and wide,
With want and woe on every side ;
And they work well who take some part
Of sorrow from a single heart ;
And they work best whose work in love
Shall meet the Master's praise above.

HUNGARY.

1848.

IF tears were medicine for wo,
    Then were it well to weep;
For Hungary has fallen—fallen low
        Before her foe,
    And slavery's legions sweep
Across the plains where Liberty descended.
    The unequal strife is ended;
And man, oppress'd and foil'd, sinks down
        Beneath the frown
        Of proud and cruel lords.
    The patriot swords,
Drawn in defence of liberty and right,
And gory with the blood of valorous fight,
        Lie in the dust,
        Discolour'd with the rust;

The tyrant's steel
Has touch'd a vital part;
His heel
Is set on Hungary's quivering heart.

Oh! hapless land,
Bestead by fire and brand!
Her mothers and her maidens refuge seeking,
Their garments reeking
With blood from the accursed rod,
That tears their flesh while they are shrieking
In agony to GOD.
The homes where hope had lighted
Her promise-fires are desolate and blighted:
The winds, melodious once with freedom's song,
Groan with the piteous plaint of causeless wrong:
The sunlight falls on blasted fields,
Whose soil no recompense to reaper yields:
The stars look tearfully on hopeless men
Who have no heart to look on high again;
But stricken, humbled, broken, crush'd—
The nobler voices of their being hush'd—
They bear the heavy chain,
Or gnaw in silence at its links in vain.

Shall it be ever so?
Heaven and earth together answer No!
But, sure as the eternal heaven stands,
The LORD will break the bands
Wherewith the tyrants fetter Freedom's hands.
Freedom is but a little child of days,
And yet a child immortal as the truth;
When tyranny shall totter in its ways,
That child shall show the lusty strength of youth;
The rusty shackles from its limbs shall fall,
And down to ocean's deepest depths shall go;

The oppress'd in all the earth shall heed the call,
    And join the strife against the common foe.
O day of glory and of triumph too!
    O wretched foes, accursed of GOD and man!
Where will ye hide when heaven and earth pursue,
    And Truth and Freedom lead the battle-van?

THE FALLING HOUSE.

WHO dwells within this mansion hoary,
    Crumbling, tottering, soon to fall;
The tokens of whose former glory
    Linger faintly on the wall?

The windows, dark and stain'd and dusty,
    Dimly light the inner room;
The hinges of thy limbs are rusty,
    Lonely sitter in the gloom!

Is there no voice in thee abiding,
    Accent tremulous or strong,
To tell the passer-by some tiding
    As he wanders here along?

The watcher at thy gate of hearing,
    Dull and drowsy, heeds no sound,
The outer world to him appearing
    Silent as a burial-ground.

Oh! why art thou so unreplying,
    Inmate of this ruin gray?
Alas! I speak but to the dying;
    Lo! the soul has pass'd away!

Deserted, dark, disfurnish'd dwelling,
    Empty utterly and riven,
Thy lifelong tenant now is swelling
    Psalms and hymns and songs in heaven.

And thou, in beautiful expansion
    Built again, no more to fall,
Shalt be the soul's immortal mansion
    Who here tenanted thy hall.

LINCOLN.

SO deep our grief, it may be silence is
    The meetest tribute to the father's name:
A secret shrine in every breast is his
    Whom death hath girt with an immortal fame;
And in this dim recess our thoughts abide,
    Clad in the garment of unspoken grief,
As fain the sorrow of the heart to hide
    That yields no tears to give our woe relief.
But death is not to such as he, we cry:
    His tongue is mute; his heart may pulse no more:
Yet men so good and loved do never die;
    But while the tide shall flow upon the shore
Of time to come, a presence to the eye
    Of nations shall he be, and evermore
Shall freemen treasure in historic page
This martyr-hero of earth's noblest age.

REMEMBER THE POOR!

REMEMBER the poor!
 It fearfully snoweth,
 And bitterly bloweth;
Thou couldst not endure
 The tempest's wild power
 Through night's dreary hour,
Then pity the poor!

Remember the poor!
 The father is lying
 In that hovel, dying
With sickness of heart.
 No voice cheers his dwelling,
 Of JESUS' love telling,
Ere life shall depart.

Remember the poor!
 The widow is sighing,
 The orphans are crying,
Half starving for bread;
 In mercy be speedy
 To succour the needy,—
Their helper is dead!

Remember the poor!
 The baby is sleeping,
 Its mother is weeping,
For woe's in her breast;

Her cheek, wan and hollow,
Betokens she'll follow
Her husband to rest.

Remember the poor!
To him who aid lendeth,
Whatever he spendeth
The LORD will repay;
And sweet thoughts shall cheer him,
And GOD's love be near him,
In his dying day.

THE EDITOR SAT IN HIS SANCTUM.

THE editor sat in his sanctum,
In a hapless plight was he;
Fain would he fall in a thinking fit,
For he was at the end of his wit
As to what his leader should be.

He had reap'd his brain so often,
The soil seem'd barren grown;
The forest of wit was fell'd to the stump,
The flowers of fancy were gone, save a clump
Where the seed had lately been sown.

He fish'd in the river of knowledge,
But his angling-line was short:
"Surely there's plenty of fish in the sea,
But 'tis as plain as a herring," quoth he,
"In deeper waters they're caught."

19

He dived to the bed of his ocean,
  Where the pearls did erst abound;
He raked and sifted the briny mud
That lies below the emerald flood,
  But not an oyster he found.

"Ah, what shall I do!" he murmur'd:
  That imp will rap at the door:
Methinks his tones on my ear-drum stir,—
'The men are all waiting for copy, sir,
  And they are growling for more.'"

"It hath been quoted often,
  With a full meed of credit,
The maxim Witherspoon spake in his day,
'Never to speak till you've something to say,
  And stop when you have said it.'

"Ah, good advice to a parson,"
  He sadly went on to say;
"But I would ask, who ever said it, or
  Hinted such thing to a brain-worn editor,
    From his birth to his dying-day?"

He rose in his mental anguish,
  And turn'd the key in his door;
The messenger came, and loudly did knock,
But the editor sat as still as a stock,
  And the imp then knock'd the more.

The editor lean'd on his patience
  As on a cushion'd chair;
And he sat him down, and he rock'd away,
While fancies began in his mind to play,
  And thoughts to nestle there.

He neither swore nor curséd,
  He hated a word profane;
(Ah, verily, he who curses and swears
But adds to his sins and adds to his cares—
  And the vice is mean and vain.)

The editor and the devil
  Maintain'd the skirmish-strife;
For the inky imp kept sturdily knocking,
While the editor was incessantly rocking
  And thinking as for his life.

His fancies came like a morning
  In the beautiful time of May;
And thoughts, like the rays of light, shot out,
And tremblingly glimmer'd and twinkled about,
  Till his mind was as clear as day.

The imp was drumming and drumming
  A rat-a-tat on the door;
The editor cared not a whit for his thumps,
But quietly finger'd his ideal bumps,
  Till the flood began to pour

Down to the tip of his fingers,
  When he caught the paper and pen,
And beautiful things from the bodiless air
Were call'd into being, and written down there,
  A blessing to true-hearted men.

Truth shone on the face of the paper,
  And the editor's heart was light:
For noble the man among noble men
Who fears not to ply a truth-telling pen
  For GOD and for human right.

He sprang to the door of his sanctum
  As swift as a Grecian winner
When reaching the goal in Olympian race,
And the copy he push'd in the messenger's face,
  And thankfully went to his dinner.

LIFE ERAS.

A FOUR-YEAR, prankish and dumpy,
  In time long, long ago,
Like Cupid, fat and stumpy,
  With a skin as pure as snow;
And a cheek that round its dimples very
Much resembled a honey-cherry
That had blush'd through all the month of June
'Neath the kisses of sun and stars and moon;
  With hair that straggled everywhither,—
    So light that a puff
    Of wind was enough
  To waft it freely hither and thither.
    His eyes were blue,
And sparkled like drops of tremulous dew,
And winks of love and flashes of fun
Flew from the lids like shot from a gun.
    Yet oftentimes a serious shade
    Of thought across his forehead stray'd,
  And so he said to himself one day,
  "Shall I be happy as I am now,
  When one-and-twenty summers shall lay
    Their sign upon my brow?"

I think he was a curious child
To deal in queries so odd and wild.
He may have had presentiment
    Of times of sighs and sorrow:
Forewarnings may to-day be sent
    To arm us for to-morrow.

Anticipation's hot desire
    Urges Time to speed his race;
But he, as if in sullen ire,
    Steals along with lazy pace.
So, like a colt that prances round
The prairies' endless pasture-ground,
The frisky boy danced wild and free
In fancy o'er the life to be.
       He took to his book,
          And laid up of lore
      By hook and crook
        A plentiful store.
The sea of knowledge open'd wide
      On every side.
      He launch'd his ship
      And made a trip
    Upon that quiet sea,
      Till on a far isle
      He fell by the wile
Of the siren Poesy.
Now gracious, now coy
Was she to the boy:
She taught him that ever-
Continued endeavour
    Alone could obtain
A place in her palace:
That draughts from the chalice
    Of piety, patience, and pain

Must purge from his spirit
  Its earthlier dross;
And he must inherit
  The crown through the cross.

———

The man of five-and-forty see,
The father of a family
  And husband of a wife;
With lacs of love at interest,
But little of (what's more in quest)
  The golden gear of life;
A little house, and comfort in it;
  A little library, all too small;
Of idle time he's scarce a minute,
  Thought and labour filling all.
A little garden, where the sun
  Lingers lovingly and long,
Where his children lightly run,
  Full of mischief, play, and song.
A little silver in his hair;
  A sacred sorrow in his heart;
A corner with a vacant chair;
  Some little trinkets set apart;
    A little mound
    In holy ground,
That he tends with loving care.
Work by day and rest by night
  Interweaving warp and woof
Of his life, now dark, now bright,
  Love is queen beneath his roof.
As the stone rolls down the hill
  With an ever-growing force,
Running faster, faster still
  Near the ending of its course:

So his life hastes on apace,
  Fleeter-footed day by day:
Give him, JESUS, helpful grace
  To live for GOD and man alway.

THE WAR-FIEND.

A SHADOWY spectral shape:
    The form of a man,
    But haggard and wan
  And hideous as an ape.
    His substance was thin
  As clouds that crawl
  Up the side of a mountain wall
    By forests hedgèd in.
  And airier wings the dragon-fly
  Never display'd against the sky.
His eyes were set as if carved in stone,
And, never winking, gazed right on,
With a stolid stare, leaden and drear,
That struck onlookers with ghastly fear.
His cavernous jaws wide open stood,
And his lips were all a-drip with blood,
And yet seem'd parch'd by hunger's rage
That mountains of victual could not assuage.

  He spread his pinions, and quick as light
Over the land he sped his flight,
Over the length and breadth of the land
From Maine away to the Rio Grande,
Halting a while o'er hillocks green
That show'd where the din of battle had been.
He stopp'd and scented the hospital air
As an odorous dainty rich and rare;

The sighs of the dying tickled his ear,
And he flapp'd his pinions to show his cheer:
He grimly chuckled in wild delight
Where brothers fell in the mortal fight:
He laugh'd while widows and orphans wept
And flames around the homestead swept.

"Ho! ho!" quoth he, "never in hell
Have I feasted so lusciously and so well!"
And, folding his wings, he sat him down
Beside the ruins of a town
Where Death stood waiting by Despair,
And pestilence defiled the air.

Yet glowing bulletins over the land,
　From fields of slaughter gory,
Made shouts arise on every hand
　Of "*Victory and glory!*"

TO A FRIEND.

NO news to tell.　The lightning's fire
　　Flashes it all along the wire,
And every wonder now grows old
Before 'tis fully heard or told;
Indeed, some folk know what is done
Before the hour the thing's begun.
And every day we're growing wiser;
And sure a keener man than I, sir,
'Twill take to tell where we shall stop
In our immense progressive hop.
Ere many years—quite likely soon—
We'll find the way to reach the moon,
Or take a summer-jaunt upon
The locomotives of the sun.

It may be, Sam, the child is born
That shall behold a flaming morn
Whose splendor shall eclipse our light
As mid-day sun the stars of night.
—Tut! what's my trickish muse about,
To caper so when she's let out?
But give my muse a slacken'd rein,
She scampers wildly o'er the plain,
When in a most familiar way
I seek to troll a simple lay.
Nay, say not, Sam! "'Twill be, perchance
Like sprites of transcendental trance,
So dim, impalpable, and thin—
The shadow of a spectre's skin—
That when a critic seeks to find
Some real creature of the mind,
A dubious mist he faintly spies,
Which like a morning vapour dies
Ere he can wink his wondering eyes
Or mark its texture, shape, or size."
Though poets, in these loose-shod times,
Sow seeds of brain-confounding rhymes,
And raise a crop of wordy stuff
Luxuriant as a fungous puff,—
A thunder-clap of sense will come
And strike each jargon-grinder dumb;
Then men shall say he was an ass
Who, by hydrogenated gas,
Got in the clouds above the steeple,
Dumbfounding for a while the people,
Till, tumbling from that giddy pitch,
He fell in vile Lethean ditch.
But lest you set me down a bore,
I'll hie to bed and write no more,
And dream of Sam and schoolboy days,
The days of fun, and tricks, and plays.

THE LATEST BORN.

A MERRY babe and beautiful is this our latest born !
  Her cheek is soft as silky threads that overlay
    the corn;
Her eye is like a tiny spot of heaven's serenest blue
Imbedded in the fleecy clouds, with starlight flashing
    through.

Her voice is but a little voice, and yet it enters in
My bosom with a welcome that a monarch could not
    win:
I love the rill that down the hill comes dancing with
    a song,
But more I love her liquid notes that trickle all day
    long.

Her hair is not a silver white, nor yet of golden hue,
But of a colour cunningly compounded of the two:
'Tis not a flimsy gossamer that glistens in the sun,
But like the richer fabric from the multicaulis spun.

With mother-love and patient skill, there's one who
    strives to teach
Her guileless tongue the simple sounds that form our
    human speech:
She looks up in her mother's face, as if in wonder why
Her lip should speak the tender things once spoken
    by the eye.

'Tis but a year and seven months she's dwelt among
    us here,
And yet has she become to us an object passing dear;

'Tis wondrous that a love so young should twine its
    tendrils so,
As make us fear our hearts would tear before they'd
    let it go.

She enters on the race of life with tottering steps and
    slow,
And often trips upon the floor from overhaste to go:
Thus infancy has ups and downs as well as graver
    years,
But bears them with a lighter heart, if not with fewer
    tears.

A thousand mothers in our land may fold within their
    arms
A babe as beautiful as this, or sweeter in its charms:
The blessing of our loving LORD be on these bosom-
    flowers;
And may their bliss in them be such as we have found
    in ours!

LET'S SIT DOWN AND TALK
TOGETHER.

LET'S sit down and talk together
    Of the things of olden day,
When we, like lambkins loosed from tether,
    Gayly tripp'd along the way.
Time has touch'd us both with lightness,
    Leaving furrows here and there,
And tinging with peculiar brightness
    Silvery threads among our hair.

Let's sit down and talk together;
   Many years away have past,
And fair and foul has been the weather
   Since we saw each other last.
Many whom we loved are living
   In a better world than this;
And some among us still are giving
   Toil and thought for present bliss.

Let's sit down and talk together;
   Though the flowers of youth are dead,
The ferns still grow among the heather,
   And for us their fragrance shed.
Life has thousand blessings in it
   Even for the aged man;
And GOD has hid in every minute
   Something we may wisely scan.

Let's sit down and talk together;
   Boys we were,—we now are men;
We meet awhile, but know not whether
   We shall meet to talk again.
Parting time has come: how fleetly
   Speed the moments when their wings
Are fann'd by breathings issuing sweetly
   From a tongue that never stings!

THE HOWLING STORM AND THE WONDROUS CALM.

WHILE sailing on the sea of life,
  I saw a storm arise;
The troubled waters met in strife,
  And lightnings rent the skies.

My fleet and fragile bark above
  The tossing billows roll'd;
My utmost store of hope and love
  All garner'd in its hold.

The winds blew mightily, and swept
  My fearless vessel on,
While murky clouds the sky o'ercrept
  Till sun and stars were gone.

My heart upheld its steadfastness,
  As if 'twere stone or steel:
The deeper horrors of distress
  'Twas needful I should feel.

The darkness of the night came down
  And on my soul it lay,
As if my righteous Maker's frown
  Were gathering round my way.

The darkness cover'd all the sky,
  And cover'd all the sea:
I madly cast the compass by,
  And steer'd uncertainly.

20

My bark was rack'd, its sails were rent,
  I heard the rudder break;
The hungry ocean seem'd intent
  My very life to take.

I said, "Why should I longer strive?"
  I lay me down to sleep,
And let my bark at random drive
  Along the fearful deep.

High on the utmost billow's top
  'Twas for a moment seen,
But more impetuously to drop
  Deep in the gulf between.

As lonely as if I alone
  In all the earth were left,—
As helpless as an infant-one
  Of mother's care bereft,—

How swift and sure had been my doom
  Had CHRIST forgotten me!
A voice arose amid the gloom,
  "Thy Saviour loveth thee!"

Immediately there was a calm,
  A calm without, within;
For JESUS wrote upon my palm
  Full pardon of my sin.

The inward tempests rage no more,
  The spirit's sorrows cease,
When JESUS stands upon the shore,
  And gently whispers, "Peace!"

SONNET RHYMES.

RAINY APRIL.

THE wind still blows from the north-eastern
    quarter,
  Full charged with chills, and coughs, and sniffling
    sneezes!
  Let poets sing of April's balmy breezes,
'Tis my belief that Spring's a wayward daughter,
Whose parentage is found in clouds and water;
  Or she is Nature's washerwoman, splashing
  The earth's old clothing—suds around her dashing.
At all events, I wish her reign was shorter.
  The weathercock awhile turns to the north,
  The long-imprison'd sun comes weeping forth,
His eyelids fringed with diamond drops; when, lo!
  The wind returns to its accustom'd place,
  And blows the clouds directly in his face,
And turns their watering-pot on man below.

NOON IN THE COUNTRY.

'TWAS Sabbath noon. I sat me down upon
    A fallen tree, beside a little rill
That ran along the bottom of the hill
And sang upon its way. The summer sun
    Beam'd hotly down; but 'neath the shadowing trees
    My bosom felt the coolness of the breeze.
A noise and silence seem'd by turns to reign;
    The squirrels nimbly pranced along the fence;
    I harm'd them not, nor feign'd to scare them
        thence,
For who could put such merry things to pain?
    Upon the ground came lightly down a bird;
A frog was gravely sitting by the rill;
But far from me was thought to affright or kill,
    And quietly I sat and saw, and quietly I heard.

HAPPY CHILDHOOD.

THE birthright of a child is love; and be
    The portion his, without a stinted measure:
    O may his bosom be brimful of pleasure
Aflowing from affection's treasury.
    A happy child is beautiful to me:
Let others praise the picture-limner's art,
    Mine eye prefers the quick reality,
Whose living beauty thrills upon my heart.
    Then let him taste a little while that earth
    Hath yet a cup of blessedness and mirth.
Soon will he learn the falseness of the world,—
    The selfishness of man,—the hateful strife
    Of brothers, and the tyrannies of life—
And see his childhood's castles into ruins hurl'd.

THE COMING OF SPRING.

THE gentle Spring comes knocking at the door;
    And surly Winter gruffly bids her wait;
Her timorous foot she places on the floor,
    But Winter growls and shows his wrinkled pate,
And she, affrighted, swiftly flees away.
The southern winds invite her steps to stay,
    And she returns and softly knocks again,
And nature smiles and beckons her to enter.
Around her pathway flowering beauties centre
    And pleasure overfills the hearts of men.
The Spring arrives at Summerhood in June.
    When flowers are young and beautiful and bright,
And brooks and birds troll out their sweetest tune,
    And longest is the day, and balmiest is the night.

EARTH'S NOBLEST MEN.

SOME men are born t'endure the toil and strife
    And heavy burdens of the earth. They are
The pillars in the temple of this life,
    Its strength and ornament; or, hidden far
Beneath, they form its firm foundation-stone.
In nobleness they stand distinct and lone,
    Yet other men upon them lean, and fain
(Such selfishness in human bosoms swells)
    Would lay on them the weight of their own pain.
Where greatness is, a patient spirit dwells;
    They least repine who bear and suffer most:
In calm and stern endurance they sustain
The ills whereof ignoble minds complain;
    And in their lot they stand, nor weakly sigh nor boast.

"THIRTY."

"AT thirty wise, or never!"   So 'tis said;
    How wisely said, the poet sayeth not:
  I'm thirty now, yet scarce am I a jot
More grave than when less years sat on my head.
But life is not so beautiful as then;
    Its opening scene was lovely to my view:
Then earth was heavenly, and the race of men
  I deem'd its angels while the scene was new.
I'm wiser now, or better taught.   I've found
The world to be a sin-polluted ground.
    Man crushes man; GOD'S image lies in chains;
And Pride looks down from her unstable throne:
    Unpitied Misery weeps amid her pains,
While few indeed are they who live like CHRIST alone.

"MAY I COME UP?"

"MAY I come up?" the waking germ inquires;
    "All winter long, the fearful frost has bound
  Above my head a mass of icy ground.
I've slept in silence, till the solar fires
    Have driven away the frost; the soften'd earth
  Invites me now to claim the right of birth.
Oh may I come, and see day's sunny smile?"
    "Not yet, not yet.   'Tis past the time of snow,
  But frosts may come, and nipping winds may blow.
'Tis safe for thee to bide a little while
    Within thy cell: ere long shalt thou arise,
And GOD thy life wilt keep."   The April hours
  Soon weeping come, with warm and genial skies;
The germ springs up, and bears a crown of buds and
      flowers.

THE BABE ASLEEP.

THE babe is sleeping.   Hist ! no footfall here
 To jar the placid air.   Cease, singing-bird,
 Thy melody; and, puss! no mewling word
To grate upon the little sleeper's ear.
 How still she lies! and see that dimpled curl
About her lip, as if some pleasant thought
Were in her heart, from heavenly angels caught.
 GOD's blessing rest upon my baby-girl!
Were I to give my frolic fancy play,
 I'd sing of her as some angelic sprite,
 Who, wandering from her native home of light,
Fatigued, had fallen asleep upon the way;
 I'd fear to wake her, lest she'd plume her wings
 And soar away from me and all sublunar things.

THE EARLY ICE.

THE ice has come!   The cold-lipp'd Frost has
 kiss'd
 The waters while they slept at night; his breath
 Has laid them in a torpor, as of death.
Nor shrub nor flower the midnight ranger miss'd,
 But on them all he press'd his fatal fingers.
He touch'd the trees; and when the sun comes forth
 And warms the leaves, they fall in many a shower;
 The midnoon-rays, like sudden joys, o'erpower
 The feeble health that in them faintly lingers.
The blast is keen this morning from the north;
All tender things are dying day by day;
 Soon, soon will they be gone, and seen no more,
 And we shall stand on nature's wintry shore,
The gentle dreams of summer having pass'd away.

TO JOSEPH R. CHANDLER, ESQ.

GRAVE potentate of scissors and the quill!
　　Few days agone I sent thee sundry rhymes,
　Befitting well the temper of the times,
And wrought with all the printer-poet's skill.
Though daily since, I pored thy lucid sheet—
　　The inner columns and the outer side—
Nor line, nor word, nor syllable did greet
　　My eager gaze or gratify my pride.
My curious wits are at a loss to know
Why thou hast used thine humble servant so.
　　Deep in my heart a spring is bubbling up
Of thoughts most sweet and pleasant unto me;
　　And when I dip and proffer thee a cup,
Wilt thou, untasted, cast it far from thee?

THE PUBLIC PARK.

I LOVE the spot where GOD'S great trees have room
　　To spread their branches far on every side,
　And lift their tops in pristine forest-pride
As in their own domain, and bud and bloom
　In vast variety; while round their roots
The grassy spires the unctuous mould o'erspread
And fragrant clover shows its honied head,
　　Or buttercup or violet upward shoots.
Awake from slumber, drowsy dreamer! wake!
　　Inhale the healthful breathings of the sod;
Night's sickly bonds from thy dull being shake,
　　And while the birds are piping praise to GOD,
Lift up thy heart—in gladness lift thy voice:
When nature sings, let man with her rejoice.

HORTICULTURAL EXHIBITION.

WITHIN old Eden's walls methinks I stand,
  While sin is not, and innocence and love
  Make earth the counterpart of realms above,
And streams of joy flow through the happy land.
  The blooming beauties of earth's varied climes
Together here in sisterhood have met;
  Their Latin names would spoil my English rhymes,
Else I might have them all in order set.
  These fruits and flowers of every shape and hue,
And bees, and honey in its virgin comb,
  And peaches, pears, plums, grapes, and apples too,
I fain could wish were in my larder home.
  Oh that an Eve would wander near my seat,
  And bid me rise, and freely pluck and eat!

FATHER IS COMING.

"HURRAH! here father comes!" the children
  shout,
  While standing at the door at set of sun
  They see him in the distance. Down they run
To meet him coming. Gathering round about
  His weary feet, they wildly romp and race.
One hugs his knees, the others clasp his hands,
  While tottering Will, for want of better place,
With glad and laughing look behind him stands
  And grasps his outer garment's pendent tail;
  And thus their weary parent they assail.
He kneels, and Will climbs up his back, and throws
  His arms around his neck. With Ella, sweet,
  And Agnes, in his arms—the others round his feet—
Beneath his lovely load the father gateward goes.

THE BROTHERHOOD OF MAN.

IF any man must fall for me to rise,
　　Then seek I not to climb.   Another's pain
I choose not for my good.   A golden chain,
A robe of honour is too poor a prize
　　To tempt my hasty hand to do a wrong
Unto a fellow man.   This life hath wo
Sufficient, wrought by man's satanic foe;
　　And who that hath a heart would dare prolong
Or add a sorrow to a stricken soul
That seeks some healing balm to make it whole?
　　My bosom owns the brotherhood of man;
From GOD and truth a renegade is he
Who scorns a poor man in his poverty,
　　Or on his fellow lays his supercilious ban.

THE POET'S MISSION.

EACH mortal being hath a mission here:
　　'Tis mine to travel soberly along
The track of life, and sing, perchance, a song
That ringeth sweetly on some listening ear.
　　A fellow-traveller jostles me at times,
And scorns the music of my simple rhymes;
But still I sing; for soon will come the day
　　When mental hunger will his breast annoy,
　　And love of gold and sensual things will cloy,—
And then he'll bow submissive to my sway.
　　My life is not an idle one.   I sing
And work together.   When my time is o'er
　　My frame—like some old harp whose every string
Is gone—will be worn-out, to labour here no more.

ANOTHER GONE.

THE hasty mail hath brought me heavy news!
　A friend is dead.　Of distant kin, yet very near
To me in love was JOHN.　The tribute-tear
Mine eye, that seldom weeps, may not refuse;
　For I shall see him here no more, and we
Perchance shall long be parted from each other.
The love between us was the love of brother.
　He was alone; nor wife nor child had he,
　Yet all the world were of his family,
For he had love for all, and love supreme
　To GOD his Maker, Saviour, Comforter.
My brother-friend! his death oft seems to me
The strong delusion of a morning dream,
　And makes the tenderest strings in my sad bosom stir.

THE SICK BABE.

OUR child is very ill.　She sigh'd and moan'd
　Through all the night.　I press'd her to my breast
And sang a hymn; but still she found no rest;
And while she wept my spirit also groan'd.
　The house was still as when one lieth dead.
All faint and sorrowful, the mother slept,
Exhausted by the vigil she had kept.
　I held the babe, and paced the floor, my tread
Re-echoing through the silent house.　She threw
　Her trembling arms around my neck, and laid
　Her burning cheek on mine, and softly said,
In broken speech, "Dear father, I love you."
　I pray'd a speechless prayer; and when the morning
　　broke,
　She sank away in sleep.　'Twas long ere she awoke.

THE PRINTER.

A MENTAL lamp hung out by life's wayside;
    Unnoticed; yet his unpretending ray
  Shines clearly on man's intellectual way,
And proves to pilgrims an unfailing guide.
He hath within a worthy sort of pride,
    And knows his worth, though some allow it not.
  A heart and thinking mind above his lot
'Mong men are his.   His coffers ill-supplied,
    Yet want and virtue seldom ask in vain.
  Nor is his life exempt from various pain;
Few days are his: the rose that freshly bloom'd
    On boyhood's cheek assumes the hue of death;
  The oil of life within him soon consumed,
In life's supremest prime he yields his vital breath.

THE THOUGHTS DWELL WHERE THE HEART IS.

M Y mind to-day is ever homeward turning;
    Amid the cares of business, every thought
  With an intense anxiety is fraught,
And homeward, homeward still, my heart is yearning.
    There, wearily a loving daughter lies:
By day the fever-heat prevents her rest;
By night the cough doth rend her quivering breast;
    And meekly doth she bear it all.   The sighs
Of our sick hearts we hide from her; for she
Appears endued with quiet constancy.
    I would not speed Time's swiftly-moving wings,
Yet how impatiently the day's decline
My soul doth long for, when I may entwine
    My arms around my child, and soothe her sufferings.

FANNY FORESTER.

O FAIR and fanciful Fan Forester!
 I wish I knew her—honestly I do!
A brotherly regard have I for her,
 She is so natural, sisterly, and true.
There is no cant in her : her feelings rise
 From Nature's fountain, like a crystal stream
 Upspringing from the depths,—love's sunny beam
Reflected there,—and glistening in our eyes,
 As if pure diamonds over beds of gold
 In liquid torrents all around her roll'd.
Would it were mine to leave the world's confusion,
 And live in love in some hill-hidden nook,
 Like Fanny's green, romantic Alderbrook,
And sing, like her, lifelong in my seclusion.

JUVENILE REMINISCENCE.

WHEN we were boys, my brother Will and I,
 The night before, were wont to tie together
 Our largest toes at two ends of a tether,
To wake us early on the Fourth o' July.
 We loved the dawning light of Freedom's time ;
 We loved to hear the bells at daybreak chime,—
Those hundred bells, that o'er Manhattan sent
 Their wild and mingling clangour, till the air
 Seem'd charged with music full as it could bear,
And joy's vibrations shook the firmament.
 Through the warm night I guess we suffer'd some ;
If either moved, he pull'd the tether'd toe,
And many a sleepy, simultaneous " Oh !"
 From our unquiet lips all night was heard to come.

21

SEPTEMBER.

I BEAR a special love to sweet September:
   Though people say partialities are wrong,
From youthful Janu'ry to old December
No month I love with love so true and strong.
   The year hath got its richest ripeness then,
Like womanhood when in its perfect prime
And comeliness, before the hand of Time
   Hath lined the forehead with his telltale pen.
September's lap is full, and plenty reigns
To recompense the toiler for his pains
   And feed the poor. A pleasant look hath she,
Such as the children love to see upon
Their mother's face, when they her smile have won :
   Let others choose their love—September give to me.

DRAWYERS CHURCH, DELAWARE.

A DOWN in brave old Delaware there stands
   An ancient church amid a field of dead;
The trees implanted by its children's hands
   Now cast deep shadows o'er their peaceful bed.
This church hath long borne witness for its GOD,
   And He hath had a people here, to praise
   His blessed name, for sevenscore years of days.
Four generations here have risen, and trod
   Life's changeful path, since first the sod was broken
To lay therein the corner-stone, and build
This temple which His Presence oft hath fill'd,
   And where His grace hath set its sealing token.
Here reign, our GOD! till time shall fade away
Into eternity, like night in morning's ray.

SNOW-STORM SONNET.

OLD father Winter's powdering o'er his hair:
　Grim Vanity! he's gray enough already;
　For one so old, he ought to be more steady,
Yet he's as fickle as the springtime fair.
　But yesterday, his was a balmy breath;
To-day he blusters, sending out his frost
　To nip the buds, and smite with sudden death
The early flowers that ventured forth to peep
If cruel Winter yet had fallen asleep:
　The daring act their gentle life hath cost.
Thus died Louise, our tenderest summer flower,
　So meek, so mild, so beauteous in her bloom;
The blast of winter howl'd around her bower,
　She shrank away, and hid within the tomb.

THE WANE OF LIFE.

THE world around me groweth gray and old:
　My friends are dropping one by one away;
　Some live in distant lands—some in the clay
Rest quietly, their mortal moments told.
　The lightness of my youth is gone; the veil
That hid from me the selfishness of man
Is lifted up, and I have learn'd to scan
　The world with wary look.　My cheek is pale;
A dimness often stealeth o'er mine eye,
And many furrows on my forehead lie;
　And when my children gather at my knee
To worship GOD and sing our morning psalm,
　Their rising stature whispers unto me
My life is gently waning tow'rds its evening calm.

OUR BABE.

WE have at home a cunning babe.   Her eyes
    Are blue and beautiful, and flash out gleams
  Of changeful light, much like the trembling beams
On frosty winter nights from starlit skies.
Her cheeks are tinted with the blushing dyes
    Which Heaven, so wisely bountiful, bestows
    In virgin freshness on the mossy rose.
When, worn and sad, I seek the spot where lies
    My lovely all—that infant's budding charms,
    As she disports within her mother's arms,
Dispel my sadness, and her winning wiles
And crowing shouts provoke unwitting smiles,
    Till every care is from my soul beguiled:—
    Blest is the man who loves a little child!

HEART LONGINGS.

I LONG to be beloved.   My bosom yearns
    Tow'rds all that's pure and beautiful; and fain
    Would find a recompense of love again.
My pensive soul with ardent thirsting turns
    To heaven and earth to seek its fill of love.
    Beyond the sun's domain, in realms above,
Abide full many whom I loved on earth;
    My father liveth there, and there my mother;
    My sister there, and there my elder brother;
For coldness rests on our paternal hearth.
    Though kin and friends remain who love me well,
I long to hear again my parents' voice,
With early loved ones fain would I rejoice,
    And in GOD'S presence re-united dwell.

THE COMET.

LOW in the west—the early night begun—
   A silvery streak appeareth in the air.
   'Tis neither star nor planet; but some fair
Attendant at the palace of the sun.
   It shineth clearly when the deeper night
Pervades the skies, and all the stars appear
Upon the ramparts of the upper sphere,
   Like heavenly watchmen, with a torch of light.
Perchance it comes a messenger in haste,
   On embassy from the extremest bound
Of some immense, immeasurable waste;
   Or it may be a chariot on its round,
Wherein the angels fly with news of grace
And loving-kindness to some distant race.

LOVE FOR LITTLE THINGS.

I KNOW where bloom some violets in a bed
   Half hidden in the grass; and crowds go by
   And see them not, unless some curious eye
Unto their hiding-place by chance is led.
   I often pass that way, and look on them
With loving, lingering gaze. I know not why
My heart doth love such humble things; but I
   Esteem them more than robe or diadem
Of priest or king. A babe, or bird, or flower
Has o'er my soul a most despotic power.
   The tearful eye of infancy oppress'd,
A flower down-trodden by the foot of spite,
   Awaken sighs of sorrow in the breast,
Or nerve the arm to vindicate their right.
21*

THE SICK MAN'S SONNET.

THROW wide the shutter! Let me see the light,
　And feel the cooling breeze upon my face.
So long have I been hidden from my race,
Sweet nature's aspect seemeth doubly bright.
These many days I've lain upon this bed,
　And turn'd my weary frame and sought for rest;
　But strong disease hath gnaw'd within my breast,
And throbbing pangs have rack'd my fever'd head.
　The long, still nights have brought to me no sleep;
I've counted all the hours until the morn
Hath broken in the east; and, weak and worn,
　I've pray'd my Maker for a heart to weep.
The pitying Father hears the child's request:
My sins rebuked, He gives me perfect rest.

THE OLD BLIND VOTER OF PINE WARD.

MAKE way, ye generous freemen! let him come
　And cast his ballot into Freedom's urn!
His arm, perchance, once aided to strike dumb
　His country's foes; and still his feelings burn
With all their ancient warmth for liberty.
　Approach, old man! We honour thy thin locks—
So white, so few—that tell thy lengthen'd age.
The time thou liv'dst hath been a glorious page
　Of human history, and proudly mocks
All former times. It hath been given to thee
　To see the virgin flag of Freedom flung
Abroad to float in every breeze; while he
　Whose head in humble abjectness had hung,
Did heavenward lift his eye, and strike—and dare be
　　free!

THE BUTTONWOOD STUMP.

WHENE'ER I walk in Third, near Willing's alley,
  I mark the spot where that old buttonwood
Beyond the memory of man had stood
As proudly as if in Missouri's valley.
  I mourn its fall, as of a pleasant friend
  Whose useful life hath met a hasty end.
The ruthless axe that hew'd its silver'd trunk
  Struck at the ties that, tendril-like, had bound
My love unto the tree; and when it sunk,
  My heart sunk with it, grieving, to the ground.
Old men are doubtless living, who, with me,
  Bewail its doom; who, in its grateful shade,
Some threescore years ago, in boyish glee
  With glad companions innocently play'd.

THE PATH OF LIFE.

THERE is a pathway leading to the skies;
  'Tis strait and narrow, and the travellers climb
  With songs and sighings toward its height sublime,
Where faith discerns a bright, immortal prize.
The aged man uplifts his failing eyes,
  And presses on to reach his welcome rest;
The man of sinew shouteth fearless cries
  To animate the youthful pilgrim's breast;
And ever and anon the voice of song
Or prayer uprises from the heavenward throng.
  Angelic watchers compass all the road,
And aid the travellers when their spirit faints;
  Till Death comes near to bear to CHRIST'S abode
The holy hosts of His elected saints.

LONELINESS.

ALONE! My soul doth never feel alone!
From tender childhood to this hurrying hour,
GOD hath indued me with a potent power
Of calling spirits from a realm unknown,
   With whom I hold communings sweet and free.
This life hath never been a cumbrous chain
For me to drag with heaviness and pain;
   But Time hath sped on feathery wings with me.
My thoughts to me are sweeter than my bread;
And while my lips have lack'd, my mind hath fed
   Luxuriously, as if it were a king.
And when the LORD hath smiled upon my way,
I've walk'd in heaven on many a glorious day
   While yet on earth my feet were wandering.

THE GREAT DAY.

THE shiver'd skies flee fast away; and flame
And smoke burst out, and horrid noises roar
   As if a burning sea surged on the shore,
And rack'd old Nature's perishable frame.
   Creation shudders; and the trembling sun
Turns red like blood, and casts a crimson glare
Throughout the heaving billows of the air.
   The moon and stars, as if affrighted, run
In wild confusion; while the trump of GOD
   Resounds, and all the dead are call'd to life,
And—hush'd at once the elemental strife—
   In solemn stillness men await his nod.
Ah, day of doom! Redeemer on thy throne!
Oh let thy robe of grace be cast around thine own.

THE MOTHER.

WHATEVER be the language of the skies,
    There is no fitting word that I can find
To express the affection of a mother's mind
When roguish smiles play in her infant's eyes.
    The cherub has a passport to her heart;
A key that opens nature's fastest locks;
A natural skill of witchery that mocks
    The wise professors of the mystic art.
Thanks be to Heaven that man is once a child;
    That once our nature wears the guise of all
That's truthful, loving, lovable, and mild;
    That tones of childhood to our thoughts recall
The rapturous times when in a fond embrace
We clasp'd our mother's neck, and kiss'd her cheerful
    face.

PENITENTIAL PRAYER.

I DO acknowledge unto thee, O GOD!
    A child of wilful waywardness I've been;
In crooked paths of selfishness and sin
These many years my wandering feet have trod.
    But, oh! be merciful! The world I've loved
    Like Sodom's fruit of bitterness has proved;
And I, repentant, bleeding at the heart,
    Would find a Helper in this time of wo;
    And, save to thee, I know not where to go
To find a balsam for my bosom's smart.
    Be merciful, O GOD! Let Him atone
Who died for wretched men like me: no plea
    My anguish knows but this last plea alone!
For His dear sake, my GOD! oh spare and pity me!

A SPRING SONNET.

THE maiden-hearted spring has come. The weeping
   And smiling skies alternate o'er us reign;
The grass is springing verdant on the plain,
And little germs that long time have been sleeping
Beneath the sod are timidly up-peeping;
   Sweet buds and blossoms thick are putting forth,
As if in confidence Heaven's sure keeping,
   And fearless of the threatenings of the north.
The flowers will soon be here, and bees will come;
   The notes of spring and summer birds will ring,
   And winds, and brooks, and birds in concert sing,
And make the human soul leap up in gladness,
   Save the sad hearts who, in their des'late home,
Do weep the loved and lost, though not in hopeless
   sadness.

HUMAN PORCUPINES.

SOME men are cruel in their nature—rough
   In mind and manner—burly sons of strife;
So coarsely wrought of nature's coarsest stuff,
   With them there's nothing delicate in life.
Were man a tree, they were the outer bark;
   Were man a wood, they were the brier-bush:
But *now* they're snarling porcupines, that mark
   With scratches all who 'gainst their prickles push.
They've little love for any living thing;
   Their hearts are barely big enough to hold
   Affection for themselves and for their gold;
Perchance a little for their dog or mother,
Which selfishness has not had time to smother;
   To all the world besides, they only live to sting.

TO A FRIEND.

HAS death, my gentle brother, pluck'd a bud—
　　An opening bud—from thy sweet tree of love?
And did the depths of thy fond nature move,
Until thine eye pour'd forth a scalding flood?
　　If it were so, I could not blame thy grief;
But I would sit beside thee in thy wo,
And bid my tears to thine responsive flow,
　　Till He who smote should bring thy soul relief:
My tongue would words of consolation say,
And lead thy thoughts from this sad world away;
　　And tell thee of the land beyond the tomb,
The gardens beautiful, where JESUS' hands
　　Have planted thy sweet bud, to grow and bloom,
And gladden thee and thine, while heaven eternal
　　stands.

A CHILD AT A WINDOW.

BUT yesternoon my curious eye espied
　　A child out-looking through a window-pane:
Urgent my haste, yet as I onward hied,
　　I turn'd to gaze upon the child again.
Her face was fair, her eyes were bright and blue,
　　Her hair hung loosely with peculiar grace
Of curl, and all uncertain was its hue;
　　But whether more of mirth were in her face,
Or innocence, or modesty, 'twere not
　　An easy word to say. A sweet red spot
And dimple beautified her cheek, and lent
　　A comely aspect to the child. She wore
No gaudy dress, nor golden ornament;
　　In her own native self her chiefest charm she bore.

THE TEA-TABLE.

HOW beautiful the sight!—the tidy table
   Set out for tea—the buckwheat cakes all smo-
     king,
The steaming urn, the watering mouth provoking;
The girls and boys, with eating powers able,
   Awaiting father's grace ere they begin
   To lay a store of mother's good things in.
The knife and spoon they ply with artless grace:
   To chide their eager haste, the mother cries
   In gentle tones, and warns them that "their eyes
Are bigger than their stomachs." Every face
   Grows big with wonder as to what she means.—
The tea-time o'er, the children say their prayers,
And go to bed and sleep devoid of cares.
   Would that our land were studded with such scenes!

JOSEPH C. NEAL.

HOW fast the living fade away around us!
   Some in the spring, and in the summer others:
   Autumn and winter smite our human brothers,
And snap the tendrils that to them had bound us.
   It seems but yesterday I saw his face;
And now I sit in silence and alone,
And ask in doubt, "And is he surely gone,
   And pass'd to his eternal dwelling-place?"
Fallen in his prime, like an unwither'd leaf,
The pen is poor to phrase our speechless grief.
   Of gifted mind and gentle in his spirit,
And kind and tender as a very dove,
And fill'd with an exuberance of love,
   A long remembrance richly doth he merit.

A POET AND HIS SONG.

H E was a man endow'd like other men
　　With strange varieties of thought and feeling:
His bread was earn'd by daily toil; yet when
　　A pleasing fancy o'er his mind came stealing,
He set a trap and snared it by his art,
And hid it in the bosom of his heart.
　　He nurtured it and loved it as his own,
And it became obedient to his beck;
He fix'd his name on its submissive neck,
　　And graced it with all graces to him known,
And then he bade it lift its wing and fly
　　Over the earth, and sing in every ear
　　Some soothing sound the sighful soul to cheer,
Some lay of love to lure it to the sky.

ON SEEING THE PICTURE OF A CHILD.

'T WAS but a little child; and yet I felt
　　Unutterable thrills arise within :
I thought on what my infant days had been,
When I before my mother simply knelt,
　　And clasp'd my hands and said our Saviour's prayer,
A happy boy, with blue and playful eye,
And flaxen hair, and cheek that might outvie
　　The crimson of the rose.　But toil and care
Have done their wonted work.　Ah me! how strange
That years so few should bring such wondrous change !
　　This pallid cheek—this calm and serious air—
This quiet eye—this weary, weary frame—
　　Can these be his whose promise was so fair ?—
With growing hope of heaven, the being is the same!
22

THE SPIRIT'S AILMENT.

FOR many days I walk'd beneath a cloud
  Which no sun-ray found any passage through:
The mid-noon like the depth of midnight grew,
And my faint soul was in the darkness bow'd.
Uncomforted, I wander'd mid the crowd,
  Where all were busy, eager, earnest, gay;
Some idly chatting, others laughing loud,
  And friend saluting friend along his way.
Amid them all, I was alone—alone;
  A yearning man, and with a human heart,
  From other men set seemingly apart;
Mine ear receiving not a friendly tone,
  Mine eye perceiving not an answering gleam;
  And life was nigh become a dim and dreary dream.

THE SPIRIT'S REMEDY.

WHEN overcome with darkness and dejection,
  And wintry clouds o'ercast the mental sky,
'Tis good to stir the ashes of affection,
  And gather up love's embers ere they die,
  And breathe upon the coals, and add new fuel.
The fire of love needs, frequently, renewal;
Supplies of tenderness and deeds of kindness,
  And tones of sympathy and gentle meaning;
  A brother's faults benevolently screening,
For love is nurtured by a purposed blindness.
Thrice blessed he who finds it in his heart
  To follow CHRIST! Then sadness spreads her wings,
  And pleasantly the soul within him sings;
And of the good he does, he shares a double part.

POSTHUMOUS FAME.

DEATH sanctifies the poet. While he lives
   Men seem to think he is an idler here;
And cold and heartless often is the cheer
The world to him in wanton measure gives.
Perhaps he asks too much when he has sung
   A lay that long shall humanize his race;
For him—a mortal with an angel's tongue—
   Perchance the earth has no befitting place;
   Perchance too soon he lives—perchance too late;
Or he is poor, or lacks a family name
Renown'd for glory or renown'd for shame;
   Perchance—too great to murmur at his fate—
He toils, and dies a toiler at the oar:
Then men remember him, and his sad fate deplore.

THE POOR BOY.

WHENE'ER I meet an orphan boy, I say
   Within my heart, "LORD! bless this desolate
      child,
And be his guide in all his heavenward way:
   Oh, bid the winds to this lone one be mild,
And burning suns to gently beam on him:
Let lowering clouds make not his pathway dim;
   May stony ways be soft beneath his feet,
   And bitter waters to his taste be sweet!"
A waif of heaven, cast upward by the sea
   On this drear shore, how pitiful his lot!
Nay! heavenly watchers bear him company,
   And help and cheer him, though we see them not;
For GOD a Father sits upon the throne,—
The poor and fatherless are specially his own.

MAN'S STEWARDSHIP.

ALL men are stewards of some gift or grace,
And must account to Him who lent the boon;
Some use it till old age—some, in the noon
Of life are call'd to stand before His face,
And give to Him their reckoning. None so poor
But hath his work to do in peace and love,
Which, rightly done, shall in the world above
Place in his hand a palm that shall endure.
The field is wide; each labourer hath full room
To improve his talent, and secure the word
Of glad approval from his gracious LORD;
Some barren heart his love may bid to bloom,
Some wretch may cease his weeping at his voice,
And in hope's restful bosom gratefully rejoice.

MY SABBATH SCHOLAR.

A CHILD came in our school on Sabbath-day,
A little one, whose years were very few:
I sat me down, as I am wont to do,
Beside her, saying, as I'm wont to say,
"And what's your name, my dear?" She look'd
at me
And meekly said, "My name is Mary, sir."
I felt a yearning of my heart to her:
"How old are you, my child?"—Then answer'd she
Her years were only four. She had no brother,
But lived alone at home, she and her mother.
"Tell me what is your father's name," I said.
"My father is in heaven," was her reply,
And silently she lifted up her head.—
Ought I be deemèd weak if tears o'erfill'd mine eye?

OCTOBER'S COMING.

THE prudish maid October's coming down
  From her accustom'd visit to the north:
Of her approach the signs are putting forth:
I hear the rustling of her russet gown;
  Her voice rings shrilly on the frosty air.
The forest leaves are blushing red and brown,
And Nature wears a dark, forbidding frown,
  Intensely vex'd that she's no longer fair.
October comes! her nose is sharp and blue,
  Her temper changeable: at morning cold,
At noon she tries to smile, then, like a shrew,
  At night she's lowering, turbulent, and bold.
Ah! how unlike the pregnant months, that pour
In our rejoicing bosoms their abundant store!

TO A RAT IN THE PRINTING OFFICE.

THOU long-tail'd, ebon-eyed, nocturnal ranger!
  What led thee hither 'mong the types and cases?
Didst thou not know that running midnight races
O'er standing types is fraught with imm'nent danger?
Did hunger lead thee? didst thou think to find
  Some rich old cheese to fill thy hungry maw?
  Vain hope! none but a literary jaw
Can masticate our cookery for the mind.
Perchance thou hast a literary taste,
  A love for letters, and that sort of thing;
  But why, thou wire-tail'd imp—thou vermin-king!
Didst thou but yesternight devour our paste,
  And throw our types in pyramids of *pi?*
  Thy doom's decreed!—here, Towser! at him fly!
22*

THE POET'S VISITER.

I SING for mine own pleasure, more than name
  Or money's worth: and he who lists may read
  Or not, as pleases him: my gospel-creed
Allows to all the equal rights I claim.
  Within the inner chambers of my mind
There cometh oftentimes a visiter,
  Whose loveliness surpasseth human-kind:
I sing the mysteries that I learn of her.
  I'm captive to her beauteousness; her spell
Is potent. Miserable man were I
  To slight a being whom I love so well,
Or pass her wooings unregarded by.
While my Great Maker sends me such a guest,
I'll tell what pleasant thoughts she wakens in my
      breast.

UNCEASING PRAYER.

THE voice of prayer upriseth constantly
  From mortal man to his Redeemer, GOD:
  Where'er the sun, in shining sandals shod,
Speeds o'er the busy land or lonely sea,
  Some chosen ones, awaken'd by its light
  From soothing dreams and slumbers of the night,
Leap from their couch, and bend to Him in prayer,
  Adore His mercy, and confess their sins.
The lip of one is scarcely silent, ere
  Some brother-worshipper his plaint begins.
The slave looks up with mute prayer in his eye;
  The worn and weary pray; yea, everywhere
The LORD inclines to man's imploring cry;
  And earth is girdled alway with a zone of prayer.

ON HEARING A SERMON.

AGAIN mine ears drink in the flowing tide
  Of tones more sweet than if an angel spoke:
In days long gone, that voice my spirit woke
  From dreams of folly, vanity, and pride.
The chain that bound me to earth's pleasures broke,
  Which once I loved as if there were none other,
  I learn'd that man to every man was brother,
And on my neck CHRIST laid his easy yoke.
  New life was mine: a holier course begun,
I loved—and love—my teacher as a son.
Let coward Slander rear its venom'd crest,
  And seek to sting in some unguarded place,
Still GOD's good hand shall shield him by his grace,
And they shall love him most who've known him long
    and best.

OH! HIDE THY FACE.

OH! hide thy face from all my sins, good LORD!
  I cannot answer for them, no not one,
  But mutely stand before thy righteous throne,
And dare not ask thee justice to award.
  Grace—grace through CHRIST—unmerited by me,
  This, this I crave, most Merciful! from thee.
These many years a fitful course I've trod,
  Running or halting, leaping or groping on;
  Yet all the hours, as they have come and gone,
Have brought some blessing from thy hand, my GOD.
  But I have made such recompense of ill,
Ashamed am I to look up to thy face;
  So weeping o'er my sins, yet hoping still,
I hide my erring soul beneath thy robe of grace.

TAM'S FORTNIGHT RAMBLE.

TAM INTRODUCED TO THE READER.

MOST gentle Reader ! *Tam's a friend of mine*—
  A bosom-friend : I long have known him well :—
I pray thy grace and courtesy benign
  While he in words of verity shall tell
The story of his travels. Sit with him
  An evening hour ; and should his strain bedim
Thy tender eye, or cause thy heart to swell,
  It may be, Reader ! also thou shalt find
  Refreshment in it for a thirsty mind,
And joy with thee a welcome guest shall dwell.
  I stand aside, like one who bears the bowl
Whereof his friends partake ; and if the draught
Afford delight to those by whom 'tis quaff'd,
  A kindred pleasure shall pervade my soul.

T. McK.

RHYMES ATWEEN-TIMES.

TAM'S FORTNIGHT RAMBLE.

CANTO I.

I.

'TWAS Christmas time. From over-toil and thought
My spirits droop'd like wheat-ears in the rain,
And moody whimseys brooded in my brain
As evening fogs brood in low meadows fraught
With dew. " I'll go," in suddenness I said,
"And see again the place where I was born,
And where I had my schooling ; where I shed
The early bitter tear of one forlorn,
When Death appear'd before the accustom'd time,
And smote my parents in their midlife prime.
I'll stand again where once I stood of yore
And gazed with wondering and asking eye
Far out unto the dim, uncertain shore
Of time to come, where boyhood's mysteries lie."

II.

Still mine the memories of the boyish days
When young delight went hand-in-hand with hope,
And life to come was but a sunny slope,
Where roses bloom'd and birds sang merry lays.
What though the experience of my wiser years
Has proved that heaven is not of earth, and he
Who would inherit bliss that ever cheers
Must work in love, and love unselfishly;
Yet, pleasing still the fantasies remain
Of careless times, when trustfully I dream'd
Of years with naught but pleasure in their train,
And paradise in coming manhood seem'd.
Those hours illusive long have pass'd away,
But, bright for aye, ye memories, with me stay.

III.

I took the cars, and went to New York city:
'Twas Sat'day night, and ere eleven o'clock
The ferry-boat had brought us into dock
Across the Hudson. ('Tis somewhat a pity
The cars can't drop us in the town; 'tis very
Uncomfortable thus to cross the ferry
On winter nights. It makes a mortal shiver
To leave the cosey cars, and face the blast
That whistles frozen notes in rushing past.
Ugh! how I hate that voyage o'er the river!)
I went to bed, and got up rather late
Next morn, for I had lain till nearly eight:
I kiss'd my friends; my lips with love did quiver;
And then I kept the Sabbath with becoming state.

IV.

Were I to judge from every towering steeple
That rises grandly o'er their city round,
I'd say the Yorkers are as pious people
As anywhere upon the earth are found.
On Sabbath morn I went to Dr. Potts's,
(He who had wordy jousts with Dr. Wainwright:
Which one of these good men was in the main right,
If I should say, I'd get as many shots as
My literary vestment could contain:
And so 'tis wise my dictum to refrain.)
The doctor preach'd an apostolic sermon,
As orthodox as plain folk wish to hear,
Strong Scripture common sense; and on mine ear
It fell refreshingly as dews on Hermon.

V.

The music witchingly my cares beguiled,
Echoes of heaven amid a world of sin!
Like mother's crooning to a sobbing child,
It calm'd the tumult of my thoughts within.
Nature ne'er meant that man should be a Quaker;
And though the Friends are students in her school,
They follow not each clearly written rule,
Nor in her full harmonic teachings take her.
Life without music is night without a star,
Day without sunshine, bud that never blows,
Eye without lustre, cheek that never glows,
Home without inmate with the door ajar.
Music on earth for me, besides the promise given
Of music and of hymns high in the courts of heaven!

23

VI.

I walk'd alone upon the Battery,
And look'd upon the waters as they roll'd—
A crystal sheet, with many a crumpled fold—
Up through the Narrows from the distant sea.
Vessels in multitude lay safe in port;
And some were outward bound with flowing sails,
And others, stain'd and batter'd by the gales,
Yet full of treasure, came to pay their court
To the proud island city by the sea:
While shell-like skiffs were skurrying everywhere,
Skimming like sea-birds most capriciously,
As if now on water,—then as if in air.
The scene so varied, once so old to me,
Like a rare master's picture, held me gazing there.

VII.

Twice I received a wholesome castigation
For stealing to the Battery to play
Without parental leave and approbation;
I'll not forget it to my latest day.
I told a rather hesitating story,
Not quite in keeping with my course in youth;
It may have been a crooked allegory,
And did not run in straight lines with the truth.
I bless the rod, and bless the hand that wielded,
Although it made my youthful shoulders tickle.
'Twas thus I learn'd a rod was in the pickle
For me when I to wilful follies yielded.
This was the moral I shall long remember—
Prune in the early year for fruitage in September.

VIII.

Both long and brief beseem the varied years
That have since then departed; joy or sorrow
Coming to-day and vanishing to-morrow:
All fitfully as April, hopes and fears
Bore changeful sway.   Now heavy care depress'd
My sinking soul; anon a sudden flow
Of wondrous pleasure overran my breast
Like sunlight after storm, till in a glow
Of ecstasy I gazed upon a stone
And loved my Maker more because He made it.
But there's no brook that has no tree to shade it,
And dim the dancing diamonds that shone
Upon its sunlit waters.   So, I ween,
The experience of the most of men has been.

IX.

There was a period of my young existence
(Far in the misty past, while yet the haven
Of manhood glimmer'd in the uncertain distance,—
My cheek still dimpled, and my chin unshaven)
When o'er my mind unwittingly came stealing
A tide of deep and melancholy feeling.
Up-bubbling fancies sparkled, and then broke
And sank away, and were forever gone.
Softly I breathed the while the spell was on,
Nor moved my lip, nor audibly I spoke.
I strove to catch each evanescent thought
That, like a meteor in the August sky,
With sudden brilliancy oppress'd mine eye;
But long—oh! long—my strivings were for naught.

X.

Words may not tell how hopelessly I've lain
Upon the floor, while seeking to give vent
To fancies that, like molten lava pent,
Surged madly in my wild, chaotic brain;
Till passionately I cast my pen from me,
And, like an infant wearied with long weeping,
Resign'd myself to thoughtless apathy,
And lay supine as if in quiet sleeping.
Then love stole slyly in; and she was first
To bid my fancy own a conqueror's sway:
The barriers of the flood were swept away,
And wild and rude the hurrying numbers burst.
O'erwhelming and exuberant was the joy
The rough-shod rhymes imparted to the boy.

XI.

Nor may I paint the years that follow'd after,—
The thoughtful hours—the hours of melancholy,
Commingling with the days of joy and laughter,
That led me oft to moralize on folly.
From fame's illusion, in my sober view
Unworth a struggle or a suffering pang,
I turn'd aside, and, with earth's simple few,
Life's simple themes in simple words I sang.
Within my soul religion shed her grace,
And cast her pure irradiance on the lyre;
The glow of peace illumed my pallid face,
And kindled all my better passions' fire;
My haughty temper melted in the flame,
And o'er my chasten'd breast a meeker influence came.

XII.

Idle it were to pile a pyramid,
Or seek a place among the sons of fame,—
To grave on rock the letters of a name,
And tell the world of what one said or did.
In poet's lore, and sentimental story,
It seems as 'twere this life's supremest aim
For heroes to achieve what men call glory,
And die intoxicate with earth's acclaim.
Ah me! how little care the dead for breath
Of vain applause that saved them not from death.
Could fame immortalize the human frame,
And fix undying bloom on beauty's cheek,
And cancel guilt and memories of shame,
Then were it well the precious boon to seek.

XIII.

True fame and dignity are born of toil:
'Tis so ordain'd by Him who saw it good
That man by thought and toil should earn his food.
Ev'n the brown'd delver in the yielding soil,
Who draws from earth the sustenance of life,
Has more of nobleness than he who slays
His fellow-man on fields of bloody strife,
And bears a weapon stain'd in mortal frays.
The world and CHRIST have different measurements:
While He has said, that *Blessed are the meek*
Who in forgiveness their avengement seek,
The world applauds the coward who resents
A scornful word—whose craven spirit fears
His Maker's anger less than man's disdainful sneers.

23*

XIV.

A wrong avenged is doubly perpetrated;
Two sinners stand where first had stood but one:
But wrong forgiven is wrong annihilated;
The sin is almost as 'twere never done.
Oft, love and mercy and their gentle train
Appeal to man's hard-heartedness in vain:
Mercy and love, in holiest incarnation,
Once dwelt upon the earth; but hate arose
And fired the fury of their deadly foes,
And smote them in the Prince of our salvation.
Yet He who felt the fiercest stroke of malice,
And, 'spite its wrath, man's full redemption wrought,
Ev'n He takes from our hand revenge's chalice,
And bids us hold a cup with loving-kindness fraught.

"Vengeance is mine,"
Saith GOD:
"Not thine,
Child of the sod.

"I will repay
The wrong,
Though long
My time delay."

Ye wronged and crush'd,
And weak,—
Ye meek,
Whose plaint is hush'd

By fraud and power,—
Hope on!

The hour
Will come anon,

When Heaven shall strike
Your foes,
And like
Untimely snows

They'll melt away,
And ye
Shall be
No more their prey.

Who stings a heart,
The sting
Shall bring
To him a smart.

Ye who in heaven
Would live,
Forgive,
To be forgiven.

Who suffer loss—
And take,
For sake
Of CHRIST, His cross,—

Pray for your foes,
Do good
To those
Who long have stood

Across your path,
And glared

      ·   In wrath
    To see you snared:

    And when your time
          To die
          Is nigh,
    In strength sublime

    Your souls with hope
        Shall wait:
        The gate
    Of heaven shall ope,

    And voices sweet
        With love
        Shall greet
    Your flight above.

                    XV.

The test of worth is wealth, it seems to me:
Too often in this world a fearful ban
Is on the poor.   Nay, tell me not "a man,
If honest, is respected, though he be
A dweller in the vale of poverty."
When he would rise, the meaner sort combine
And lift a heavy heel to push him down;
And if the noble struggler do not drown,
'Tis not because they show no base design
Or purposed negligence.   At any rate,
He rises in despite of Mammon's hate, ˙
And his own hand his hard-earn'd bays entwine.
Were Heaven to add ability to will,
Nature's man-children Pharaoh-like they'd kill.

XVI.

When haply some more generous spirit lifts
A child of promise from the vale obscure,
Who else had died unknown among the poor,
And cheers him with his sympathy and gifts,
"A miracle!" the astonish'd public shout,
And laud him loud and lavishly because
The man obeys the Almighty Father's laws,
And like a brother throws his arms about
His lowlier brother's neck.   Oh, blessed lot
To be possess'd of wealth and of a heart
So heavenly made that it refuses not
Of its abundance freely to impart!
Our Saviour says the blessedness of giving
Is better than the pleasure of receiving.

XVII.

To waste this life in selfish pleasure-taking,
To have it on the book of heaven printed,
"He feasted and he died, nor ever stinted
His revel-nights or days of merry-making
To wipe the dews of grief from brows of sorrow,
Or cheer the soul that sat in gloom of night,
Nor bade it look with hope for a to-morrow
When GOD should give it a supernal light"—
To noble natures how contemptible!
For such a life the vial of scorn is full.
Who gives a cup of water in GOD's name—
The water of affection—to the lip
Of some sad one who scarce has strength to sip,
Shall have a vast reward, and heaven shall know his
    fame.

XVIII.

While impudence, like weeds, will thrive apace,
Genius is child-like, and so sensitive
It scarce can find a fit abiding-place;
And love must tend it, or it cannot live.
Neglect and contumely have destroy'd
Full many a man whose spirit long was buoy'd
By the fond hope that yet would come a day
That should repay him for the pain he bore:
The world's unkindness, like a canker, wore
Into his heart, and life escaped away.
'Tis sad that earth should lose so suddenly
Her gentle ones, and few be left behind
To temper the impetuous selfish mind,
And pour affection's oil on passion's furious sea.

XIX.

So let it be—it has been ever so;
For since the world's foundation-stone was laid,
And sin brought "death and all our mortal wo,"
Suffering has been the ransom-money paid
For man's redemption.   Precious lesson taught
By suffering JESUS!—Murmuring heart, be still!
Enough for thee that 'tis thy Maker's will.
Then let thy work in faithfulness be wrought:
Thy weary toil shall fit thee for thy rest.
Thy grave more welcome—quieter thy sleep—
If round thy coffin many sigh and weep,
Who but for thee had lived and died unblest.
GOD grant to thee, my soul—GOD grant to all—
Ripeness in faith and works before our time to fall.

CANTO II.

I.

THE Utica was steaming up the Hudson;
  And we (some friends and I) took passage in her,
And reach'd Peekskill in ample time for dinner.
The mountain trees had neither leaves nor buds on,
Yet beautiful the haughty Highlands stood.
Oh blessed land of rivers, plains, and mountains!
Beyond all regions Heaven has made it good!
More precious than the golden-bedded fountains,
Or diamond stones of India or Brazil,
My country is my Holy Land. I love her!
The purest, brightest skies are spread above her,
And heavenliest beauties cover vale and hill;
Her lakes are oceans, and her mountains hide
More secret wealth than all the earth beside.

II.

(Reader! forgive the muse's transient rapture—
Thy heart is cold if thou forgivest not.)
We gazed on Tarrytown, the famous spot
Where three militia-men made noble capture
Of André, the adventurous English spy.
The man was hang'd, and bravely did he die.
Some years ago the British sought his bones
And placed them 'mong their famous worthies. We
Once lost a hero worthier than he;
And still he lies beneath the unnoted stones
Where he was buried. I have ever kept
A corner of my heart for Nathan Hale
To live in; and until my days shall fail,
I'll honour him whose fate a lonely mother wept.

III.

He ask'd them for a Bible e'er he died:
He had been taught to love it in his youth,
And now he sought the solace of its truth
In his last moments,—and he was denied!
The Britons swung him 'twixt the heavens and earth,
As if he were a dog; nor scarcely gave
A shred of time to fit him for the grave.
(Howe! noble merely by the chance of birth—
Thine is the sin, and thine the ignoble fame!
I loathe to stain my verses with thy name.
I hold thee forth as one of vermin-breed,
That men may scorn thee as they scorn a lie!)
Hale grieved—let freemen ponder as they read—
"That for his country he but once could die."

IV.

The envious tell us, " We are base-begotten—
A mongrel nation, born in Time's declension—
Plebeian people—sellers of corn and cotton,
Unworthy high and honourable mention."
Well, be it so.   The lusty strength of youth
Is better far than proud decrepitude.
With mind and might and fortitude endued,
We stand erect, and fight for present truth.
We're in the young delight of new existence;
The ardent blood leaps lively in our veins;
The dim traditions glimmering in the distance
We scorn, for objects worthy manly pains.
We tread a path our slanderers never trod,
And as we choose, we serve and worship GOD.

V.

It ill becomes our brethren thus to mock.
Their homesteads once were also ours; and we
Have well upheld the family dignity,
Nor proved degenerate scions of the stock.
Let all the earth produce a parallel
To this good land wherein our people dwell.
'Tis ours to show what man, most free, can be:
The mission is not given to us to pore
O'er cobweb'd tomes of well-forgotten lore;
Progression is our law and destiny.
We lead the van of battle, well begun
By Sidney—Hampden, Cromwell, on the field,—
And glorious Milton, who a pen did wield
That glow'd with light from mind's unclouded sun.

24

VI.

Oh, that the blind seer's mental mantle might
(Like the rapt prophet's) fall upon this land,
Which owes its freedom partly to his hand,
That dared betimes the fearless truth to write.
The man immortal of our father-isle,
His fame is also ours.   'Twere well all men
Should sit like children at his feet awhile
And wisely learn of him.   All nations then
Would show their giants.   I wish in vain, I fear.
When he was old and blind, they gave him ten
(They promised twenty) pounds for his great poem,
And let him die.   And 'twould be so again.
Thus angels sometimes on the earth appear,
But till they fly to heaven the world seems not to
        know 'em.

VII.

If I believed in canonizing men,
I'd canonize John Bunyan.   But, indeed,
My faith is in a stern and simple creed,
The "excellent way" Paul taught by tongue and pen.
And so the tinker may content himself
To take a place upon my mental shelf
Beside John Milton.   Twelve full years was he
A guiltless prisoner held in Bedford jail;
And, companied by his daughter, blind and pale,
Manlike he bore the wrath of bigotry.
"'Twas time to curb the license of his speech;
They had not sent him," thus the prelates reason'd:
"In their own tenets he had not been season'd,
And strange 'twould be to let a tinker preach."

VIII.

'Tis hard to hinder bitter thoughts from rising—
To keep the word of scorn unspoken—when
I read the cruelties of these mitred men
Who seem t' have thought that man-anath'matizing
Was a far holier work than man-redeeming.
But Bunyan was beyond their power: nor cords
Nor bars could bind the immortal thoughts and words
His genius hid beneath the guise of dreaming.
He stands alone in his peculiar glory,
Sole sovereign of the realm of allegory.
Two hundred years have pass'd; yet brightly beams
(Such fascination in his necromancy)
On us the radiance of his brilliant fancy.
What wondrous sleep was his that had such glorious
    dreams!

IX.

Thou, too, stand up, Noll Cromwell! Take thy place
Among thy country's mightiest; for thou wert
The sturdy champion of thy suffering race;
And thou didst battle, ev'n to thine own hurt,
For man and truth and GOD. They slander'd thee,
The minions of the second Charles. The dirt
Of slander now is dried, and, verily,
Like good old Bunyan's pilgrim, thou art girt
With brighter glory. Godless cavaliers
Made merry of thy manly spirit's heaving;
Thy sighs and groans, thy prayers and flowing tears
Were mocking mysteries to the unbelieving
And scoffing followers of the bigot-king,
Whose velvet fingers hid the accursed sting.

X.

The first and faithless Charles (since falsely named
The Martyr) sat on England's throne, and sought
To set aside the precepts wisely framed
To guard the freedom of man's word and thought.
He maim'd the men who spoke the unwelcome truth,
Imprison'd some, and some the tyrant fined;
In pillories stood stern martyrs of the mind,
Yet all the people show'd them kindly ruth.
A reckoning-day was coming. Cromwell! thou
And thy true cousin Hampden scorn'd to bow
Before the pride of monarch, priests, and lords.
Humanity arose in arms; and dire
And awful were the mortal hate and ire
When tyranny and freedom measured swords.

XI.

The Arm divine o'erthrew the foes of men:
The death of Charles a small atonement made;
And tyranny sneak'd to its murky den,
And tiger-like lay watching in the shade.
'Neath thy protectorate, old England's fame
Grew great and glorious. Thy simple name
Sufficed to keep a turbulent world in awe;
And people great and small securely dwelt
Beneath the shelter of the equal law;
And at their wont the high and lowly knelt
And worshipp'd GOD. When death to thee came
          near,
Still trustedst thou in Him who died to save.
Thou hadst thy faults; but who, alas! is clear?
Immortal memories sanctify thy grave.

XII.

Short time it was that thou hadst been entomb'd
When tyranny came howling for its prey;
Thy sacred corpse was savagely exhumed,
And on a gibbet swung in open day.
They cast thee in a pit: thy mother dear
And thy sweet daughter too: and many more
Of pure and holy ones.   The atmosphere
Shook nightly with the bacchanalian roar
And horrid riot of the royal court;
And freedom's wail afforded royal sport.
I can no more.   Let future writers tell
The faithful story of those murderous times,
The merry monarch's shameless tricks and crimes,
Whose merriment provoked the laugh of hell.

XIII.

Old Europe bends beneath her load of crime:
Her catalogue of guilt is written down,
And Justice waits, with ever-deepening frown,
To smite for sins of past and present time.
The lordly few eat up the land; the poor,
Vilely earth-trodden, sullenly endure
The hunger-pang; and foundling infancy,
Unfather'd and unsponsor'd, marks the shame
Of unwed mothers—babes without a name.
The cry of man uprises to the LORD—
Of man oppress'd, and moaning helplessly;
And shall not He fit recompense award
To those who spurn Almighty GOD's decree
That man in very deed a man should be?

24*

CANTO III.

I.

THE rugged head of Winter on the lap
  Of Autumn lies. His snowy locks he flings
Upon her bosom. His chill arms enwrap
Her shivering form, until her quiverings
Subside in death. His voice breaks forth in wild
And piteous howls, as if he mourn'd the death
Of the meek one who perish'd at his breath.
On his stern brow the angry clouds are piled,
And bitter are his rage and vengeful spite;
And seamen on the rocky coast at night
Fall victims to his ire. At times he seems
To put away his wrath, and melting tears
Run down his icy cheeks in copious streams;
But soon anew they freeze, and all his rage appears.

II.

Yet nature in her barrenness has charms;
And men of cheerful hearts may even see
Some beauty in a brown and leafless tree,
While silently it stands, with naked arms
Appealingly uplifted tow'rd the skies.
The man has dim and uninstructed eyes
Who never finds the precious gems that lie
Beneath his feet wherever he may tread;
And he who bears a high and haughty head
Will pass unseen GOD's works of wonder by.
The flowers may all have gone, the birds departed,
And babbling brooks be changed to speechless ice,
Still nature's winter aspect may suffice
To fill with tender thought the pure and earnest-
    hearted.

III.

The man who looks around him as he walks
Sees objects strange and wonderful and new;
And he who thinks while his companion talks
In time may grow the wiser of the two.
An open eye—a quick, attentive ear
Will lead the mind into the ways of knowledge;
For all the world's a universal college,
And every one may be a learner here.
Experience is the teacher: dear, indeed,
Her charges are to thoughtless folk and fools;
But all'who follow carefully her rules
The various tongues of nature learn to read.
Thought adds to thought; and soon the mental pile
Uprises heavenward, like a coral isle.

IV.

Who seldom sows his mind shall reap but little;
Weeds quickly overspread the fallow soil;
The toiler may be wearied by his toil,
But it shall yield sufficiency of victual,
Enough for his own use, and much to spare.
To him who hath, abundance shall be given;
From him who squanders wastefully his share,
All that he has shall righteously be riven:
The world shall make a proverb of his name,
And he shall fill a sepulchre of shame.
Work waits for every man; and he who fills
The measure of a working Christian here,
Shall little heed life's ordinary ills,
And calm content his life and death shall cheer.

V.

In our humanity the LORD has hidden
Things richer and more beautiful than lie
In Colorado's mines; and we are bidden
To seek and find. We live below the sky,
Yet we may lay up treasure even there;
Yea, life immortal to the pure in heart—
Similitude to GOD, in that we bear
Our Saviour's image in our better part—
The taste and thirst for knowledge failing never,
But strengthening in us ever and for ever,
While depths of love and goodness we explore,
And wondrous mysteries of His working learn
In the grand worlds that in the distance burn,
And find new cause to praise Him evermore.

VI.

This present life seems full of mysteries;
The vulgar mind, to superstition prone,
In nature's movements fearful omens sees,
And shrinks aghast from terrors of its own
Imagining.   Despotic is the power
Of ignorance; and thousands live in fear
And die unnumber'd times before the hour
That Heaven has set to end their strivings here.
The trustful, quiet, mighty thinker seeks,
In loving faith, the unknown orderings
Of the Great Former of created things,
And GOD to him in guiding accents speaks.
Still, in the dealings of the LORD with men,
Are mysteries far beyond our human ken.

VII.

Some dwell in palaces, and some abide
In huts; some languish from the lack of toil,
And others wait the hour when they may hide
Their over-weary bodies 'neath the soil.
Some men go hungry all the day; and some
Do turn away with loathing from their food,
For Heaven has given them multifarious good
Until satiety has overcome
The natural craving.   Some have friends to spare;
And some, the prey of loneliness and grief,
Have none to bring them comfort and relief.
Some sink in trouble, some have naught to bear;
Some soar to power, and some are trod in dust;—
Can lots so various 'mong equal men be just?

VIII.

Were death annihilation—were this life
A lamp extinguish'd, never to be relit,—
Then words of deep despondency were fit;
Then man perchance might lift his arm in strife
Against his LORD.   Were blessedness of mind
Dependent on the vastness of the heap
Of gold and gems the schemers 'mong mankind
Could gather, then 'twere virtuous to weep.
But 'tis not so.   Infinity of time
Is yet to be.   Beyond our vision lie
Eternal realms ineffably sublime
And beautiful.   Nor heart, nor ear, nor eye
Of man has known what things are laid up there
For all who love Him and His spirit share.

IX.

The mourners of the earth there mourn no more;
The sigh, the tear in heaven is unknown:
They walk as children round the Father's throne
Who in their mortal life were spurn'd the door
Where Sin and Mammon reign'd within the dwelling.
Unselfish bliss their raptured breasts is swelling,
And all are brothers there.   None rolls himself
In dust of gold, and lifts his head above
His fellow worms because the glittering pelf
Sticks to his slimier coat.   The law of love
Is perfectly obey'd.   The innumerable throng
Have separate tnemes of thankful joy; yet all
Unite in hallelujah and in song,
And GOD's benignant smiles on all the brethren fall.

X.

And there is rest,—the full and perfect rest
Of unfatigued activity: not such
As lulls awhile the languid mortal's breast
When he has thought or labour'd over-much;
Not such: but more, immeasurably more,
That needs eternity to tell it o'er:
A ceasing from infirmity and sin,
From envy, lust, and hate, a banded crew,
That, through its oft-unguarded doors, let in
Upon the soul a cursed retinue
Of evil spirits:—rest in the love of GOD,
The garment of His grace His people covering,
Their feet with sandals of his goodness shod,
And clouds of blessing ever o'er them hovering.

XI.

And has this various life a change so fair
And glorious? May man, his death-sleep o'er,
Awake angelic? Then who would not bear
And suffer long, and wait in patience for
Deliverance?—O weeper on the way!
Do many sorrows on thy bosom prey?
Dost feel thy burden heavy? Lift thine eye
To CHRIST thy strengthener. If from thee He take
No burden, still He helps thee at thy cry:
Who bear His yoke, their back shall never break.
And oh, ye poor! contemn not GOD'S decree:
If poverty, a bitter medicine, cure
The soul's distempers, blessed are the poor;
Yea, if ye are CHRIST'S poor, thrice blessed men
    are ye.

XII.

If plenty pall the palate of the rich,—
If appetite be lacking at the feast,—
If honours lose their magic power to 'witch,
And when obtain'd, are loved and worshipp'd least,—
It is that man should heavenward aspire,
And seize the substance, while the shadows pass,
Dim images reflected in the glass,—
Should warm his spirit with the sacred fire
Of love to GOD and man, and day by day
Work in the good LORD's field as well as pray,—
A follower in the path of Providence,
Cheering the halting on life's rougher way,
The orphan's helper and the widow's stay,
Till GOD shall call his willing servant hence.

XIII.

Uprightly stand, then, brothers of my race!
And manly meet the troubles of the way:
A trustful hope in our Redeemer place,
And lovingly and kindly as ye may
Assist some weaker ones who meekly bear
A weight of which your arm should take a share.
Whate'er your station, ye are call'd of Heaven
To do a generous work among your kind:
Into your trust a talent has been given;
It may be wealth of gold or wealth of mind,—
It may be large, it may be very small;
But use it well, and ye shall surely hear
The Master's voice in gracious accents call
Your souls to dwell in an immortal sphere.

XIV.

There are some bosoms, all the wide world over,
That flow with what is call'd the milk of kindness;
And though I've not been an extensive rover,
Yet I were chargeable with moral blindness
Did I not see and own the winsome grace
That Heaven has given to many of our race.
The image of the Highest may be seen
Borne brightly in His children on the earth.
No claim make they to a patrician birth,
Yet in their loving tone, their peaceful mien,
Their faith and works, and self-denying spirit,
They give us strong assurance they inherit
The temper of their LORD, who, on the Mount,
In matchless words man's duty did recount.

XV.

The heart of kindness seldom sours or curdles;
The cream of love is in it pure and sweet:
With every charm that human nature girdles,
And every grace of gentleness replete,
The man who has a kindly heart is most
In pattern like his LORD; for where the law
Of kindness rules the heart, the virtues draw
Together in companionship, and post
Themselves around that citadel of love.
The kindly man doth always kindly prove:
He has a word of sweetness for the child—
Of pity for the poor—of sympathy
For all who mourn; and truly glad is he
When through his generous care some sorrowing face
     has smiled.

25

XVI.

There's music always in the kindly soul,
For every deed of goodness done awakes
Its chords of pleasure, till the harmonies roll
(Sweeter than man's most cunning finger makes)
In waves of joyance o'er the happy breast,
Like the blest home whose gleeful daughter's singing
Sets bells of gladness through its halls a-ringing.
How foolish they who seek in biting jest
Amusement at a weaker brother's cost!
The wanton anguish man inflicts on man
Is written down—it never shall be lost;
Some coming day 'twill meet GOD's righteous ban.
Be ours the grace to breathe our daily breath
In kindliness, and die the good man's death.

XVII.

Old Peekskill village has a goodly share
Of kindly men and women. ("Women! I pray!
Use softer term, Sir Poet! *Ladies*, say."
The proudest name the gentler sex can bear
Is WOMAN, simply woman—bosom-mate
Of hardier man, and sharer of his state.
And 'tis, besides, the name bestow'd by Heaven:
I'll use it till a better word be given.)
How big the human heart! How much 'twill hold
Of love! In it the blissful stream may pour
Continually, and yet there's room for more.
Should I be spared till I am gray and old,
I'll not forget the freshet of affection
That met me there and drown'd my mind's dejection.

XVIII.

Brother and I together took a ride
To Shrub Oak Plains. There cousin John alone
Is lying—friend nor kinsman by his side.
His resting-place is noted by a stone
Of whitest marble: truthful words are those
Inscribed thereon. The scene of his repose
Befits his life: 'twas beautiful and calm.
In meekness and in love he went his way,
Uprightly walking—filling up the day
With useful deeds. He often pour'd the balm
Of healing into wounded breasts; nor sought
The praise of men in doing good,—for he
Had been a learner at Gethsemane,
And he remember'd well what his loved Master taught.

XIX.

Dear John! 'Twas but a little while ago
When he beside me, pensively and still,
Wander'd among the mounds at Laurel Hill,
And sought the grave of one he loved. The snow
Had melted from the fields, and spring was coming;
And southern winds blew with a gentle humming.
He left me for his northern home. The flowers
Of summer bloom'd and faded; autumn came,
With setting sun that gleam'd like golden flame.
Then winter brought long nights and stormy hours.
But John the autumn or the winter days
Saw not; for, call'd of GOD in summer time,
He pass'd away in his and nature's prime.
A nobler pen than mine might worthily write his
    praise.

XX.

There also dwelt another godly man ;*
But there he dwells no more; he too has cast
Aside mortality, and lately past
Into the heavens.   His life was but a span
On earth; and yet 'twas long enough to win
The crown that waits the victor over sin.
"I have one hope—one only hope," he said,
"My precious Saviour!"   And as thus he spoke,
Death's darkness gather'd slowly round his head;
And from the invisible world a brightness broke
On his new-given spiritual sight.
The morning of the Sabbath had arisen,
And earth was resting when his soul took flight,
And heavenward sped, like bird escaped from prison.

XXI.

In after-time I stood beside the grave
Fresh open'd for the youngest of my love,
My latest born.   Affection vainly strove
Most earnestly the dying boy to save.
'Twas otherwise decreed.   Were I to say
How pearly pale and beautiful he lay
Within his coffin, one might think it were
A sin to hide him in the sepulchre.
I touch'd his forehead and his tiny hand;
How cold they were!—the chill went to my heart,
And wellnigh caused the pent-up tears to start;
But stern composure came at my command,
And silently I stood, and loved the more
The child who, dead, look'd lovelier than before.

---

* Rev. DANIEL BROWN, pastor of the Second Presbyterian Church.

XXII.

We bore him to the grave while yet 'twas morn,
The winter sunlight shining on his coffin:
The weight of grief was heavy to be borne,
And the salt tears rose in our eyelids often.
We slowly walk'd in mutely sad procession,
The pitying people freely making way;
And the blest child, yet guiltless of transgression,
We softly placed between the walls of clay.
We sang a hymn—we bow'd our heads to pray;
And GOD, who had our bitter grief appointed,
Sent also strengthening grace by lips anointed.
With lingering steps we left him as he lay
In angels' care; and when we homeward went,
We felt his home was better 'yond the firmament.

XXIII.

The old clock in the hall is slowly ticking;
And hour by hour it tolls a funeral chime:
Its ever-going and unhurried clicking
Denotes the speed of the old traveller Time.
It is a solemn voice.   Who hath an ear
To hear its warning accents, let him hear,
And preparation make to meet the day
When he shall lie alone upon the brink
Of human life, and death shall bid him drink
The hemlock cup that none can put away.
What though man turn from the unwelcome theme,
Will Time sit still for man's forgetfulness?—
To watch betimes were wiser than to dream
And wake at last to wo remediless.

25*

XXIV.

" 'Tis time we should be going," Socrates
Said to his judges; " I to die, and you
To live: the better which, is known unto
The gods alone." Happy for him who sees
'Tis time for him to go about his work
And finish well the allotted part before
The set of sun, when labour-hours are o'er,
And night descends in mantle damp and murk.
In reckless mood, some waste their morning-time,
And, like an idiot gathering straws, they clasp
The gewgaws of this world with earnest grasp,
While life slips on; till, past its glorious prime,
With trembling steps they carry down the road,
Hugg'd to their breast, a perishable load.

XXV.

Spring for the youth, and summer for the man,
And autumn-time for him whose head is sere;
But when one meets the winter of his year,
Then should he rest, and well and wisely scan
The tenor of his life, and lessons give
How younger men may well and wisely live.
I loathe to see the old man dabbling in
The turmoils of the world. Like one apart,
Turning aside from Mammon's work and sin,
Be his the holy task to teach the heart.
In the midway between two worlds he stands:
His foot is lifted; when he steps again,
He passes from the dwelling-place of men,
And a new stage of life begins in other lands.

XXVI.

Thus earth goes forth in constant emigration
To the good land of Heaven.   And evermore
The angel who stands sentinel on the shore
Proclaims, "Another from the lost creation!"
The sea of death continually is dotted
With barks of spirits voyaging across;
And all whose guilt the grace of CHRIST has blotted
Sail swiftly on, nor meet with harm or loss.
True, darkness to the natural eye may cover
The still and dismal waters, and alone
Each vessel ploughs a sea before unknown,
Yet o'er the track invisible angels hover;
And the death-hidden, from the darkness waking,
Beholds the morn of day-eternal breaking.

CANTO IV.

I.

THE Singsing stage up to the door was driven;
    I was the only passenger that day,
And sadly, gladly pass'd I on my way,
My wavering heart by varying feelings riven,
And, like a pendulum, swinging to and fro.
From dear and loving friends I grieved to go,
Still fain was I to turn my wandering feet
And hasten homeward to affection's seat.
St. Anthony's Nose blew forth a bitter blast,
And pierced my bosom with the sharp-edged cold:
All snugly wrapp'd in many an ample fold
Of cloak and fur, I held them close and fast,
As o'er the wild romantic road I sped
Whose winding way along the river led.

II.

The Dunderberg sat silently beneath
The snowy clouds, that form'd a vapory wreath
Above its peak.   The Hudson swept along—
'Tis not in me to paint.   Had I a pen
Endued with master gifts and genius, then
Might I aspire to tell its praise in song.
But I'm an humble bard, without a name,
Who tunes his straw in praise of homely things:
If gentle hearts are touch'd by what he sings,
He is content, and thinks it noble fame.
All mistily let transcendentals sing,
And soar to realms of sense-confounding fog;
So that my rhymings have a natural ring,
In common pathways be it mine to jog.

III.

Of human things my muse delights to tell—
Of home and hope—of gentleness and love,
That sink like oil into the deepest cell
Of selfish hearts, and make the hinges move
More readily to let sweet mercy in.
There's poetry bound up in every life
Whose years with love and usefulness are rife,
For poesy and love are sister-kin.
The affectionate glances of a happy wife—
A husband's tender tones—an infant's smile—
The voice of childhood merrier than a fife—
With themes like these 'tis good an hour to while;
And so, when musing on a lonesome way,
With things of common life my thoughts are wont to
    play.

IV.

And thus it was the woof and warp of thought
Into this web of ballad-lines were wrought:—

MARY'S HOLLOW.

A shady dell beside the road,
   Sequester'd, cool, and grassy:
A pleasant brook anear it flow'd,
   Its current pure and glassy.

And Mary's home was on the hill,
   Up in the farm-house yonder:
But in the dell so cool and still
   It was her wont to wander.

Her father's sheep the tender maid
   Her steps had taught to follow,
And friskful lambs around her play'd
   Down in the grassy hollow.

And there she sat on summer days,
   Her nimble fingers flitting
Through many an intertwisting maze
   In curious arts of knitting.

And there she sang some simple song
   Or hymn learn'd from her mother:
The hours to her were never long—
   Each moment chased the other.

A native quietude of mien
  So graciously became her,
The maidens on the village-green
  With honour loved to name her.

The peaceful meekness of her brow
  Awoke no special wonder,
Though like a brook beneath the snow
  A stream of thought ran under.

And oftentimes a sudden smile
  Her countenance stole over,
As flitting sunbeams dance the while
  O'er fields of blooming clover.

The very angel of her hearth,
  Her mother's hand caress'd her:
She changed her father's care to mirth,
  And silently he bless'd her.

On Sunday, in the village choir,
  Her pure, sweet voice, outpealing,
Struck up in listening hearts the fire
  Of deep and holy feeling.

When sorrow's burden fell upon
  Some soul too weak to bear it,
She bent her willing shoulder down
  And kindly sought to share it.

The great wide world was all astir,
  And heaved in toppling billows;
But all was calm as heaven to her
  Beneath the drooping willows.

As life ran on with silent pace,
   Her meek and pious spirit
Grew meeter for the holy place
   The pure in heart inherit.

And when the leaves were turning red,
   And autumn winds were sweeping,
Sweet Mary with the blessed dead
   Beneath the grass was sleeping.

The neighbours, still, who pass that way
   Where Mary's sheep did follow,
Remember her; and to this day
   They call it Mary's Hollow.

v.

I pass'd the homestead of a rancorous Tory,
Who fought against his country in the years
Of our old revolutionary glory.
He well deserved a cropping of his ears,
But Britain pension'd him.   His neighbours round
Gave him a pension too—of hearty scorn.
Of freeman's powers he by law was shorn,
Yet was he wont to come upon the ground
Where freemen met to vote.   His very name
A jest-word on the tongues of men became.
"Ho! ho! sir patriot! will you cast a vote?"
They cried with biting tone and lip upcurling.
"I'd rather have," he mutter'd in his throat,
"Two hundred fifty pounds in money sterling!"

VI.

This was the sum the British paid him yearly:
And Judas-silver 'twas that nation did owe
To such as he. They gave it to his widow
When he was dead. Methinks 'twas earn'd too dearly:
The smiter of his fatherland for gain
Deserves the doom of the old murderer Cain.—
What germs of wild romance here go to waste!
What ripen'd memories cluster on the stem
Of old tradition ! Who shall gather them
But one whose line's with some ancestor graced
That sow'd the heroic seed? Chivalric tales
Might be rehearsed of these grand hills and vales.
Had the mute rocks a voice, what poet's verse
Might even feign the deeds they would rehearse?

VII.

The times of Seventy-six and after-years,
Till freedom on our hills sat peacefully,
Were times not often given to earth to see,
When men, triumphing over natural fears,
And with a courage bonds nor hunger broke,
Wrench'd from their country's neck the rasping yoke
Of foreign sway. It was not meet that they—
The hardy tamers of a continent—should give
Their birthright to their kinsmen far away,
Who dwelt upon an island in the sea;
A haughty isle, yet so diminutive,
That, were a giant, in a sportive sally,
To toss it in our Mississippi Valley,
'Twould seem an infant on a Titan's knee.

26

VIII.

'Twas kingly tyranny and priestly rule
That drove our fathers from the homes and graves
Of their ancestors.   In staunch Freedom's school
They learn'd man's dignity; and crouching slaves
In mind or body they could ne'er become.
They cast the price, and sternly paid the sum
Their ransom cost.   They took their venturous way
Over the sea, and set their feet upon
A free wild land beneath the western sun.
The GOD they served was their unfailing stay;
And busy towns and villages arose,
And peace and plenty dwelt within the land,
Till in a fateful hour the Briton's hand
Fell heavily on them, and brethren turn'd to foes.

IX.

The men of Seventy-six in their good arm
—Hoping in GOD—reposed a manly trust;
O'er all the land was sounded war's alarm,
And victory crown'd the valour of the just.
The fire of liberty fell down from Heaven
Till from our shores the enemy was driven;
And freedom, with the land's redemption shod,
Her benison flung o'er every hill and plain.
None of that band of noble men remain;
The death-roll sounded at the word of GOD,
And they were laid in honour's sacred fane,
Their toils repaid by o'er-abounding gain.
While love of home the freeman's breast shall fill,
Their fame shall cause the freeman's breast to thrill.

X.

Dear brethren, friends, and country of my love!
"The lines are fall'n to us in pleasant places:"
A newer blessing every moment chases
Some previous blessing sent us from above.
Our cup is full, and rich as Heaven can make it
For lips of man unworthy.   Brethren, take it,
And let us quaff it with a grateful spirit.
Its fulness will remain; and while we drink
Of bliss surpassing nectar, let us think
How great and pure was our forefathers' merit.
Let thankful thoughts, like morning's fragrance, rise,
Whene'er to us returns our natal day;
And He who smiles upon us from the skies
Will guide our country in a righteous way.

XI.

—Our coach got in too late.   The waiting stage
Had started on the way to Tarrytown;
So at an inn my driver sat me down.
Folly it were to fall into a rage,
And so I paid the fare and kept from strife.
The sun was to its winter zenith risen,
And forth I went to visit Singsing prison,
Where some have berths for years, and some for life.
A thousand live in company, yet alone,
And earn an honest meal by quarrying stone.
The prison stands along the river shore;
It has no outer wall; but men with guns
Keep watch, and shoot the felon if he runs;
And rogues, in silence, learn to steal no more.

CANTO V.

I.

THE tide of time is stealing up the shore:
  A wrinkle's on my temple, and my hair
Is not so brown as in the days of yore;
And my complexion (ruddy once and fair)
Begins to show the trace of work and wear:
And several children clustering round my chair
(One is in A, B, C; the others read
In languages: they're very apt indeed)
Look up to me with fond respectful air:
Yet sober truth impels me to declare
My heart will not grow old; but, full of joy
And sportiveness as when I was a boy,
With mischief and with mirth my bosom teems,
And still I take a part in childhood's fun and schemes.

II.

I give this merely as a fond excuse
For all the whims and fancies of these papers:
If graver people, liable to vapours,
Object, and say, " The poet is a goose!"
Why, let them say it. Well enough I know
That living springs in April overflow;
But who'd refuse the limpid stream to quaff
Because the waters, as they run along,
Dance over stones and sing a cheerful song,
And whirl and purl a sort of aqueous laugh?
Methinks my verses human life betoken;
Sadness and mirth mix'd curiously together,
Like clouds and sunshine in the spring-time weather:
What cheerful heart that has not nigh been broken?

III.

In summer-time the fleet-wing'd shadows skim
Trippingly o'er the hills and vales of earth:
So transient shades flit o'er the face of mirth,
And casual tears the brightest eyes bedim.
For instability and change are written
On us and all our works. The loveliest things,
When full of promise, oftentimes are smitten;
And sweetest roses foster sharpest stings.
The world, if loved too well, is prone to pall,
And the poor fool who set his heart thereon
Beholds his idol into ruin fall,
Its frail foundation undermined and gone.
May thus a mortal utter his complaint,
When faith is weak, and spirit worn and faint?
26*

IV.

" I weary of this wosome world, O GOD!
My languid spirit sinks; my nerveless hands
Have lost their wonted skill; my feet are shod
No more with diligence.   Like one who stands
Supine and listless at his journey's end,
Or like a beggar who has naught to spend,
There is no relish in this life for me.
For I have sought for kindliness and ruth
And brotherhood among my human kind:
But I have found the visions of my youth
Unreal fancies of a dreaming mind;
And fame and riches false and fleeting be.
The twig may thrive when sever'd from the tree,
But all my comforts die when I am far from Thee."

V.

Yet good's in every thing save only sin;
And even sin itself makes virtue seem
More beautiful.   Pain is of brother kin
To pleasure.   Night adds brightness to the beam
Of day.   The spring is balmier for the cold
And bitterness of winter.   Budding trees,
That long seem'd dead, are pleasant to behold.
In tropic heat, more grateful is the breeze.
Thirst makes mere water sweet: to hunger, bread
Is heavenly manna; and the weary head
Contented rests upon a bed of straw.
The goodness of our Maker may be found
In every place the wide creation round:
His daily providence proclaims this blessed law.

VI.

How warmly we are loved, we seldom learn
Till pain and sorrow take our strength away;
Then, hearts too long estranged to us will turn,
And be at peace, as in a former day.
Our true and loving wife more loving grows;
Our little ones in pitying wonder stand
Beside the bed and clasp our fever'd hand;
Their glistening eye the tear of feeling shows;
And it may be, when evening calls to rest,
They meekly kneel beside their mother's chair,
Their silvery voices blend in simple prayer,
And for their sire they make a child's request.
The times of anguish are not vainly given
That lead a family to unity and heaven.

VII.

An urchin said, "If he were rich, he'd swing
All day upon the gate." And witless people
Oft nurse the vain conceit that it would bring
All heaven to them, if they could climb the steeple
Of their desires. They clamber up full high,
But still the goal seems far off to the eye;
For as they rise, ambition grows the stronger;
Insatiate longings prey upon their mind;
And while they seek what they can never find,
Death intervenes, and lets them seek no longer.
Their day and dream of life together past,
Aside their kinsmen lay them in the tomb;
A passing thought upon their fate is cast,
And myriads still rush on to meet a similar doom.

VIII.

And is this all of life?   Is bursting bubble
Or Sodom apple all that man may gain?
Like a lone partridge wandering mid the stubble,
Must he so wander o'er life's barren plain?
Sowing for happiness, and garnering pain,
Is this his portion?   Selfishly alone,
Shall he supremely ever seek his own,
And leave the suffering one to weep in vain?
Is all that heart requires accomplish'd when
A heap of wealth is gather'd at our door?
How thirsts the yearning soul for something more,
Some good that lies beyond its keenest ken!
And must that thirst forever be unslaked?
Shall suicidal dreamers never be awaked?

IX.

For man immortal, it is wisdom's way
To make this life the pathway to a better;
To do to all as kindly as he may,
And love as well in spirit as in letter.
Let man achieve a victory o'er himself;
Let him observe the blessed Master's teaching,
And turn aside from trickery and o'erreaching,
Nor grind his fellows for the sake of pelf.
Oh let us take each other by the hand,
And help the weaker o'er the rougher places:
Sure, GOD will bless so brotherly a band,
And gift our souls with high and holy graces.
What is there here worth living for, if it
Be not to work in love, and grow for heaven fit?

X.

The book of human nature is a tome
Most strange and curious. He reads it ill
Who sees not man's perversity of will
Written on every page. Eschewing home
And all its quiet joy—neglecting all
The little tender acts that fill love's measure,
And, like the dews that on the prairies fall,
O'erspread the heart with fragrant flowers of pleasure,
And seeking good wherein no good abides,—
Is't strange that disappointment man betides?
What though the earth has thorns, the roses grow
Among them. Hapless is the lot of one
Who goes through life and never finds it so.
For him the pitying muse bids these quaint numbers
  run:—

  The happy man is he,
  In city or countrie,
  Whate'er his lineage be,
  Who liveth lovingly
  Amid his family;
  Whose heart is like a tree
  That flowereth beauteously,
  And beareth seas'nably,
  And yieldeth fruitfully;
  Whose mind from guile is free;
  Who followeth equity;
  Who scorneth flattery;
  Who showeth charity;
  Who toils with industry;
  Who walks in constancy
  And true humility;

Who loveth minstrelsie
And natural poesy,
And trees and shrubbery,
And brook, and bird, and bee;
Who serveth reverently
The LORD of land and sea;
Who honoureth the decree
Of the heavenly chancery,
And uncomplainingly
Resigns mortality;
Whose faith in CHRIST'S a key
To ope eternity,
Where, while the ages flee,
He'll dwell immortally,
And wondrous glories see
Unveil'd by Deity.
Be this the destiny,
Reader! of thee and me.

XI.

I went from Singsing in the afternoon
And rode to Tarrytown, and willing pains
The driver took to get in to White Plains
To reach the cars; and he was paid a boon
In welcome coin.—The alarm-bell shrilly rang,
The steam-horse all impatient to be gone:
The passengers in sudden hurry sprang
And took their seats: and we went dashing on.
All nature seem'd to be with legs endow'd:
A circling race the trees began to run;
The hills, the rocks, the fences joined the fun,
Creation hastening past us in a crowd.
In plainer phrase, along the rail we flew
Till Manahatta's city open'd on the view.

XII.

I met a man—I may not tell his name—
His face was frank and fair: but one who gazed
Into his eye might see that he was crazed;
His wife had crazed him by a deed of shame.
He sat beside me in the flying car;
I know not why he told the tale to me,—
Perchance he saw and felt the sympathy
I had for him whose soul had such a scar.
He dwelt in peace in his own home afar,
And love and quietness abode with him;
And in that heaven his wife was as a star,
Until a cloud arose and made it dim.
A villain stole her heart; and what was left
To comfort him when of her love bereft?

XIII.

She left his dwelling, and she bore away
Their only child—a blooming boy, but blind:
The blow was fatal; and his anguish'd mind
Totter'd like some half-rooted tree, whose stay
The hurricane has rent. He sallied forth,
And on the wretch he plied the stinging stroke
Until the rod in useless fragments broke;
And then he took his journey to the north
To seek the child. "I would not take his life,"
He calmly said, "though he beguiled my wife:
Who sits upon the cloud beheld the wrong
I suffer'd—He will make it right." We parted
And met no more; but in my memory long
Shall bide the look of one so wan and broken-hearted.

XIV.

Within the cars were various sorts of people:
Some sat in couples—others sat alone;
Some softly spoke, and some in boisterous tone.
A churchman told of his new church and steeple,
And rightly show'd a warm regard for both;
A fellow near, who GOD nor man regarded,
His low and vulgar language interlarded
At intervals with an emphatic oath.
He claim'd to be a gentleman, no doubt;
Methinks he was alone in that opinion;
A common swearer's Satan's meanest minion.—
'Twas dark when we got in; and I got out:
To brother's dwelling I went hastily,
And quietly with friends sat down to talk and tea.

XV.

Delightful is an evening's cheerful chat
With pleasant friends, especially to one
Who has been long away.   The minutes run
With speed that all the talkers marvel at.
So much to talk about—so much to tell—
So many sleeping memories to awaken—
The various fates that absent friends befell—
Whom time had spared, and whom the grave had
    taken
The tear to shed for those who pass'd away—
The sigh to breathe for those who went astray—
Our times of darkness, and our days of light—
Our purposes and plans for coming years—
Our heavenly hopes, our earthly human fears—
And lo! 'tis time to say, "Good-night, dear friends,
    good-night!"

XVI.

Now seek we balmy sleep.   How happy he
Who folds his arms upon his peaceful breast,
And calmly takes his 'custom'd nightly rest!
But some sad soul is sighing wearily:
The eye is dull, yet sleep the lid forsakes;
The ear is quick to catch the faintest noise;
The clock's dull tick the drowsy spell destroys,
And on his couch the sufferer lies awake.
All sleep but him—all in the silent town,
And lonelier grows the still and lonely night.
The stealthy cat, with footfall fleet and light,
Along the stairway patting up and down,—
The cricket in the hearth,—the creaking door,—
But serve to make the silence deeper than before.

XVII.

And thus the hours in solemn stillness roll,
While plaints, like rifted clouds, drift o'er his soul:—

I lay me down, but cannot sleep;
My thoughts unwilling vigil keep;
I turn in weariness and pain,
And, lo! I hear the sentry's strain—
    " Twelve, and all is well !"

The air with noise no longer stirs;
Still as the place of sepulchres
The sleeping city is, save when
The sentry's voice is heard again—
    "One, and all is well !"
27

How solemn is the night!—the eyes
Of heavenly creatures light the skies:
They glimmer o'er the ancient tower
Wherein the sentry marks the hour—
  " Two, and all is well !"

Does any other wake with me,
Dear brother in infirmity?
Does any homeless wanderer hear
The tones that fall upon mine ear,—
  " Three, and all is well !"

Sad heart! how wearily and slow
The long and lengthening moments go!
When will the darkness pass away?
Why tarries so the coming day?—
  " Four, and all is well !"

Yes! all is well!   Though now I weep,
I know my GOD will give me sleep;
The morning light is in the skies,
And slumber softly shuts mine eyes—
  "Five, and all is well !"

CANTO VI.

I.

'TIS Sabbath in the town.   The calm of rest
  Is in the souls of men.   The sound of bells
The hour for holy convocation tells;
And sacred aisles by worshippers are press'd.
Mean Mammon hides within the deepest cells
Of the mean hearts wherein he wonted dwells.
The rich man's day—he feels his poverty,
His need of grace bestow'd without a price:
The poor man's day—he learns his high degree,
That he is noblest who has least of vice:
The gathering-day around a Father's table,
When brethren from their wandering-places come
And sit in peace like children at their home;
An Eden of the soul, outspringing from a Babel.

II.

The day is past. Another morning breaks,
And man again to wholesome labour wakes:
Labour, mother of rest; the discipline
Of love; the doom most merciful and just,
That keeps the soul uncanker'd from the rust
That else would eat it with the tooth of sin,
And let innumerable sorrows in.
The stillness of the Sabbath—passing sweet
It was—has given place to various din:
The hammer's clang, the rumbling in the street,
The sound of many voices, hurrying feet,
The massive stroke of ponderous machines,
All these, and countless more, the listener greet,
And magical appear the city's wondrous scenes.

III.

The blind man groping cautiously his way
Along the crowded pavement of a city,
Has natural claims upon our tender pity.
Whether 'twere night, or whether it were day,
Would seem to make small difference to him
Whose days and nights alike are ever dim;
Yet still the tramp of human feet, and hum
Of human voices, sweetly fill his ear;
The surgings of the tides of life appear
Like the deep sounds that from the ocean come
At midnight to the list'ner. Pity's glance
Upon his form instinctively I throw;
And while some sadness clouds my countenance,
To GOD I pray to save me from such wo:—

IV.

"Thine earth, O LORD! is beautiful. Mine eyes
Have seen—my heart has felt it so. Thy hand
Has set its mark of glory on the land,
The sea, and every thing beneath the skies.
The earth was bright to me in early days,
Ere dimness fell on me. O Father GOD!
Thou know'st that I its hills and vales have trod,
My bosom full of love to Thee, and praise.
I love the earth because 'twas made by Thee,
And made so fair. I still would look upon
Its face when lit with radiance by the sun,
Or by the moon or paler stars. To me
'Tis beauteous still, the earth and all its kind:
Then spare me, gracious LORD! and let me not go
    blind!

V.

"About my hearth, five little ones are playing;
Their mother sitteth with our last-born near:
What hand shall feed them, and what voice shall
    cheer,
If I am smitten blind? LORD, I am praying
For these my children whom Thou gavest me,
And her, more loved in my extremity.
I kiss the rod that smiteth me. Thy will,
Thy sovereign will, be done! But yet I pray,
Oh! spare to me the pleasant light of day,
And let me look upon my kinsfolk still.
The face of man to me is very dear;
Then set me not alone, where I shall see
My human kind no more, and ever be
A dweller in a land all lonely, dark, and drear."

VI.

More pitiable is the man whose mind
Is darker than the ancient night that fell
On Egypt, (as our holy Scriptures tell,)
And who has never learn'd that he is blind.
In rank and saucy speech he calls to task
The Great, the Wise, the Holy All in All!
With questions such as he alone dare ask,
He mocks Infinity!   The lightnings fall,
And scath him not—he scorns the Thunderer!
He swells in pride, a little deity,
Nor heaven nor earth shall make his spirit stir!
Fool were a word as weak as word can be
To brand his brow:—Ah no! the man is blind:
The GOD of grace illume his darksome mind.

VII.

From Manahatta may be seen Long Island;
It lies between the river and the ocean,
And interposes many a verdant highland
Between the city and the sea's commotion.
There, near the beautiful Gowanus bay,
Is Greenwood Cemet'ry, the place of rest
Of mouldering men whose souls are with the blest.
With loving friends I wander'd there one day,
A winter day, such as we sometimes see
When old December, hoar with age and rime,
Relents its rigour in its dying-time.
The snow lay here and there; and spots of green,
Amid the snow, diversified the scene,
The emblems of a life beyond mortality.

VIII.

In after-time, when musing on that hour,
My thoughts fell captive to the muse's power:

Were I to choose where I would rest
　　When all my care is o'er,
I'd bid them lay my silent breast
　　Beside Gowanus' shore.

In Greenwood's vale should be my grave,
　　Or in its shady steep;
The ceaseless singing of the wave
　　Should charm my peaceful sleep.

I'd rest on nature's dreamless bed,
　　Beneath the smile of GOD;
His hand of love beneath my head,
　　And cover'd with her sod.

I'm weary, weary now, and long
　　Have weary, weary been;
And melancholy tunes my song
　　When sadness reigns within.

Yet so I work His gracious will,
　　And so my LORD approves,
I'll bear my daily burden still,
　　Till He its weight removes.

When GOD shall bid me enter on
　　The Sabbath of the dead,
He will not leave me all alone
　　The silent way to tread.

Confiding as a child I'd lie,
   And slumber on his breast;
Who sleep in Jesus never die—
   They rest in living rest.

IX.

On Monday afternoon—it lack'd a quarter
Of five o'clock—I like to be exact
In days and dates, and other things of fact—
I bade my friends good-by, and cross'd the water
To Jersey City, and took the homeward cars.
The evening shades set in, and soon the Night
In silentness put on his crown of stars.
The moon came up, and sprinkled o'er with light
The rifted clouds.   Of all the stars, mine eye
Chose Sirius, the glory of the sky:
It pointed to my home; and then a rhyme
Rose in my mind, and cheer'd the lagging time.
Thus lovingly I rhymed, while tasting only
The luxury of lounging languidly and lonely:

RHYME IN A RAILROAD CAR.

Afar from home for many days,
   I cried, "More swiftly move,
Ye cars, upon your iron ways,
   And bear me to my love."

The wintry day had pass'd, and night
   Put on his jewell'd crown,
And from the moon the beams of light
   In silver showers came down.

A single star appear'd at first,
   And twinkled near the moon,
Undimm'd by all the host that burst
   Around its pathway soon.

The steamy engine, like a bird,
   Skimm'd o'er the level rail;
'Twixt mountain-heights it wildly whirr'd,
   And leap'd along the vale.

But still the star sped on before,
   As if to lead the way:
"Perchance my love within our door
   Beholds its silvery ray;

"And peace comes softly in her heart,
   And dark and troublous fears
Beneath its cheering light depart,
   And hope dries all her tears."

And then methought the eye of GOD
   Doth ever shine upon
The darksome way in patience trod
   By every suffering son.

And comfort, like a sinless dove
   Soft brooding in its nest,
Nestled within my heart, and love
   O'erfill'd my quiet breast.

Deep silentness was all around,
   The mid of night was o'er,
When mine own faithful love I found
   A-watching in our door.

X.

Anon I thought, at home 'twould not be ill
To set up for a poet—get a sign,
"Tam, Poet—and Commissioner for the Nine,"
And tack it to an office window-sill,—
Procure a desk, a library-case, and chair,
And then put on a literary air,
And cross my legs and wait for customers,
As legal men and medical doctors do.
I'd send my card to liberal publishers,
Thus, "Office hours from 10 o'clock to 2."
A quid pro quo I'd always render; that is,
The merit of the poetry should be
Proportionate to the bigness of the fee
The editors and album-ladies gratis.

XI.

Ah! what a revolution would be brought
About in things poetic! Then no more
Would scribblers dwell within starvation's door,
Supping on words and breakfasting on thought,
Till, like frost-bitten plants, they wilt and die:
No Motherwell or Chatterton be mated
With lean and hungry want: no more be fated
To live midway betwixt the earth and sky
'Neath attic rafters. Crowns of tinsel glory,
A foremost place in babbling men's esteem,
The puffs that give a transient name in story,
And daze their wits as in a drunken dream,—
All these were theirs who'd take their pay in kind
And cast away the birthright of their mind.

XII.

Pah! pah! I'll none of it.   I'd rather stand
Nobly among the poor, than soil my soul
And stain the palm of my unsullied hand
With Mammon's glittering and dear-bought dole.
If I possess a fairly-founded claim
To add the poet's title to my name,
Let me sing on as nature teaches me:
Let virtue's signet be upon my words;
O let me touch in human hearts the chords
That vibrate in completest harmony,
And waken music in the souls that sit
Afflicted and disconsolate in their door,—
Till far from them the evil spirits flit,
And in their desolate hearts joy bides for evermore.

XIII.

But oft I have no heart to make a rhyme;
'Tis scarce worth while to tell the reason why.
I cast my verses negligently by,
And lay them over for a happier time.
"Why should I seek with earnest care to find
A jewel, worthless in the eyes of many,
Who set a higher value on a penny
Than on the purest diamond of the mind?"
When thus I ask, awhile my spirits fail;
But better thoughts and purposes prevail:—
I'm but a man amid a world of men;
Among them all, a few may haply listen,
Until their hearts grow soft, and eyeballs glisten
With tender tears awaken'd by my pen.

XIV.

Then my own heart grows stronger, and I feel
That GOD has given us naught that is in vain;
That simple herbs may cure acutest pain,
And gentle words a bosom-sore may heal.
Then sing I on in hopefulness and faith,
And close mine ear to what the scoffer saith;
Nor heed the cold, unsympathizing stare,
The haughty look, the dull, ungainly grin
That marks some faces, as 'twere printed there
In living type, "There is no man within!"
Oh, that my rhymings, like a living rill
That slakes the thirst of mortals worn and weary,
May flow in pure and crystal streams at will,
And make the heavy-hearted light and cheery.

XV.

Somehow another train ran off the rail,
And thus were we consid'rably belated,
And longer kept than we anticipated
Upon the road.   At midnight we made sail
Across the Delaware.   Few minutes more,
And I was standing safely in my door.
A warm embrace soon told me all was right;
In arms of Love our lives had all been hid.
I kiss'd the children :—'bove the coverlid
Their bright blue eyes twinkled like stars at night.
If breasts e'er gladly throbb'd, our bosoms did!
Kneeling to Heaven our grateful vows to plight,
In fearless trust our weary eyelids closed,
And softly, sweetly, soundly we reposed.

NOTES AND ADDENDA.

Tam's Fortnight Ramble.—Pages 261–324.

This piece was written for *Neal's Gazette*, and published under the pseudonym of Tam.

PAGE 265.

On Sabbath morn I went to Dr. Potts's,
He who had wordy jousts with Dr. Wainwright.

An allusion to the famous controversy between these clergymen occasioned by a remark in an oration made by Mr. RUFUS CHOATE, that "New England in its settlement exhibited the striking spectacle of a church without a bishop, and a state without a king."

PAGE 300.

And to this day
They call it Mary's Hollow.

A locality near the village of Peekskill, Westchester County, N. Y.

PAGE 91.

Then the people, if unmournful,
Said, "Poor Norah's dead!" unscornful.

HONORA POWER, known as Crazy Norah, was for many years a notable character in the streets of Philadelphia. The *Sunday Dispatch* gave the following reminiscences of this strange woman:—

The dress of Norah was as fantastic as her speech. Strangely enough, too, considering her antipathy to men, her garb was usually more than half masculine. A man's hat, long boots, and curiously-cut plaid coat, secured around her waist by a broad leather belt, formed her usual costume. At times Norah bedecked herself with fanciful ribbons and flaunting finery, and with a bootjack or some equally uncouth utensil in her hands, she paraded the streets, stopping occasionally to make a speech, in which fantastic thoughts were clothed in strange verbiage.

From our earliest days, the wild fantastic garb and the coarse though not unhandsome features of poor Norah have been associated with our recollections. We remember well, at a time when we could scarcely shape a sentence with our juvenile lips, how Norah would take us by the hand and compel us—under fear of her displeasure—to repeat after her, word by word, the Lord's Prayer and the Creed of the Catholic Church. If we obeyed her directions cheerfully, and betrayed no fear of our wild monitor, a reward was sure to follow. Norah invariably carried with her a capacious bag, well filled with little odds and ends, which she had gathered in her wanderings, and a recitation of a creed or a prayer would certainly be rewarded with a bit of broken china-ware, a fragment of looking-glass, or perchance a piece of red tape or gay ribbon. Norah had a strange jargon of her own, and she made odd speeches. Her grandmother was mixed up with the prince of darkness most singularly in all her orations; and his satanic majesty and her aged relative invariably figured conspicuously in connection with the trash she bestowed upon good children as a reward for their proficiency in the matter of creeds and prayers.

PAGE 109.

What is death to one that liveth
In the love of our dear Lord?

The *Philadelphia Inquirer*, on December 22, 1863, published the following tribute to the memory of ANNA MARIA ROSS.

In the first hours when the call was made for woman's labour in the cause of patriotism, Miss Ross took her position as nurse and principal of an institution for the suffering soldiers, and from the moment when she first undertook the onerous duties appertaining to the position she has never faltered, never wearied. Day and night found her at her post; no disease was too dangerous, no wound too loathsome for her hands to minister to; no sufferer was too rude for her gentle sympathy; no discouragement too great to unnerve her heart; and when the way was opened for the foundation of a Home for the discharged soldiers, her whole energy and life were thrown into the enterprise. She visited all who could give aid or influence to the scheme, travelling over the State, canvassing the city, and, while still constant at her old position, her earnest endeavours were ever bent toward the forwarding of the noble scheme.

The perfect self-sacrifice of her life can only be appreciated fully by those who have watched her course, been taken into a place in the same warm heart that cast no one out, and marked the daily and hourly toil for the beloved object. At last the work was near completion. Aided by noble and patriotic friends, sustained by the citizens of Philadelphia, and encouraged by every well-wisher of the disabled soldier, she saw the building opened for the reception of furniture, took her position as Vice-President of the lady managers, and worked still faithfully to bring all to perfection, till worn down by almost superhuman toil, and utterly exhausted by her unparalleled exertions, she laid down her life on the very day when the Home for which she had given it was dedicated, her words of parting being, " I did not think my work was done, but GOD has willed it so; His will be done."

Anna Maria Ross, after a life of devotion to others, has gone to meet the reward awaiting her at her Master's hands.

She has spent her life in earnest seeking after God's will, and resolute efforts to fulfil it faithfully; every charity found in her an active and untiring co-operator; her hand was ever ready to minister to the suffering and needy; her warm heart was ever open to loving charity, and her pure Christian words always waiting to pass the portals of her lips.

PAGE 110.

On the field of battle, mother,
All the night alone I lay.

Founded on a line in a soldier's letter to his mother, " When you meet together, tell my little brother and sister that I died to save my country."

PAGE 113.

Let me kiss him for his mother,
Ere ye lay him with the dead.

A young man from Maine, hale and ruddy from his native hills, was seized by the yellow fever in New Orleans; and the tender care and nursing of the Howard Association failed to save his life. When the coffin was about being closed, " Stop," cried an aged woman who was present, " let me kiss him for his mother !"

PAGE 136.

Methought the graves again appear'd,
Neglected, as of old.

The beautiful Park in Philadelphia, known as Washington Square, was in former times the public burial place, or potter's-field.

PAGE 147.

For many days our eyes have seaward wander'd
As if to search the ocean o'er and o'er.

The beloved and honoured HENRY REED, Professor of
Literature in the University of Pennsylvania, on the twentieth
of September, 1854, embarked at Liverpool for New York, in
the United States steamship Arctic. Seven days afterward, at
noon, on the twenty-seventh, when almost in sight of his native
land, a fatal collision occurred, and before sundown every
human being left upon the ship had sunk under the waves of
the ocean.

PAGE 189.

Forget mine ancient friend, my Neal!
" Nevermore !"

The witty and amiable JOSEPH C. NEAL, Editor of *Neal's
Gazette* in Philadelphia, who died suddenly a day or two after
his marriage to one of the lady contributors to his paper.

PAGE 73.

Oh for a spell of the former time,
When I dwelt beside the river of rhyme,
And the frequent thought would over me steal,
" Shall I dip a bowl of its waters for Neal ?"

Many pieces in this volume were evoked by the kind en-
couragement of Mr. JOSEPH C. NEAL, the well-known editor.
The author's literary connection with the *Gazette* began with
the series of jocular rhymes here appended :—

"THERE IS NO POETRY IN A HAT."

Neal's Gazette.

THE editor says, " No poetry in a hat!"
　　I throw the gage to him on his assertion:
　　I'll prove it but an undeserved aspersion—
I'll make the editor " get out of that."
　　" No poetry in a hat!"   His hat, I s'pose,
He means—and then perchance 'tis true;
But sure 'twould be a pretty how d'ye do?
　　For him to stand in other people's clothes,
And say they have no poetry in their hats.
　　Some hats and trunks are lined with poetry,
　　All printed fair, and beautiful to see;
And hats are used by some as mental vats,
　　Wherein they pour the brewings of their brain:
　　And curious 'twere to taste the beverage they contain!

A hat's the dome, the steeple-top of thought—
　　The attic room, the cockloft of the head—
The hive where fancy's honey-bees are caught,
　　Which, else, beyond the memory's reach had fled.
A hat, well-brush'd, 's a cap-stone to the man;
　　Corinthian column he, with cap to match—
A column it were poetry to scan,
　　And with a glance its fine proportions catch.
A crownless hat lacks poetry; and he
　　(Whoe'er the miserable man may be)
Whose tangled hair stands peering through the crown,
Far from the graces hath he tumbled down:
　　Sans hat, sans coat, sans character, sans all—
　　Who thus hath fallen, how fearful is his fall!

" No poetry in a hat!" (my strain is growing
　　Perhaps too sombre—so I'll change the theme:)
Who ever saw a poetaster going
　　Forth to the fields, in ecstasies to dream,
Without a hat upon his head?—not one!
Were it by day, the fervid noontide sun
　　Would quench his fire with floods of perspiration:
Were it by night, mosquito, bug, and gnat
　　Would place him in a painful situation,
And make him long for e'en a napless hat.

" No poetry in a hat !"   Behold the Quakers,
Who always wear their hats, except in bed ;
    Of all mankind, they are the keenest takers,
For poetry and common sense enshrine each placid head.

Now, here I'll stop :—I hope that you will own,
Dear Mr. Neal, your charge is overthrown :
    If you won't yield, why, I must try again
What virtue still abideth in my pen.

The editor stoutly denied that he said there was no poetry in
a hat : his assertion was that there was

"NO MUSIC IN A HAT."

I PRAY your pardon, gentle editor :
    You have me on the hip, and I am smitten
    As dumb as lead for what my pen has written.
I see not how it was I said it, or
    How my good specs misled me as I read
    " No poetry," when " no music" 'twas you said.
But so it was :—man often double sees ;
    And sometimes sees what is not to be seen ;
    And, when he is particularly green,
Is made to see what his tormentors please.
    But still, methinks, I was not much in wrong ;
A hat I heard of which had music in't,
    (At least, so thought the hero of the song ;)
The way was this, as I have read in print :—

There was a man (for thus the story goes)
Who always wore a claret-colour'd nose ;
    Some bees once took it for a gaudy flower,
And settled in a swarm upon his face.
    A horrid fear the wretch did overpower !
(A wretch is any man in trouble ;)—he
    Stood like a stone in his perplexity,
For bees can sting more keenly than a gnat :
    But soon a thought came with a sudden grace.
With steady hand he lifted high his hat ;
    The bees mistook it for a hive, and flew
Straight into it, and fill'd it to the brim :
Methinks, the hum from that old hat to him
    Was sweeter music than the spheres can " do."

(The rhyme just made is good—the English bad.)
'Tis said the razor-strop man oft doth tell
A story to the point—of what befell
A wretched man who drunken habits had.
(I pity him who, in this better day,
For alcohol will give his soul away.)
His shoes were toeless, and his elbows out;
His face was puffy, and his tangled hair
Evinced no daughter's love nor sweet wife's care;
And in the breeze his hat-crown flapp'd about,
And made a music that an owl would scout,—
(Queer music that, but music still, no doubt.)
A few more lines, and then I'll cut the thread
That draws the rhymes in couples from my head.

There's many a hat, on every pleasant day,
That's full of music and of poetry;
And any man the truth of this may see
Who leisurely will saunter on his way
Through Chestnut Street, or in the verdant Square,
And mark the foreheads lit with intellect:
In every glance, a poet may detect
The life of poetry indwelling there;
And from the mouth of our true-hearted girls
Soul music issuing 'tween the rows of pearls
That stand like sentries just within their lips;
The sweet sounds dying when they close the mouth,
Belike the moon last night, when in the south
Her mild, fair form was hidden in eclipse.

Whenever woman's brow her beauteous bonnet bears
A hat of music and of poesy she wears.

Besides many others, the *New Orleans Delta* now took part
in the fray; whereupon the Rhymer conferred with Editor Neal
as ensueth :—

TO EDITOR NEAL.

WE'LL drive that interloper off. He's poaching
Upon our grounds. We have pre-emption right,
And we must show our spunk, and give him fight.
That Oregon is ours. We'll suffer no encroaching.

'Tis ours from centre to circumference,
Throughout its utmost, universal bound,
From pole to pole, or water, ice, or ground,
   E'en up to nature's last, extremest fence!
But, by-the-way, I wonder if a hole
Into the earth is found at either pole;   ·
   For if there is, we claim the world inside
(Its mines of diamond wit—its golden piles
Of thought—and all its coral fancy isles)
   As well as all upon its outer tough, rough hide.

You squatted first, and I sat down beside you,—
   You Daniel Boone, and I his nearest neighbour;
   You set the stakes, and I partook the labour;
Now, I'll stick to you, let what will betide you.
   We fell'd the trees,—we clear'd the brush away;
   The minx, the coon, the beaver felt our sway,
And yielded us the crown.—Shall Delta come
   And shoulder us aside? Shall he apply
Unto his nose the tip end of his thumb,
   Twiddling his fingers, with a winking eye?
He shan't play Yankee game with Indian folk:
   We'll hold our own, like Prussian miller bold,
   Who loved his homestead more than Fred'rick's gold:
We'll keep the hat, undaunted by his joke.

A pretty pass sure things are coming to
   When you and I can't hoe alone our row,
But every little cockadoodle-doo
   Must flap his wing and imitate our crow.
The hat—the whole hat—nothing but the hat!
Ha, Mr. Delta, what d'ye say to that?
   So, now be off, and go t' the Nile, and climb
The Pyramids, or seek the Sphinx's nose,
   Or learn if it is true, that, at the time
Of morning-light, old Memnon music wakes.
But pray don't come where we have planted stakes,
   Or we may tread on one another's toes.
So take the hint, or Mr. Neal and I
The virtue found in stones at your expense may try.

The *Delta*, nothing daunted, sang in this wise:—

" We say, Sir Tam, the hat is all our own,
As by a thousand reasons could be shown;
    But what of that ?
By our retaining it we feel
We would be tempting you to steal—
    So take ' our hat.' "

TAM'S SAY TO THE DELTA.

WE do not want your hat; we'll keep our own;
    We're much obliged—your article won't fit.
And what's a hat, unless a head of wit
Is underneath?   As well present a bone
    Denuded of its marrow.   We've a head—
The editor and I—that " can't be beat;"
Full grown in size, and stored with mental meat
    Of various sorts, and literary bread;
    And from its garners hungry folk are fed
With wholesome food that satisfies the mind,
And nurtures thought, and makes them wise and kind.
    The busy beaver's neither snared nor dead
Whose fur shall form a hat that will compare
With that which we on Saturdays do wear !

Ha! " take your hat !"   You 'mind me of the days
    When I went courting.   Happy days were they !
    One freezing night I beau'd my lady gay
To hear some singers warble lovely lays
    Composed by Handel (or perhaps by Haydn.)
My hat I placed upon a bench near by,
    My soul entranced by music and my maiden;
A man of warty face and squinting eye
    Approach'd my hat, and set himself beside it.
    With sidelong look I watch'd what might betide it.
He moved, and moved, and still kept moving on,
    And when he moved, he moved my hat along;
    My mind was caught a moment by the song,
And when I look'd again, the man and hat were gone.

Not gone—but going quickly to the door !
    I follow'd fast.   " That hat is mine " I said.
    "Oh! ah! is't yours?" exclaimed the warty head;
"I thought 'twas mine !"   I took my hat once more.

The warty squinter pick'd up from the floor
A furless thing made in the days of yore,
And bore himself away as well he might.
—Thus Mr. Delta, fancying our hat,
Quick whips it up, and thinks he has it pat;
But we, forgetting not the concert night,
And conscious that we have the legal right,
Arrest the culprit and reclaim the prey.
We lecture him, and let him go his way;
And he, ungrateful, claims the hat—the wight.

During the hat controversy in *Neal's Gazette*, some curious
persons sought to fix the identity of Tam. Hence the following

"ASIDE" FOR THE EDITOR'S EAR.

THEY ask who Tam is? Pray don't whisper it
To any one. Enough that you and he
Are cognitive of his identity.
He's rather modest; and he loves to sit
Behind the curtain of his pseudonym
And throw his rhymings in the midst of men:
Like some kind fellow who, from some odd whim,
Ensconces him from all observers' ken
Behind a wall, and pitches apples out
Among a hungry crowd: they take and eat,
And while they munch the food, they look about
To ascertain who throws them in the street.
They praise his fruit, and vote the man to be
A clever chap, and say, " Pray who is he?"

He's neither Parson, Doctor, nor Professor Tam,
Nor Lawyer Tam; nor even does he claim
(So deep his scorn of humbug and of sham)
To add Esquire to his simple name.
His home is in a place where Providence
Has set him. Neither very rich nor poor,
His bread and water have been ever sure.
To man or brute intending no offence,
He seeks to live, and die, in peace with all.
Years three times ten (and more) he's trudged along
The lane of life, and sometimes humm'd a song
To cheer him in a heavy interval.
He bears a burden equal to the might
That Heaven has given, and hope has made it light.

Then let him travel on his quiet way;
   Ask not his name, his whereabouts, and so forth.
   If 'tis his wish incognito to go forth,
And gently touch the doings of the day,
So let him do; and let him have his say.
What reasonable man will answer Nay?
   Expect him not to kick at every cur
That snarls behind his heels.   He has an aim
More noble than a thirst for vulgar fame:
   The better feelings of man's heart to stir,
His dearest purpose.   If to fun he bends,
   It is to wisely win the multitude,
   And lure the mirthful to a thoughtful mood,
And thus accomplish high and worthy ends.

ELECTROTYPED BY MACKELLAR, SMITHS & JORDAN,
PHILADELPHIA.